While glancing out of a window

an anthology

by Northants Writers' Ink

edited and introduced by
Michael J Richards
Chair, Northants Writers' Ink

New Generation Publishing

A good short story crosses the borders of our nations and our prejudices and our beliefs. A good short story asks a question that can't be answered in simple terms. And even if we come up with some understanding, years later, while glancing out of a window, the story still has the potential to return, to alter right there in our mind and change everything.

– Walter Mosley

Contents

Humour and Whimsy

Science Fiction

Love and Romance

Introduction

by Michael J Richards

While glancing out of a window is Northants Writers' Ink's second anthology. While the pieces in its first anthology, *Tales of the Scorpion*, had a common theme, this does not.

The 45 short stories, nine poems, two scripts and one essay in this anthology are grouped by subject or theme: Crime and Drama; Ghost and Horror; History and Myth; Humour and Whimsy; Science Fiction; Love and Romance.

* * * * *

While **Gordon Adams** has contributed three science fiction stories, his love story "A Perfect Match" reveals his continuing growth as a writer. Full of wit, it shows off a wry humour and charming lightness of touch.

Of **Pat Aitcheson**'s six pieces, her longest story, "Out of time", is also her most mysterious. Its basic premise is initially unexplained but, with close attention, is not difficult to divine. Although the narrative moves slowly, it builds piece by piece to a thrilling, enlightening climax.

Deborah Bromley offers three pieces, all concerned with death or other existential planes. "A Dance to the Death", which opens this anthology, is an excellent introduction to her view of the world. Skilfully constructed, thoughtfully written.

Beth Heywood always writes unflinchingly of the darker side of everyday life. Her four pieces in this anthology follow that path. The longest of them, "A new beginning", deals with the less fortunate people in contemporary society, showing that they, like the rest of us, grab their happiness how and where they can find it.

1

Nick Johns contributes 17 short stories, in some cases "very short" being more accurate. Nick specialises in flash fiction, most of it quirky, off-the-wall and in many cases, really quite disturbing. However, his longest piece, "Who's There?", is the most haunting, made all the more so because of its tightly controlled, chillingly reasonable writing.

Jason McClean gives one story, "Was it worth it?". It examines the question in the title from several points of view – school, lone parenting, sterile domesticity, crime – coming to, in all cases, morally ambiguous conclusions. A provocatively philosophical exploration of the dilemmas each of us faces in our daily lives.

Elizabeth Parikh revels in comedic writing. Three of her four pieces exhibit this to the full. "The rap before Christmas", though, is arguably the best. Certainly the most fun, it screams out, "Perform Me!"

Michael J Richards presents four pieces – three short stories and the only essay in the volume. He says "Cowboy's lament" and "it is most mad and moonly" are among his best.

In 16 pieces, **Allan Shipham** gives us a mixture of forms – poetry, song, script, short story. But among all this, "Excerpt from *The Malford Chronicles*" stands out as probably the finest piece he has written to date. Tactile and grounded, it transports us effortlessly to the mythic Celtic world of the late seventh century.

More details about the contributors can be found at the end of this volume.

* * * * *

Formed in October 2013, Northants Writers' Ink is a writers' group based in Wellingborough, Northamptonshire, England.

New members can find more information and how to join
at www.northantswritersink.net,
by emailing northantswritersink@outlook.com
or by going to www.meetup.com.

Michael J Richards
Wellingborough, Northamptonshire
August 2016

Crime and Drama

A Dance to the Death

a short story by Deborah Bromley

It was dark in the wet, ill-lit street. Smoke hung in the air and filth littered the ground. Shadowy characters sneaked into doorways or scuttled down narrow alleys.

A hunched figure drew his cloak tighter as he clung to the corners of buildings and pressed his slight form into the gloom, making his way over the cobbles.

"Ere, get yerself outta my way." A doorway tart flashed her cheap red satin to accompany her complaint.

The figure crept backwards to avoid a confrontation.

"Just keep yerself away from me – you look poxy."

He skulked away to prevent any more unwanted conversation.

Further along, the darkness deepened until it seemed to absorb the man. He moved silently, using shadow to conceal his passage. A hidden doorway breathed rank, stale air and he paused to inhale, then darted in.

The rickety staircase creaked as he climbed to the top floor. His footfall went unheeded as competing noises, the noises of crammed-in humanity in all its vile forms, clamoured from within other rooms on the landings. His arrival went unnoticed. His key in the well-oiled lock turned sweetly. The door clicked quietly shut as he closed it; his hand on the doorknob was tender. Silence was his friend.

He shrugged off his cloak and laid it reverently on the single chair. His hunched frame unfurled to reveal a soft leather holster which he unbuckled deftly and set down on the table. There would be time to take bread later. Perhaps when his long-suffering landlady could be persuaded to part with some broth and chunks of a dark loaf. But, for now, his attention was focussed on his holster, his tools. It was time to give them the care they deserved.

7

* * * * *

"You off again, mister? Another of your errands, no doubt. And you never stop to eat, it seems. Let me scrape out the bottom of my stew pot for you. And a little bread to mop it up with?"

A slow smile spread across the man's face.

"Yer don't look after yerself, I don't know how you live and breathe. And what if I had no leavings today, then what'd yer do?"

He shrugged his bony shoulders.

"It'll be in the room when you come back. Mind it's not late, though. Don't want my stew to turn. And don't forget my rent!"

But he had gone out into the darkness.

He walked with careful, measured paces, light on his feet, the heel first, then the weight held back until the sound of his foot was muffled on the cobbles. He moved purposefully but noiselessly. When the street ahead glowed with sulphurous air, he hung back, clinging, limpet-like, to the shadows. Then bold. A gentleman of means, freshly fed and watered, looking for company, loitered ahead, unafraid of the pools of yellow light. A knife appeared and a throat was cut. A white-gloved hand clutched the air. Blood spread out like spilled wine on the wet street. The killer crept away.

* * * * *

The darkened room closed in around the figure at the table. The cloak hung on a solitary peg by the sideboard bearing the crumbs of his humble repast. The man sat at the table with a single candle, just a stub, hardly lighting the room. A pile of gold coins and a stack of paper money lay on the table. Several knives, a garrotting wire and a length of lead pipe were on a cloth in front of him. He cleaned and polished his tools. He removed the blood and tissue from his longest knife and placed it carefully on the table. He then examined all the gleaming blades before him, taking his time to sharpen them to a lethal edge with his block of oilstone. He coiled and wrapped the wire in a clean rag. The lead pipe, satisfyingly weighty in his hand, was encased in a tube of black cloth. He caressed his knives with a lover's tender touch before sheathing them in the soft leather holster.

The candle guttered and flared, briefly. His face lit up to show a man in love with his work. There was pride and pleasure in his expression, despite the pitiful housing and the absence of any home comforts in the room. His hand hovered over the stack of money. He spread the coins out and re-formed them into three piles. The notes he fingered, reaching for a glass to magnify the words. The man sighed. It was a sound conveying, to anyone who might be listening at the door, true satisfaction with his lot. Then he picked two coins, caressing them with his fingers, before dropping them into a worn cloth bag which he placed on the sideboard.

* * * * *

"Are you in there, mister?"

Another loud knock rattled the door in its frame.

"I wants me crocks back, I'm comin' in, hope yer decent."

The woman withdrew a bunch of keys from her skirt and peered at them. She selected a key and unlocked the door. The room was empty. Cold and bare and unadorned. She shuffled over to the sideboard to retrieve the used bowl and plate. The gravy had been wiped clean from the bowl. Her hand covered the money pouch and scooped it up, secreting it furtively into the ample pocket in her skirts where she hid anything of value from anyone who might want to take it from her.

"A good man, you are. And I see you enjoyed my stew."

She paused, casting her curious eyes around the room. It was much as she had rented it to the man. She sniffed the air. She could detect the faint sense of occupation. The tang of the body rather than of damp and the mildew. The scent of clothing, woollens, leather. And another smell. One she only knew subconsciously, but it startled her.

She set about examining the room more carefully. Touching the table. Yes, this table knew what she was after. The back of the chair, the underside of the thin rug. Then the sideboard, empty but for a few meagre sticks of cutlery. The hard iron bedstead stood in the corner with thin grey blankets – neatly made – and, although she had little hope of finding a hidden packet, her efficient and inquisitive fingers twitched in expectation. Her hands crept under the mattress. Methodically, she explored every inch without leaving a trace.

* * * * *

The crunch of well-shod feet echoed around the empty alley. All former occupants had scattered. There had been no requirement for dogs. They knew where they were going. There had been a tip-off.

An authoritative knock on the door produced a scruffy woman, hands crossed over her chest, voluminous skirt swishing like the tail of an angry cat. She bared her broken teeth in what might pass for a smile.

"Top floor," was all she said before retreating to her rooms to wait out the night.

* * * * *

Another man stood solemnly at his office window, watching the carpenters working in the yard below. The finishing touches were being put into place. Nails countersunk as per the usual orders. He had to crane his neck from time to time to see around the bars. He took a gold watch out of his pocket and observed the time. There were other preparations to be made. He walked away and signalled to a younger man standing guard in the corridor.

A nod was all that was required. He now wished to be left alone.

He opened the door to a room with a window high above and no view except for the sky. A long solid table, blackened with age, occupied the centre. A wooden cupboard stood open in the corner. A long coil of good rope awaited his attention. But first he would dress. It was unseemly to commence this ritual improperly attired. He selected a clean white shirt and stiff collar. Dark, heavy trousers added formality. A thick leather belt, wider at the back, was secured around his waist. He would tighten it later. He sat to put on black shiny boots, the soles reinforced with hobnails. These boots had been his father's. His long jacket was draped carefully over a chair while he went to work.

But before continuing he paused for a short prayer. It was his custom.

He turned his attention to the task. His hands and arms moved in a fluid sequence of coiling and knotting and tugging until, finally, he was satisfied. It was his duty and his pleasure to fashion the noose. He would not trust anyone else to make it. As he turned his work slowly around, checking for any loose coils or faults in the rope, he was reminded of his father's words.

"The act of taking a life is a great burden, my son. But a necessary one. It will be your responsibility to despatch the convicted soul with dignity. When you take care over every little detail, it will ease your conscience, knowing you did your best."

He took a moment to reflect on the words. When he was content that his heartbeat had slowed and his mind was calm he stood again, then brushed a few specks of lint from his trousers.

Outside, a dull dawn was breaking. The sounds from the carpenters had ceased. Further along the corridor, murmured voices and shuffled footsteps alerted him to the closeness of the appointed time.

It was not his job to judge. That had already been done

to the satisfaction of the law of the land. But he knew of the prisoner. It would have been difficult to have avoided that knowledge. A hardened footpad who was in the pay of anyone who cared to hire him. It was rumoured he was leaving the police with all the details of his career. It was likely that the repercussions of the case would strike fear into those who had hired him. And some names were straight out of the society pages. Well, there would be busy times ahead. Not that he wanted more work. But it would not be right to hang this man if his employers did not face justice as well.

* * * * *

The prisoner waited for the priest to say the final words. It confused him, the desire of the authorities to bless him before they killed him. But it seemed to make them feel better so he went along with it. He was not frightened of death. He had witnessed so many deaths in his time that he understood what was coming. He ascended the scaffold. He observed the structure, the joints, the solidity, workmanship. He nodded his head with satisfaction.

The hangman mounted the scaffold. He was soberly dressed in black with a good jacket, a starched collar and a top hat. The sound of his sturdy boots on the platform echoed around the yard. The prisoner observed the hangman's hands. They were good strong hands, clean, with nails cut short. Cared for hands. The prisoner looked him calmly in the face. It was an unremarkable face, a forgettable face. But it gave an impression of dignity and respect. A hard thing to achieve for such a man. Their eyes met. Neither flinched or looked away. Then the hangman moved towards him and held out the black bag in one hand and the loop of the noose in the other. The prisoner nodded towards the noose.

He felt the thick, heavy coil anoint his neck. It settled like an old friend. He noted the smoothness of the quality rope against his skin and the satisfying symmetry of the winding knot. He would have touched it if his hands had not been bound. It would be a pleasure to be hanged with such a noose. He smiled. The black bag was placed over his head and he waited, expectantly, for his end.

Beautiful Dreamer

a short story by Nick Johns

The flames from the shack convert my dreams to smoke and waft them aloft to float, swirling and diminishing, towards the distant horizon.

I watch from the ridge, hunched down in the long grass, imperfectly hidden but safe. My tormentors are swept up in their infectious, heady moment of destruction. Their hate binds them together in this instant. The Richards boys stand shoulder to tattooed shoulder with Billy and Asa Hardesty, egged on by other, lesser players. For this endeavour the raised weal scars across Billy's back, a tangible roadmap of their feud, are forgotten.

I worm my way backwards, not standing until the crest shields me. I brush the rich dark loam from the knees of my already stained jeans. My hands shake off the last dusty traces of this place and I set off for the road.

Walking has different tunes as well as different rhythms. Walking away is an etude, in a minor key. The notes repeat over and over. A practice piece for your future, constructed from fragments of the ballads of your past. Each step is a beat, echoing your heart, running down towards its last tick.

Eventually my thumb fishes a big truck out of the raging, smoky waters of the highway and I climb aboard, my melancholy melody now drowned out by the roaring techno beat of the accelerating diesel engine.

I lean back into the cracked leather seat and breathe in the driver's world, savouring it like a gourmet. I identify a tang of bitterness and an aroma of long lost love overlaid with the more mundane strains of tobacco and loneliness. He casts a sideways glance at me and I catch it easily.

"Where you headed?" The road warrior's standard opening.

"Second star to the right and straight on 'till morning."
My unfamiliar return gambit causes him to pause before venturing his next move.

"I guess you ain't from round here?"

"Not anymore."

"Travellin' man, then?"

"Since they burned my place down this morning."

He gives a disgruntled huff, cricking his road-stiffened neck with audible clicks while I reflect on the unsatisfactory quality of truth as a conversational medium.

After thirty minutes and a similar number of silent, awkward miles, I spot an approaching town.

"You can drop me off here."

He crunches roughly down through the gearbox, grinding my unwelcome presence between the cogs, before stopping obviously, rudely short of the town outskirts.

"Thanks. Have a safe journey." I jump down, gravel crunching beneath my feet before stepping back to avoid a lungful of diesel smoke as the truck pulls away with a disapproving roar.

I set my feet to the road. They know the routine of the blacktop. My old familiar friend and I once more reunited, we settle immediately into the companionable cadence of my resumed rootless existence.

Above me, I notice wispy shapes running before the stiffening breeze and wave the net of my imagination above me, trying to capture some new dreams, suitable for this new place.

Win Some, Lose Some

a short story by Nick Johns

Her mind was seized with a sense of elation so intense she screamed silently.

* * * * *

It had begun as just another morning, indistinguishable from most of the others since she had run away.

Her growling stomach had woken her. Millie had squirmed out from under the dumpster and tripped over the holdall, measuring her length on the heedless asphalt.

She cursed her skinned knees and the world in general before balefully regarding the cause of her fall.

Black leather, scuffed like welfare's salvaged shoes, sadly soaking up the driving dawn rain, it mocked her. The street light caught the glint of the brass zipper and her anger was washed away in a stream mixed of curiosity and avarice.

Millie grabbed the worn handles, the wet leather slimy in her grasping fingers, and trudged and splashed towards the bus station, praying just once she would find a discarded umbrella that had not already blown inside out.

An early morning sheen of diesel fumes hung heavy in the air as the first buses coughed asthmatically into life, prodded awake by their sullen drivers.

Millie's arm muscles shook by the time she could finally drop the bag.

She pulled open the zip. Wraps of green paper fell from the bag, some crinkled from the night's soaking, and swirled around her feet like a pack of damp eager puppies.

Millie fell to her knees, ignoring the scrapes, scrabbling to round up all the one hundred dollar bills, stuffing them back into the holdall.

* * * * *

"Hi, Millie? You want breakfast?"

Wayne, the night manager, called across the forecourt.

"Oh, hi, Wayne. No thanks... just got back from a night at the Waldorf – couldn't eat another thing!" She waved him away.

One hundred dollar bills... thousands of them in a bag that size!

She felt faint.

She had to get somewhere to think this through. A hotel room. No, they'd never let her in looking like this. After all, the doormen had moved her on months ago, before her wardrobe became so... street chic.

Should she buy some clothes? No. Nowhere open yet.

With that kind of cash she could get them to open.

Hell, once she was fixed up she would get a guy to pay a call on Jeff and return with interest all he had given her in the...

No. Why bother with that low life?

From now on her life was different. From here on it was all gravy, baby...

"You want to give me my bag back, sweetheart?"

Rain-slick hair, sharp suit, and sharp eyes - but the stiletto looked sharper.

Millie backed away, leaving the predator the kill for himself.

He zipped the bag and strutted off, heading uptown.

Millie's tears were indistinguishable from the rain running down her face.

Then she noticed a green corner peeking out from beneath the sole of her tennis shoe.

"Hey, Wayne! Maybe I'll have that breakfast after all – on me this time!"

Carefully peeling off the sodden bill, Millie began to whistle.

All in the Mix

a short story by Nick Johns

Life is like mixing cocktails. Adding things together make a whole new thing. A lifetime's worth of unrequited love mixed with a gallon of faith and trust is a stable compound; stir in a large dash of untraceable money and, sure as shit, it turns into betrayal, with a whiff of avarice for good measure.

The frost-rimed window distorts my view of the street, like looking through a snowman's kaleidoscope. If I stand in just the right spot, though, there is a clear patch, barely big enough to see trouble coming. But it is coming tonight, like it always does.

In the halo of the solitary working street light, I can see her waiting. Cool and beautiful as ever, she wears her designer labels like armour from the cold that she never seems to feel. As she flicks her lighter, the flame illuminates a face more perfectly painted than any Michelangelo ever captured. A face I know as well as my own. I had thought that I knew the person behind it too, but, hell, one out of two ain't bad.

It goes to show, you can't be sure about much in this world, but the one thing I am sure about lies nestled, cocked and loaded in my coat pocket.

The thing about the cold is, it carries sound – messages for the brain to turn into pictures. You can create a whole movie in your head from the evidence of your ears – if you know the back story.

The slam of a car door – no, two doors. A big car, heavy doors.

Footsteps across the cobblestoned street, slow and steady.

The screech of a reluctant gate hinge.

Bam!... Bam!... Bam!...

18

A tired, communal door shivers under the weight of the blows.

The buzz and click of the entry system. Someone buzzes a problem in – to save their door, I guess – and in the hope that it isn't their problem.

Count the treads of four feet on threadbare carpet. Thirteen steps to my floor. Unlucky for some.

Wait.

Another thirteen steps, but only one pair of feet.

A crash of a door, a scream, a slap, and silence for a heartbeat.

The floorboards creak above me. I follow them across the ceiling, the light fitment trembling briefly, then settling as the steps move to the back.

The back!

I snatch the precious carpetbag and rush to the rear of the flat to cover the old, disused communal staircase, a relic of the building's grander days.

Stamp. Stamp. Stamp.

As the echo fades from the flat above, two doors are kicked in.

One above me, one behind.

I fumble for my forgotten .38, but the hammer snags in the lining of my coat.

A sharp metallic tap tap tap bounces down the stairs.

BANG!

Blinded by the flash, I stagger back, stunned and deafened.

A blunt, brutal, blow buffets my ears and I go down like a house of cards in a winter squall, bouncing once off the wall and once off the floor.

Face down, one eye examines the worn, dirty boards closer than I ever want to.

A harsh metallic taste invades my mouth, dripping down my face and pooling dark on the floor, some running away through age-old cracks, into the flat below.

A pair of red stilettos glides into my field of vision and, using a slip of white lace handkerchief, a perfectly manicured hand reaches down daintily for the fallen bag.

As the shoes spin away to leave me to my fate, my .38 shouts from my pocket.

I see one of the perfectly formed feet disappear in a cloud of red mist.

She falls in front of me, face scrunched up and screaming. Not so pretty now, eh?

There you go, sweetheart; gunpowder, lead, and blood.

The perfect cocktail.

The Unknown Witness

a poem by Allan Shipham

Sleep you well, my sleeping beauty,
aged only six and such a cutie.
But, alas, she moves and stirs
as her beloved kitten purrs.

Disturbed is she from the street below
when the land of Nod said hello.
She gets up and goes to the curtain
to survey the cause and make certain.

Above her mum's shop she's lived for ages,
while teenagers below have brawls and rages.
It's the centre of town, no forewarning,
and always forgotten in the morning.

But this night she sees a stabbing,
blood and gore, pushing and grabbing.
Shocked is she to see this sight,
on such a dark and starry night.

One bad man wears a white tracksuit,
the other sunglasses, such a brute.
Draws a knife,
takes a life.

Three steps back she nudges her toys,
they all fall down and make a noise.
She tries her best not to wake her brother,
but the crash is enough to wake her mother.

From her bed close by Mum hears a din,
she opens the door and looks in.
Is everything alright, my sweetie?
Yes Mummy, I don't feel sleepy.

Back to bed, darling, it's the middle of the night,
by the sound outside, there's some kind of fight.
I hope you don't grow up like that,
stay here where it's warm, just like that cat.

Yes, Mummy. You know... I hope that he's not hurt badly.
Mum looks at the cat; of course she'd no idea, sadly.

The Other List

by Nick Johns

Stick close, kid, I'll show you how it's done... You do this one... Screams and tears don't bother you, right?... Good, you'll see plenty tonight... Quiet! Don't wake the others... No, the Boss don't dirty his hands, just does the nice stuff, image-conscious, see?... Hurt them? Hell, yeah, but that's kinda the point... Now for the fun part... There – that red-headed kid... Of course we have to, don't wimp out!... He's the reason we're here... An object lesson, He calls it... Yeah, I've checked twice, like always... Let's show him what it means to be on Santa's other list!

A famous villain

a poem by Allan Shipham

Are you that smell at the end of my snout?
Or the shadow I saw when the lights went out?
Are you the creak at the window I mistook for a bird?
Or the underfloor scratches I thought I heard?

Are you the presence I feel all of the time?
That makes my skin creep and makes my hair climb?
I'm learning about you, I don't like what I hear,
you fill me with dread and you fill me with fear.

They say you're a villain; you're out for our souls,
confusion and mayhem are your spiteful goals.
I think that I know you, know what you're about,
If you ever come near me I'll scream and I'll shout.

You're quick and you're vicious, but most of all mean.
You don't care who you've chosen, you've never been
seen.
When others tell lies the bells will chime.
Sick to my stomach, I feel all the time.

I imagine you know me, you're plotting deceit,
I'm hoping to God that we never meet.
You keep me guessing, you keep me thinking,
I better watch out, you'll pounce when I'm blinking.

You're the subject of stories since times of old,
you're out to destroy me like a cough or a cold.
Just when I think that I've worked you out,
You surprise me and crush me.

The famous villain is... Doubt.

Finders Keepers

a short story by Nick Johns

Is there one here tonight?

I need one.

I really do.

I scan the eager, laughing, candy apple smeared faces.

With the casual expertise of a lifetime's practice, it is possible to search even whilst squirting the gullible dwarf full in the face with my fake flower.

They roar.

They always do.

Clinging to their mummies and daddies, they rock and jump, pointing and shouting at my antics, unaware of my scrutiny.

I watch for the eyes.

They always give it away.

Towards the end of the set, just as the tyres fall off the car and the wheel comes off in my hands, I spot him.

Under the stands, in the shadows, hidden from the barkers and roustabouts, I spot two unmistakable eyes; big, round and shiny, two full moons in eclipse. A mouse in the skirting, even though ready to bolt at any moment, the Boy's eyes solemnly follow every nuance of the act.

For the blow off, I wave the bucket full of water hither and yon, teetering on the verge of a seemingly inevitable fall, yet impossibly maintaining an unsteady equilibrium. The front rows in the crowd flinch as I approach, then laugh as the bucket swings away from them, gasping once more as I lurch back towards them.

Finally, I launch the water into the audience and the screams turn to laughter as the water is revealed as glitter and falls, a sparkling, gleaming shower of deceit, into their relieved laps.

As I take my bow, pausing to kick the bowing dwarf

into an impromptu somersault, I produce a red, shiny ball from behind my ear, and flip it across the floor and into the shadows towards the Boy.

It rolls to him and, just as he reaches out a tentative hand to grasp it, it pops, transforming into a miniature replica of my car. His hand, frozen in shock as it changes, hovers above it, before squirreling it away into the pouch of his grubby, ill-fitting dungarees. He goggles at me, eyes wide with a wonder I remember but have long since mislaid.

I wink.

Sprinting across the sawdust ring, I kick my treble-sized shoes into the wings and dash for the exit. I gasp as the cool night air sticks my costume to me like a damp second skin and the dew-wet grass chills my feet.

Skipping lightly over the wire-taut guy ropes, I locate the dark patch of the Big Top, unilluminated by the lamps at the entrance, and wait.

Almost immediately a hand appears under the edge of the canvas, closely followed by an arm, a shoulder, and, with an imagined pop, the Boy's head. Like a snake sloughing off its skin, he sheds the tent. He scrambles up, bent double, hands on knees, gulping in air after his exertions.

I reach out and grab him by the scruff, hoisting him off the ground.

He flips and wriggles like a line caught trout.

I swing him round, bathing him in the flickering light of the nearest oil smoke torch.

"Well, look here, what have we caught?"

His wriggling turns to thrashing, but my arm, strengthened by years of carnie work, holds him firm.

"Where's your ticket, Boy?"

His eyes roll.

"Well? Cat got your tongue, Boy?"

He shakes his head, quietening down a little, all except his eyes; they dart here and there, seeking an escape route.

He mumbles.

"Don't tell me, you must have dropped it, eh?"

He nods.

"So, we've got a freeloader – as well as a thief."

"I'm no thief!"

"No? Well how will you explain to the Constable how you came by that little red car in your pocket?"

"...But you..."

"I what? Did your mummy buy it for you? Shall we go and ask her?"

A veil drops over his eyes and he slumps, perfectly still for the first time. I watch as a single tear tracks slowly down his cheek.

"OK, not your mummy then. I know. We'll ask your daddy. Someone in the Top must know who your daddy is. What will your daddy do about you stealing toys?"

The Boy seems to shrink in his clothes.

I know then.

This one is just what I am looking for.

Do I really want him?

Of course I do. I need him.

The others... well, it has been years since the last. If he's not the one...

My sadness doesn't show to him, my painted smile still shines, though the greasepaint is surely smeared in places, I know.

I change to my cheery voice, the one all the children love.

"Of course, this could all be OK..."

"It could?" He sounds doubtful.

"Absolutely. It could be a finder's fee for bringing me something I need."

"What did I bring?"

"Why, yourself. I need a Boy."

"Why?" His eyes narrow, calculating, suspicious.

I laugh, a bark that startles him. I've seen that look before on too many young faces.

"For the circus. All circuses are hungry for Boys. Didn't you know that?

He shakes his head.

"Oh yes. Boys and circuses. They belong together. Like magnets and iron filings. A circus is what a Boy wants. A circus is travel, adventure, a family. And Boys are what a circus wants. A Boy is fresh, energetic, questing. That's why circuses don't stay in one place; because of the limited supply, you see."

He doesn't, I can see.

"But they must be the right kind of Boys. Boys like you maybe. Are you a circus Boy, Boy?"

He shrugs.

I fix him with a stare.

"This is it, Boy. You decide. Stay and go back to... what? Your daddy? This fly speck town? Or come with me, join the circus, fly away with us."

I drop him and he slumps on the wet grass, like a string-cut marionette.

I walk away, listening intently.

"Can I keep the toy?"

"Sure. Your finder's fee. Like I said."

Oversize farm boots shuffle and then a small grubby hand tugs at my hem. I look down.

I hold out a hand and his grips mine, hanging on like the offer might slip through his fingers.

As we walk together towards the caravans, I think for a moment of all the others and what they have become, and I smile – for the first time tonight.

"Why a circus Boy can be anything. Small ones start out as rigging monkeys, but they can grow into acrobats, or jugglers, or Lion tamers, or strongmen..."

"... or Clowns?"

"Yes, Boy. Some even become Clowns."

I thrust my free hand deep into my pocket and find the smoothed, now shapeless remains of a toy car that a Clown once gave me.

The Devil's Alternative

by Nick Johns

The shooting's stopped.

I told him. He wouldn't listen.

If the army couldn't stop them, how would he, or our walls around the house?

They'll be crossing the bridge about now.

"OK, kids, time to come in now."

Only three shells left in this old pistol.

"Quiet! We're going to meet Daddy."

Lord forgive me.

Quid Pro Quo

a short story by Nick Johns

If I'd known he'd be there again, I'd have brought the money.

Guess it's bad manners to employ a professional killer then not pay him.

I'd see exactly how pissed off he was by the weapon he had brought. I reached for the switch.

"Don't touch that. Some things are best in darkness. Just like your poor wife's... accident."

My shaky hand dropped away.

"Jon. About the money..."

"I've been thinking about that. What would you say to a proposition?"

"Proposition?"

"You do something for me – and you don't need to worry about the money again."

"Do something?"

"Yes. I want you to kill someone."

"Who?"

"Me. I want you to kill me."

* * * * *

So, that's why I'm wheeling a gurney out of the mortuary at 2am.

Oh, killing Jon? That was the easy part.

I phoned him. He became an emergency admission when I was on call.

I told Geraldine, the night nurse, I'd attend to this patient. She was always looking for quiet time to write.

Jon shook my hand before I gave him the injection. By the time Geraldine heard the alarms and wandered in, Jon was dead.

She took his pulse and called me.

A massive myocardial infarction. A quick squiggle on a death certificate, job done.

"Some people just live life too hard. Tough on a fairly young guy, though."

She peered at me.

"We all pay for all our sins one day

For evil does not wash away

Though smooth the road for mile on mile

Beware the final Serpent's Smile."

"Yeah, right. Nice one Gerry."

I finished the paperwork and sketched a goodbye wave at Geraldine, still mumbling her gloomy, night-time poems.

* * * * *

I had discovered the current admin password for the clinic computer system, and, once in the basement mortuary, swapped Jon's records with another recent stiff. I pushed him out along the deserted corridor.

I checked the loading bay. Periodically we had to call the cops when some junkie remembered there were drugs inside, and figured this quiet place might be their way in.

I unzipped the body bag and gave Jon another shot.

He stirred, then sat up, stretching his recently paralysed muscles, before hopping on to the concrete floor.

I handed him the bag of new clothes.

Dressed, he reached out his hand.

"A black Dodge truck, just around the corner." I flipped him the keys. His catch showed his reactions had recovered.

"The cops will buy it?"

"Trust me. You're dead. Buried later this week."

"Thanks, pal."

He reached out his hand again.

As we shook, he pulled me towards him. Off balance, I slumped against him. His left hand snaked behind me. I

31

felt a sharp jab in my neck.

Falling away, I saw him pocket the bloody scalpel.

"Just another junkie attack. Tragic. But no-one stiffs me on a contract."

He smiled down.

"I'm a man of my word. I promised you'd never again worry about the money you owed me."

The Cleansing Fire

a short story by Nick Johns

I bury my face in her shirt, sobbing. Her scent insinuates itself into my tingling nostrils and draws me toward her, even now. I resist the siren call of her screams and let the crumpled garment drop from my useless fingers into the flames. And I step off to join it.

* * * * *

It had all started so easy; a trip to the pharmacy to replace her dwindling supply of meds. A quick in and out; no more dangerous that the monthly trip to forage for food.

I'd nailed the door shut and slid a note ringed with kisses under the weathered oak. I'd shrugged to adjust the familiar weight of my ballistic vest and checked that I was locked and loaded before dropping down the hatch and crawling out to meet the watery, winter dawn.

It had all gone to hell. Newly blocked streets had made for massive detours and delays. By the time I had all the drugs, I was running dangerously late. Lengthening shadows swarmed across every street, growing fast as the sun fled, phantom fingers reaching to pull me into the dark.

In movies in the old days, how many times did you shout at someone who got into a car in the dark without first checking the back seats? What can I say? I was in a rush to get back to her – and more than a little spooked by then. Hey! It's not like they would steal the car. They don't drive.

I jumped in and gunned the engine. The roar of the unsilenced V8 echoed off the concrete.

I felt a hand grab at my shoulder and threw myself flat on the bench seat. The hand scrabbled for a hold before falling away. I swung the shortened twelve gauge on its strap and fired blindly through the seat.

BAM! BAM!

I rolled out on to the road, and lay there, ears ringing and hands shaking from my narrow escape, gulping for suddenly scarce air. No injuries.

Jumping to my feet, I snatched open the rear door to clear away the remains of my stowaway. I should have grabbed another car, but the old sedan had been hers in happier days and I wanted to hang on to it. I dragged the shredded body out on to the road. As I turned to get back in the front, the body heaved and snatched my leg. I kicked out and, as I wrenched away, I felt nails scratch down my leg as my Levis rode up above my boots.

BAM! BAM!

The body jerked across the asphalt like a gaffed fish being landed and lay still – for now. I fishtailed away and took three tries to get the flame near enough to my Camel to light it.

The tingling in my calf started almost straight away. I rubbed it hard with the side of my boot, hoping it was just an adrenaline twitch. By halfway home, my whole leg was burning and the other was tingling. I figured I had a couple of hours at best. I needed a plan.

* * * * *

I skid to a halt on our drive and fall out of the car. My whole body feels like it has been flensed and dipped in salt. My legs are numb and I move now with their characteristic shamble. My neck tingles. I can sense her presence.

Inside, I call, "Honey, I'm home!" Like always.

"Quick, out the window, my husband's here!" comes her accustomed reply.

After bumping legs that no longer belong to me up the stairs, I lean my head against her door.

"Baby. Listen carefully. We've got a problem." My

tongue tingles and I feel like my mouth is full of dry crackers. I hear her wheelchair cross towards the door.

"What's happened?"

"One of them's here. In the house. No. I'll kill it. Remember, you've got a revolver on the dresser. Love you Babe..."

The flames from the paraffin splashed about the lobby crackles and flickers, consuming the stairs. The smoke swirls, dancing with me, beckoning me to destroy the thing that will surely kill her if I wait. I grab blindly at the laundry pile. I bury my face in her shirt, sobbing.

Was it worth it?

a short story by Jason McClean

Chapter 1

"Was it worth it?" snarled a voice behind Diane, quickly followed by a kick in the ribs. A punch caught her in the throat and another on the nose. She collapsed.

Her body was light and free, her consciousness drifting away.

Then another voice, shouting, adult and angry. "What's going on here? You three get off that girl. What do you think you are doing?"

The fists and feet stopped striking her. Diane slammed back into the here and now, pains from all over her body complementing the copper flood of blood in her mouth.

It had all started with The Retard.

The Retard was Audrey, the class anorak, complete with glasses, teeth braces and squeaky voice. She had been sitting eating her lunch under a tree when the three Year Six girls had gone hunting for fun.

"Can't afford hot dinners, Retard?" The leader Alice had poked at her. "Bread and butter is for bad girls, ones that go to prison. You done something bad, Retard?"

Diane had been walking by. She stepped in between the three bullies and Audrey. "Leave her alone."

It had all happened subliminally, automatically. It was wrong to bully.

Alice, Betty and Cara ruled the girls of the school, and most of the boys, with their iron fists and caustic tongues. They had the weight and muscle to back up anything they did and often used them, sometimes from necessity and other times for pleasure.

"Look who it is," smiled Cara. "It's Diane, 'I've got no mum,' Kent."

"I think she's The Retard's best friend," laughed Betty.

"And if The Retard has been bad, then maybe The Orphan has been bad too," suggested Alice, smacking a fist into the palm of her hand.

"Just leave her alone," said Diane, face turning red with a combination of anger and fear.

"Or what?" said Alice, face right in Diane's, breath stinking of cola and something else sweet but disgusting. "Orphan."

That was when Diane had stepped neatly back and head butted the girl straight on the nose. She had never head butted anyone before, but this was a strike of righteousness, pure justice. Alice's nose exploded and the girl fell back as if struck by a train.

That had given Diane a moment to think. "What am I doing?" In the second or possibly two that ticked by before the other two girls started punching and kicking her, she knew exactly what she had done. Something stupid, reckless and foolish. She should have walked right on by and let Audrey take a kicking.

But she hadn't.

She had taken one look at Audrey, a quiet girl who kept herself to herself. Audrey had few friends but was brilliant at anything the teachers threw at her. She was more a genius than a retard. But she was also an easy target for bullies.

So Diane had done the right thing. She had stood up for the underdog, the girl being bullied. And she had paid the price.

Miss Andrews cleared the three bullies away in a whirlwind to the headmistress's office while Mr Stone, the PE teacher, was left to administer first aid to Diane. Her nose was sore and leaking blood, her top lip split and bleeding. A tooth felt wobbly and her body was already erupting in bruises from the kicks. Her head throbbed where hair had been viciously pulled.

"What happened?" asked Mr Stone, the only male teacher at the school and normally a cool dude, dabbing the blood away from her chin with a wet cloth.

"I tried to do the right thing," said Diane, voice a little strange and thick as her lip was swollen. "They were bullying Audrey and I stood up for her."

"I see," said Mr Stone, getting a fresh cloth and discarding one scarlet red with blood. "Was it worth it?"

Diane stared at him.

"You should have gone and got a teacher instead," he said. "Look at the state of you now. I doubt you'll do that again."

That was not the response Diane had been expecting. She was rebuked. For doing the right thing. For standing up for a weaker girl. There was no sympathy or understanding. If anything, Mr Stone looked at her as if she was simple.

But his look was more than that. His eyes were filled with pity. Genuine pity for her, as though she was the lowest of the low. Not the comforting sort of pity, more the sort that came with a dose of scorn as an aftertaste. She should have known better.

A sharp tug in her stomach accompanied a raging current that was making her blood boil. It was a revelation to recognise it. She had learnt the word in English class and looked it up in the dictionary. It was injustice she was feeling.

Mr Stone finished patching her up, patted her on the head patronisingly and told her to enjoy the rest of her lunch break. Then he left her alone, sitting under the tree, staring at the dark damp patches of her own blood on the green grass. Some of it was Alice's blood and the fire inside her cooled down slightly. But she didn't feel any better. She was scared. What would the three bullies do to her when they got released from the headmistress? There was another beating waiting for her in the near future, she suspected.

Diane hung her head and fought back tears. Was it worth it, doing the right thing?

A finger tapped her on the shoulder and she jolted up,

heart racing.

Audrey was standing behind her, eyes huge behind the thick plastic glasses.

"Thank you," said Audrey in a small voice. "Are you OK?"

"I'm fine," Diane said, smiling. She wasn't fine and a blind man could see that, but it was the right thing to say. The right thing to do. Again.

Audrey smiled and understanding shone from her eyes. She knew Diane was not OK and was scared. Probably because that was the state she lived in most of the time. But it was a kind smile. It was one that said Diane had made a friend. Maybe even a real friend. Diane felt a bit better.

Chapter 2

Michael Kent watched the arrows go up and down. First the green ones flashed, then the red ones. The red ones flashed a little bit longer. He glanced at his balance on screen. It had fallen. Starting at £10,000, it said he now had £9,459.

Another second passed and this time the green arrows had pushed it up to £10,111.

He had spent six months refining his trading system. He looked away. He needed to trust the system, the one bit of advice all the gurus he read agreed on. Don't get emotional, trust the numbers, the percentages.

Michael got up and paced in his home office. It was not easy to stay unemotional when your life savings were on the line. Despite all the successful tests he had conducted in the weeks before, doing it now with real money was different.

He glanced at the clock. America, or more specifically, Wall Street, came online at 2:30pm which was only a minute away. It usually led to a spike in one direction followed by a quick retraction before it decided which way it was going to go. In forty tests, that happened thirty-six times. That was what he was counting on. The odds were heavily in his favour. If it did that today, he would make a lot of money very quickly.

But he remembered the days it went the other way. He was spread betting on stocks and shares and no matter how many times he told himself he was investing, it was really still betting. The clue was in the name, spread betting. But there was a logic behind his method. He had to have confidence in his system.

Wall Street had fallen for the previous two days. Statistically, it would be unlikely to fall for a third day, given a complete lack of bad economic news. He was expecting a quick dip down before Wall Street got bullish and the index rose.

And when Wall Street rose, so would London's FTSE100. He had set his bet at £100 a point. He only needed ten points to make £1000. He had already set a limit. It would exit automatically when he made £1000.

It was 2:30pm. His screen was flashing red and green faster than the eye could follow. If his system was going to work, it would happen within ten minutes, it always did in the tests.

He had £10,500 in his account. His finger hovered over the sell button. £500 was a good win for today. He should take it.

But he remembered his system. He needed to stick to it. He pulled back and watched it go up to £10,800. Nearly there. Small time in the big scheme of things, but a real life changer for him and Diane if it worked out.

Then the red arrows started coming thick and fast. £9,100. The market had gapped down in one big jump. Michael's mouth went dry.

He needed to trust his trading system.

Five minutes later he was on £6,400 and sweating. A news ticker crawled along the bottom of the screen. The Federal Bank in America was raising interest rates in a shock move that was destabilising markets around the world. A quarter of a per cent. A tiny increase. A correction they were calling it.

But Wall Street wasn't happy and the FTSE was following its lead downwards.

He was down to £4,800. He needed to take the emotion out. It was a temporary blip, ride it out, the chart would start to go back the other way as it usually did. It was all about the averages. Mathematically everything liked to return to the average and right now it was dipping well below the average.

Five minutes later he was on £900. He hit the sell button and sat back in his chair. Drained. Exhausted. Ninety per cent of his life savings gone in under ten minutes.

He knew what had gone wrong. He had picked the wrong day to trade. Yesterday, he would have made his £1,000 easily. He did in the dry test. Probably tomorrow he would make £1,000. But nobody could have foreseen the interest rate hike.

All he wanted was enough money to take Diane on a nice holiday, buy her new clothes and treats. They hadn't been on holiday since her mother had died. They needed a lift.

Michael hung his head in his hands and sobbed. £9,100 was a lot of money to lose for him. It was five months' take-home pay. It was what he and his wife Corinne had saved up for a rainy day. It was Diane's first car when she grew up. It was security if he lost his job.

Now it was simply gone.

He had read somewhere that 97% of spread betters lost their money. He hadn't believed it. He was lured by the tax-free earnings. He had thought himself clever enough to create a system for trading.

He had been a fool.

Then it was 3:20pm. He grabbed his car keys. It was time to pick Diane up from school.

The last thing he did was shut down his computer. He felt hollow inside.

He was nearly broke again and £9,100 behind where he

started. But he had done the right thing. He had tried to make a difference to their lives. The result was a difference all right, a bad one.

The 15-year-old Ford Fiesta started on the third turn of the key, wheezing into life. It juddered down the street and in five minutes he rolled up outside the school.

Michael hated the school. His little car was jammed up in between Range Rovers and BMWs. All of the mums were dressed in high fashion wellies and jackets that would never see the countryside. He looked behind their smiles, lips drawn upward, masking true feelings and miseries, desperately trying to get one up on each other, while their husbands worked all day and drank all night. He knew the score. They all came to his shop for food and he could see through the cracks in their make-up.

Diane came trudging out from the gate. Her face was battered and bruised. She threw her bag on the back seat and then climbed into the front. She said nothing.

Michael drove home. Silence was the third passenger. Michael didn't feel like talking. He had screwed up enough for one day and knew he couldn't find the words to say the right thing about what he had done or what had happened to her. It would end up all wrong.

Diane stared ahead and didn't meet his occasional glances. She didn't want to speak either.

Chapter 3

It was two weeks after her fight with the three bullies and Diane thought she had got away with it. They hadn't waited for her after school. They hadn't spoken or intimidated her. By contrast, Diane was a bit of a celebrity in the school with many of the other kids looking up to her and wanting to be friends.

Audrey had turned into a decent stick. She was from a nice family and they enjoyed the same music and television. They were getting on well, which was helping Diane with maths – Audrey could explain multiplication and decimals much better than her teacher.

All of Diane's bruises had healed and she was enjoying a lunch with Audrey, under the same tree where the fight had happened, when Alice, Cara and Betty walked up and stopped, less than three metres away.

Diane gulped and stood up, heart hammering to get out of her ribcage. This was the beating she had been expecting. The revenge.

"Hello, Retard," said Alice, not bothering to look at Audrey, eyes locked on Diane. "How are you doing, Orphan?"

Diane's fear turned to anger in one second and her hands clasped into fists. Alice saw them.

"Hey, we aren't here to fight, Orphan," she smiled, hands out, placating. "We just thought you two losers would like to see my new phone."

Alice was from a rich family. Everyone knew it. The teachers tiptoed around her as though afraid to say anything that might bring down the wrath of her father, a city banker.

Alice pulled out an Apple iPhone. It looked lovely and Diane's anger wavered. She would love a phone like that. It could play games, take photos, send emails, browse the internet and even make calls. Her face betrayed her desire.

"I thought you might like it," said Alice, holding it up. "It costs a lot every month but my mum and dad think I'm worth it. Where's your phone, Orphan?"

So there was the rub. She didn't have a phone; she couldn't afford one. Everyone knew she didn't have much money, that her dad was poor – or at least poor compared to their families. It wasn't going to be a kicking she received, not a physical one anyway.

She sighed and sat back down.

"No phone, Diane?" laughed Alice. "You'd have thought your dad would have got you one. After all, who else has he got to call? Not your mum, Orphan."

Audrey put her arm round Diane and shook her head.

"You are both Retards," exclaimed Alice. "But I'll

make peace, look here."

Audrey and Diane looked up and Alice pressed a button on the phone that made the sound of a camera shutter.

"See you suckers on Facebook later," laughed Alice, Cara and Betty, walking off.

A moment passed and Diane continued to eat her sandwich. Audrey kept her arm around her. "They are horrible people," said Audrey. "She doesn't deserve a phone like that."

Diane nodded. What sort of world allowed bullies to have nice phones and at the same time girls like her lose a young mother to cancer? It didn't seem fair or right. It was wrong.

After school, when Diane climbed into her dad's old car, she looked out the window and saw Alice smiling down on her from the back seat of a gleaming brand new Range Rover.

"What's up, little one?" asked her dad.

"Nothing," she said, wishing she could tell him how miserable it was having no mother. Having no money. It was the right thing not to tell him. He had worries of his own. But it felt as if everything was wrong.

Chapter 4

Michael was many things but he was not stupid. He had watched the stock market every day since his big loss and every time, it acted as his system predicted. If he had placed a spread bet on any of those days he would have made his £1,000 daily target easily.

But he hadn't.

The fact was he couldn't predict another unknown event and couldn't afford to lose their remaining savings. However paltry the £910 seemed, it was all they had. His system was proving reliable and working. But it would be wrong to use it again.

He saw Diane's friends at school in the latest shoes, designer lunch boxes and sitting in cars that cost as much as their house. He watched her look at them, not with envy, but with sadness. She knew she couldn't have the same things and didn't bother to ask him anymore. He had said no once too often. It tore at him that he couldn't provide more for her.

He watched the Range Rover speed past. The blonde mother at the wheel had bronzed skin, oversize sunglasses and looked deliriously happy as she waved at other mothers walking out of the school.

He recognised her from the shop.

"Who's that?" he asked.

"Alice."

"A friend of yours?"

"Not exactly."

"Oh."

There was a slight pause.

"Nice car," said Michael.

"Yes, she showed me her new phone today as well. It was nice too. Can I have a phone, Dad?"

He was tired of saying no and desperately wanted to cheer his daughter up. Cheer himself up. The chance to say yes rather than no presented itself to Michael. So he took it. "Yes, you can."

Diane whirled to face him, eyes shining. "Really?"

"Yes, of course, we can go and get it this weekend, nothing but the best for you." Michael said the words, really meaning them. It was the right thing to do. He felt better already.

"I want an Apple iPhone, the latest version," rushed Diane.

Working in a large supermarket meant Michael knew it was an expensive phone. £40 per month for two years. He could really use that £40 to save up for a holiday. To buy new clothes for Diane. To go out for a meal at the weekend. Forcing a smile on his face, "Whatever you want, my little one."

Diane was delighted and didn't stop babbling over her microwave dinner about her promised new phone. Michael was having second thoughts. The right thing would be to tell her the truth. They couldn't really afford it. She would understand.

But watching her face brighten with joy and anticipation, he forced himself not to snatch away her happiness.

He was bringing in a reliable wage, he was getting child support and, despite tax credits being cut, they still helped too. But he was borderline affording the mortgage each month after paying for school trips, new clothes for both of them when needed and the ever-increasing electricity and gas bills. When Corinne had been alive they had two wages to draw on. Now he was on his own and life was turning into a drudgery of survival. Financial oppression.

At 8pm, he went upstairs, dressed in his supermarket uniform and got Diane into bed. The babysitter was downstairs texting her boyfriend. She was 19, unemployed and took the £30 a night he paid her to help feed her habit for expensive clothes and vapour cigarettes. Sometimes Michael wondered if he would be better off being unemployed and spending recklessly. But he didn't have that choice. He was an adult, a lone parent.

His night shifts were only for six nights out of every four weeks and this was the start of the first block. His supermarket needed a night manager now it was open 24 hours a day in Kettering. He received a grunt of acknowledgement from the babysitter as he left.

Michael had worked his way up from being check-out operator to assistant manager. Corinne had supported him as he built a career and he missed her all the more now when he needed someone to talk to and confide in.

He was utterly unqualified to be a single father. He felt even worse now after wasting so much money betting on the stock market.

The night shift was a lot quieter than the day. He marshalled the skeleton staff into groups. Three groups would restock the shelves. One group would man the check-outs and customer services.

He remained flexible himself. He could do any of the roles, but spent most of his time browsing the customers who shopped late.

They were a broad mix of the population. There was a little old lady in a mobility scooter, charging down the aisles in a rush, her equally old husband struggling to keep up on foot.

There were policemen in pairs, shopping for sandwiches and drinks from the refrigerators near the doors.

Students tended to come after midnight, when, he suspected, they had realised that gaming and television couldn't actually contribute calories to their bodies.

It was around 10:30pm when an attractive woman strode into the store, pushing a large trolley and smiling with shining white, obviously dentist-augmented teeth. She looked as fresh as though it were morning and wore slim jeans and an expensive knitted jumper.

The security guard watched her more closely than other customers as she walked by, a smile toying with his lips as his eyes glazed over. Other men browsing the magazines at the front of the store stayed still, but eyes left pages and followed her swagger.

Women watched as well, their reactions different. Lips tightened, eyes hardened. Those with their own men stared at them to see if they were watching the new arrival.

Michael wanted to laugh out loud. He was sure there were all sorts of psychology lessons you could observe in a supermarket. Everything from jealousy through to insecurity and anything in between.

He didn't mind admiring a good-looking woman. Corinne had never cared. She knew she was the best thing for him – and he had known it too. He had always told her he might window-shop but he'd never buy or try any of the goods. She told him she would do the same. They laughed and loved each other for it.

Michael recognised the woman. She had bronzed skin that up close looked a bit too much like leather. She wasn't wearing the big sunglasses now as it was dark out, but it was the mother in the Range Rover from school. Alice's mother. The girl who wasn't exactly a friend to Diane.

Michael wondered at how quickly any instinctive sexual attraction he might have had for the woman simply evaporated. It was as though it never existed. Worse, his stomach turned and he felt revolted by her. All because his daughter and her daughter were not exactly friends.

She walked by, expensive perfume wafting. Michael walked in the opposite direction. What had been a normal evening was suddenly a little sour.

She could buy her daughter anything she wanted and Michael could barely afford a mobile phone for his.

He wandered over to the mobile phone section and located the Apple phone Diane wanted. It looked great. Much better than his four-year-old Nokia, apparently old school, according to Diane.

He had been right. The cost for a basic package of minutes and data was £40 per month on the nose. It was a lot of money that he couldn't really afford.

Michael busied himself on the customer service desk to take his mind off money problems. They seemed to follow him around like a ball on the end of a chain he could never shake off. In reality, he had a beautiful daughter, they were both healthy and he had regular income. They were comfortable. They should be happy.

But Diane wasn't happy and he knew it.

Then the blonde strode by again, trolley full as she returned to her expensive car, painted on smile still in place.

And that's when Michael had the idea.

How hard could it be?

It would be a lot easier than betting on the stock market. Had to be.

He placed the complaint papers he had been reviewing on the table and watched the woman exit the store.

He smiled.

"Couldn't afford the upkeep on that woman," said a

friendly voice.

Michael turned and nodded to his security guard, a down-to-earth man called Joe. He was always upbeat, a wise man with an insightful quip every time he opened his mouth. An observer of people.

Michael said, "I wouldn't want to spend my money on that, I don't like gold-diggers."

"True, true," said Joe.

Michael didn't move for a moment, his idea growing fast. He liked it. But it was wrong. Everything in his head and his base morality told him it was wrong.

But it was right for him. For Diane. It would be worth it. The woman would be insured. It was perfect for what he needed and it would solve at least some of his money problems. He could take Diane on a holiday. He could buy her any phone she liked.

He would rob the smiling bronzed blonde. Alice's mother.

Chapter 5

Saturday came slower than Diane would have liked.

Her new Apple phone would put her right at the front of the class. From zero to hero in a weekend.

And her dad was in good form about it as well. He was smiling more. He had a spring in his step and was kissing her on the head and cuddling her a lot. She liked that.

They drove into Kettering and parked behind the Post Office. Even that was unusual as she thought her dad would buy the phone from the supermarket where he worked. And he never parked in a pay and display car park, he always found a terraced street with free parking. But today was different.

The sun was shining, mirroring her mood.

"Why aren't we buying the phone at your shop?"

"I don't want people knowing my business there," said her dad. "And I think there are better offers from other networks."

"OK."

She ended up going for a rose pink phone. It had a big screen and came with white earphones. It had a superb camera and could download any number of games she liked. She watched as her dad handed over a credit card and signed documents. It cost £40 per month for two years. That didn't sound like much but Diane had done multiplication in school and she quickly worked it out. Twelve months a year. Two years. That was 24 months. Multiplied by 40. £960 in total.

The little box containing the phone sat beside the paperwork. She didn't really understand money, but £960 was a lot. She wasn't sure how her dad could afford it. A pack of her favourite little toy figures cost £2 and she only got them as a special treat. She worked it out. She could get 480 of them for the same price as the phone.

Diane really wanted the phone but it was prickling her. She didn't actually need it and no matter how she tried to ignore it, she knew her dad would end up struggling to pay for it. It wasn't right. She could live without it.

"Dad," she said, "can we really afford the phone? Maybe I don't need it?"

He looked at her thoughtfully. "We can afford it, my little one," he said, kissing her on the forehead. "Don't worry about it."

As they drove home, she held the box tight in her hands. She wasn't allowed to open it until she got home, so she didn't lose any of the contents. And as it was such a treat, she wasn't going to argue. She was savouring the wait.

"Will that phone be better than Alice's phone?" asked her dad.

"It's the same, I think," she said. "Maybe newer is better, though. I like my colour better."

"That's good then, isn't it?"

"Duh. Yeah!"

"Where does Alice live? Is she near us? Do you want to call in and show her?"

"No, she lives in Burton on the new estate, in one of the big houses," explained Diane. "I wouldn't want to visit her, anyway. She's not nice."

"Those are nice houses on that new estate."

Diane shrugged. She wasn't interested in houses.

They got home and she rushed into the house and tore the cellophane off the box. The phone was immaculate. "I need a phone case," she said, dismayed. "We forgot."

"We can't get one today," said her dad. "I think we've spent enough. Maybe next week?"

"But what if I drop the phone and it breaks?"

"You'd better be careful then."

Diane started her phone and went through the welcome messages and set up. She really needed a case. A pink one, with lots of flowers on it. But the niggle had returned.

They couldn't afford a case that cost £10. It seemed so small a price. Guilt was creeping up inside her, telling her that it was wrong she had the phone. She didn't need it. They needed other things much more than the phone.

Deep down she didn't know why her dad had allowed her to have an expensive phone. It was wrong. But it was very right as well. Although she didn't feel as good as she should have, it would be worth it on Monday when she went to school.

Chapter 6

By buying the phone Michael had committed himself to his plan. He needed more money.

He knew where the blonde lived and the car she drove. He would get the registration number on Monday at school and then it would be a ten-minute drive around the new estate to spot the property where they lived.

Then it would get a bit trickier.

But he was bolstered by an interview he had read in a magazine during his dinner break. It was with Sir Fred Sweet, the founder of a massive airline company.

It turned out he had started selling CDs on the street

and had ignored local licensing laws and flouted price controls to get started. He had broken the law to get a foot up and it had worked out for him. He was knighted and held up as an example of great capitalism.

Michael was going to do the same, in essence. Break the law a little bit. He was not expecting to get knighted for it, though.

He had an idea what sort of things these people owned at home. He watched them with their expensive phones at the check-outs, checking the time on their Swiss watches, taking fat purses out of Prada handbags.

If he played his cards right, he might get away with cash and valuables worth £10,000.

He had never tried this before and it was a real adrenaline rush. Life was in high definition. He was on high alert and his mind was crunching over possible problems and outcomes constantly.

The stakes were high. Much higher than the £9,100 he had lost on the stock market. That had been desensitized, he had hit a button, not actually handed cash across to another person. Robbing a home and doing it properly was going to be a lot more intense. There would be no going back.

If he were caught, Diane would be taken away and he'd end up in jail. He'd lose his job, his home, his reason for living.

That focused his mind.

But how hard could it be?

This was sleepy Northamptonshire. The woman and her family lived in a nice executive home on a new estate where neighbours rarely said hello because they were all so busy working to pay off their huge mortgages. Where all they did, he suspected, was pretend everything was brilliant and then go and slave for more money to feed their soul-draining lifestyles.

He needed a weapon. Guns were not commonplace and he had no contacts to source one. But he wanted something intimidating. Something that would get the woman's attention and hold it. Make her sweat with fear.

He had an old axe in the shed. It stood about three feet tall and had a pitted but lethally sharp iron head. He thought about that and discarded it. Too unwieldy.

He had a chainsaw. The proper type to cut through thick tree trunks. He had bought it years ago to clear trees from his small garden. It had made short work of the wood and would make shorter work of flesh and bone. It revved hard and stank of petrol exhaust fumes. Fear and confusion. That would work.

Michael took Diane to school on Monday morning and then followed the sparkling Range Rover all the way back to Burton Latimer. Famous for Weetabix and soon for an audacious robbery that was going to give him breathing space.

The bronzed blonde drove into the drive of a big new house. He went by and then turned around in a cul de sac. It gave him enough time to see her get out and enter the house. There was no other car in the drive, but a dry patch suggested one had been there relatively recently. There was a husband or partner.

Michael returned to the same cul de sac that evening on his way home from work. The Range Rover was present, but still no other car at 8pm.

Three weeks later, after checking the property at similar times of morning and night, Michael had a fair idea of what the family movements were. He was applying the same methodology he had used to create his winning spread betting system. That had failed on one occasion and then had been successful ever since. He had got that right. But it had gone wrong due to bad luck. He was determined not to let that happen here.

The husband was a short, stocky, heading for fat, middle-aged man. Given his long hours and lack of enthusiasm walking to his door, he looked to be the sort of bloke that preferred to spend time at work than at home. He had a family as an accessory, much like the new plate Mercedes coupé he drove. He normally returned home at around 9pm. Michael had even worked out why his schedule changed. It was down to the delay in trains from St Pancras. If the 7:45pm train was delayed, so was the husband.

The wife was at home from about 4pm every day. An elderly lady, probably her mother, visited on Monday and Wednesday after dinner at about 7pm. On both occasions, the wife went out for about ninety minutes to an aerobics class. He had followed her and found she went to different venues. She was trying hard to stay in shape.

The daughter, Alice, the only one Michael had a name for, went to all sorts of after-school activities and was rarely at home. She was picked up by friends or family and taken in other cars every time. She was normally home and the light in what he guessed was her bedroom was switched off at around 8:30pm. Swimming, Brownies, dancing, gymnastics and bowling were her staples Monday to Friday. He had followed her to each one. He was doing his due diligence.

Michael didn't like Alice much. She carried herself like a spoilt rotten little girl. He understood why Diane was prickled by her. There was something raw about her that was repulsive. Arrogant. Spiteful.

Underneath all that, Michael suspected something else. She was a little girl clinging on to any control she could get in a world where her father was never at home and her mother was too busy trying to keep up appearances. She was a girl that could have benefitted from a lot of love and attention. Instead, she got money spent on her and packed away to activities to keep her happy.

Michael felt sorry for her.

He settled on a day and time. Thursday evening, 8pm. The street was quiet as most families were home and tucking children into bed. Curtains were drawn as December approached. The husband was an hour away and the daughter thirty minutes from coming home from gymnastics class. He would have the wife to himself and all he needed was fifteen minutes at most.

It was a crime that would benefit his daughter. It was righteous. He knew the family would be insured against theft and loss. They would not suffer financially. He would only intimidate the wife, so the rest of the family would not be emotionally traumatised. He would be as quick as he could.

He was doing the wrong thing. He knew that instinctively.

But for the right reasons. He needed money to financially support his daughter. He needed to provide for her.

It was Wednesday night and he tucked Diane into bed and kissed her good night. She kissed him back and closed her eyes.

He would do anything for her.

Anything.

Chapter 7

Ever since she had got her phone, Diane had not been happy. It had brought nothing but misery and unhappiness. She didn't know how to tell her dad she didn't want it any more.

He insisted she take it to school and call him if she ever needed anything. She had called him the first day during lunch break and it had been exciting. But he had been busy and had to go.

Audrey had smiled at her and shook her head at the same time. She said she liked the phone but then started pulling out books and pencils to do maths. She told Diane to put the phone away, calculators were cheating.

Diane showed the phone to Alice and took a picture of her in revenge.

Alice shrugged her shoulders and walked off. "Welcome to the club," she said. "Don't bother looking me up on Facebook, we are not friends."

The games on the phone, the good ones at least, all cost money and she didn't have any cash, so she was limited to the freebies that were riddled with adverts. The adverts wanted to sell her stuff that she might have wanted but couldn't afford.

And in the last two weeks, no-one had called her. She hadn't called anyone either. The phone was useless.

Not only that, but she had seen a difference in her dad since buying the phone. He was distracted and out more often, constantly working. She had got a phone but it cost her time with her dad. She missed him and the time they spent together. What had started out so right had turned wrong.

After her mum had died, her dad had been brilliant. She missed her mum. Now she missed her dad and wanted him back.

Diane poked the phone and called her dad's number. He picked up on the sixth ring, his voice out of breath, "Hello, my little one, everything OK?"

"Where are you?"

"I'm out on my bike," said her dad. "I've stopped to talk to you."

"You never go out on your bike."

"Am I not allowed now? Is that what you called to tell me?"

"No," Diane laughed. "I just wanted to use my phone and I'm bored."

"You're at school. How can you be bored?"

"Oh, you know," said Diane. "All my friends are having hot dinners and I'm stuck here with a dull ham sandwich and no-one to speak too, so I called you." As soon as she said it, she was sorry. She sounded totally ungrateful. There was a short silence, then she said, "I do like the sandwiches and I wanted to say hello to you."

"Well, hello back," said her dad.

"Seriously, Dad, I do like the sandwiches, but maybe I could get tuna sometimes as well?"

"That's a deal. Now I better get on. I need to finish my bike ride and get home in time to pick you up from school."

"OK, see you later."

Diane hit the red button and sat back. She had the feeling she had made matters worse and pushed her dad even further away. All she had wanted to do was talk to him and even then she had put her foot in it.

Diane sighed and took a bite out of her ham sandwich.

Chapter 8

Michael had to juggle a few things that evening to cover his tracks. He told Diane he had been called in to work and would not be long, so the babysitter would be with her for an hour or so. If he wasn't home by nine o'clock, she would go to bed, but he was sure he'd be home before then.

He put his yellow waterproof top on and Diane raised an eyebrow.

"I want to try to lose some weight," he explained. "I'm doing a bit more cycling."

"You are seriously taking up cycling? In winter?"

Michael used his bike when scouting the target home as he didn't want neighbours recognising his car and number plate. He had found a bicycle route across nearby fields that took him to the estate and allowed him to see what was going on from the cover of darkness. It was the perfect vehicle for his getaway.

"Got to give it a try and the ride to work is not so far, a couple of miles each way and the inches will be dropping off my waist."

"You are not fat, Dad."

"Still, want to keep it that way."

Diane didn't look convinced. He stuffed a balaclava into his pocket, kissed Diane and told her he'd be home as soon as possible. The babysitter grunted at him as he left the house, her eyes glued on her phone screen, thumbs frantically tapping.

His heart was beating fast with excitement. It was the same feeling as when he had placed the spread bet. The fear, the anticipation. Knowing he was doing something wrong for the right reasons. He wanted Diane to have nice things. He was her dad and he was going to provide for her.

Doing the wrong thing had worked out for Sir Fred Sweet, why couldn't it work out right for him as well?

He got his bike from the shed and slung the chainsaw over his shoulder. A thrill of excitement danced through him. He could hardly believe what he was doing. It was a dark, cold evening and with every pedal revolution across the fields his fear grew, his internal devil egging him on while his internal saint told him to turn around, the risk was not worth it.

He had no lights on his bike, they would have been easy to spot during the getaway, but his night vision was good and the little moonlight shining through the heavy clouds was enough. He knew the way – he'd ridden it enough.

He got to the kissing gate by the estate in fifteen minutes. He hid the bike in a hedge and checked the chainsaw was ready to go.

He ran through his final checks and spotted the house. Lights were on, the Range Rover was on the drive, the street was quiet. Michael put on his balaclava, made sure no cars were coming or could be heard and dashed to the house.

There was a point of no return and when he rang the doorbell, that was it. It wasn't just a point of no return he crossed, it was a moral line as well.

The seconds waiting for the door to be answered ticked by impossibly slowly. It was near freezing but sweat was running down his back. He carefully took the chainsaw from his back and got ready to pull the cord and fire it into noisy, smoky life.

The door opened.

He saw the safety chain on the door was not latched. Good news. He didn't allow the occupant a moment to even glance out. He bashed through, knocking the person flying and slammed the door shut behind. He fired up the chainsaw and started swearing and shouting at the figure sprawled on the floor.

It wasn't Alice's mum.

It was Alice.

She was wide-eyed, screaming, in tears.

The blonde came running into the hallway before stopping, frozen in terror.

Alice was supposed to be at gymnastics. This was another line he didn't want to cross; he didn't want to terrorise a child. But the ends justified the means, and besides, he was committed now.

Michael stepped over the girl and punched Alice's mum in her too-perfect face.

She fell, blood spraying along with a tooth.

The hallway was stinking from petrol fumes and he revved the chainsaw again before shouting at the mother, "Get all your cash, jewellery and cards now."

Confused, she looked at him. Alice was still screaming. The beauty of these new estates was that every house was detached and well insulated. If you were on the footpath outside, you wouldn't hear a thing.

"Did you hear what I said?" Michael revved the chainsaw again and stepped deliberately towards Alice, aiming for an arm.

"No," screamed the mother. "I'll get money, anything you want."

He followed her to a desk in the kitchen where cash, wallets and cards were handed over. He stuffed them in his pockets. She kept babbling about not hurting her daughter.

He slapped her again. "Hurry up."

Alice was whimpering in a corner of the hallway, curled in a foetal position. He ignored her. It was wrong what he was putting her through. But she would get over it.

He took Alice's mum upstairs where the contents of two jewellery boxes were deposited into his now bulging pockets. He snatched a Rolex from a bedside table.

"Come on," he yelled at her, revving the chainsaw.

"What else have you got, don't make me hurt your daughter."

"Nothing, I swear," she screeched back, tears streaming. Shaking, she fell to the ground. "Please don't hurt us, we don't have much money, I've given you everything."

He stepped forward and punched her in the face.

She collapsed, unconscious.

He ran downstairs where Alice was still whimpering. He saw two mobile phones on a desk in the hallway. He smashed them under his foot and then ripped the landline out of the wall.

The arrogant spoilt little girl was long gone. She was a quivering wreck of fear. Pity washed over him fast, followed by shame. He had done this to her.

He switched off the chainsaw, threw it over his shoulder and got out of the house, slamming the door behind. He got to the kissing gate and was on his bike in under a minute.

He got home super quick, fear and excitement giving him twice the strength and speed as normal. He paused in his back garden, putting the bike and chainsaw away.

He was trembling. With excitement? Fear? Adrenaline? He couldn't really tell, but he felt more alive than anytime he could remember. He was enjoying the rush.

He took deep breaths and forced his hands to stop shaking. All the time he was listening for sirens but none could be heard. Had he got away with it?

He walked into the house at 9pm like he had promised. He kissed Diane, then paid the babysitter £20 for the hour she had been there. She left without taking her eyes off her mobile phone, grunting as the door shut behind her.

"How was your bike ride?" asked Diane.

"Good, thanks. I feel better for it."

"You do look rosy cheeked, Dad. Maybe cycling will be good for you."

"It will be, although it is a bit cold out there. Now get yourself to bed, it's late for a school night."

After the bedtime ritual of tucking her in, he deposited the loot from the robbery on the kitchen table.

His haul amounted to a second-hand Rolex that he might get £6000 for if he sold it on eBay or Gumtree. To his chagrin, he realised he couldn't value the jewellery. He had no idea if it was high or low end stuff. Still, anything was better than nothing.

There was £350 in cash and reluctantly he realised that he could do little with the credit cards despite all his great plans. They'd be cancelled before he could try to use them and he had forgotten to get the pin codes from Alice's mum.

That was it. £350 for his evening's work and some jewellery plus a watch he needed to sell.

The thought of capture pumped fear along his veins mixing with his blood.

Tears came unbidden to his eyes. What had he done? Like the spread betting it had turned out wrong.

Memories chased him. He paced up and down, eyes locked on the paltry pile of treasure.

A cold sweat took hold of him as he recalled the terror in Alice's face. The innocence he had stolen from her was not worth any amount of money. He gasped as if punched in the stomach. He was a monster. Doubling over in physical pain, he rocked on his heels for several minutes.

When he was in bed, he remembered the fear in the mother's eyes. The horror. The truth. They didn't have much money.

In reality, they were a one-parent family – just like Michael and Diane. It was predictable. The husband was rarely at home. He was away working to get the money needed for the lifestyle they lived. They had the same struggles, albeit on a different scale, to those he and Diane had.

Remorse piled on top of regret. Michael hated himself. He even thought about returning to the house and giving the stolen items back, asking for forgiveness.

At 4am he got out of bed and dressed, ready to go back.

But, instead, he washed his face and told himself to get a grip.

Doing the right thing now would be wrong. If he confessed and tried to make atonement, then he would lose his family, home, job, freedom and, most importantly, Diane, the real and only thing that mattered to him.

£350, a watch and some jewellery.

It wasn't worth it.

Chapter 9

Diane wanted her dad back, the way it used to be, before getting her expensive new phone. Since then, he had been constantly on edge. She knew it had to be from money worries. She wanted to fix that. It was the right thing to do.

"I think I am going to ask my dad if he can sell my iPhone," she said to Audrey over lunch. "I don't use it, it's such a waste, I wish I'd never got it now."

"It's a nice phone."

"It costs a lot of money."

"Yeah."

Then Alice, Betty and Cara walked by the tree where Diane and Audrey were sitting. Ever since the robbery three weeks before, Alice had been different. Diane felt sorry for her. She wasn't bullying any more and was prone to bursts of tears and wails of anguish. Diane's teacher had told the class that everyone had to be very supportive, that Alice had been through a terrible ordeal.

Their eyes met and Alice looked away. No longer commanding, but subservient. The change frightened Diane. It told her things changed and not always for the better.

The police hadn't caught whoever had carried out the brutal robbery. The attacker had broken Alice mum's nose and three teeth. The police said they were lucky he (they knew it was a man from his voice) hadn't actually used the chainsaw he had been wielding.

"Alice has got a new phone," said Audrey. "Insurance

paid for it apparently."

Diane nodded. Looking at Alice, it was clear that a new phone would never erase the memories or terror the burglary had put her through. No amount of wealth or money could make her forget. She was a shadow of her previous self.

Diane knew that by getting her own phone she had forced her dad into a bad place, somewhere he couldn't afford to be. And it was all empty. It meant nothing compared to the fun and time they spent together. A phone was a poor replacement for the love of her dad who was now so busy she hardly saw him. A new phone was a poor replacement for the innocence that Alice had lost.

She stared at Alice and wished she could tell her she understood a little bit about what she was going through. But they weren't friends and Diane was left with cold private sympathy.

Sitting at dinner with her dad that evening, Diane said: "Dad, I think it might be best if we sell my mobile phone."

He looked at her. The constantly haunted look on his face that had roosted there for the last few weeks chased away for an instant.

"I don't really use it and I know it is costing you a lot of money. I'd prefer to sell it if that helps. I really like it but I don't want us getting into money troubles. I think selling it might be the right thing to do."

Tears welled into her dad's eyes and he choked back a sob. Diane didn't know what to say. The last time she had seen him like this was when her mum had died.

"I can afford it OK, my little one," he said.

"Maybe you can, but that's not all of it. I don't use it much, Dad. I'd prefer we sold it and we spent more time together. Maybe we could go to the cinema once a month instead? The phone's great, but I don't like you working all the time."

He looked at her, eyes red and silent. The haunted look was back again.

"Please, Dad. I just want to go back to the way it was

before we got the phone."

"That's all I want as well," he whispered.

"Good. Can we sell it then?"

Another long pause. Then he said, "I have something to tell you. Something I am not proud about. But without your mum here I can't tell anyone else."

Diane nodded and reached over, taking his hands in hers over the table. She was doing the right thing, she could feel him coming back closer and closer to her.

"Your friend Alice, you know, the one who was robbed?"

"Yes, I feel so sorry for her, she's still not got over it."

Her dad nodded and looked away.

"I was the robber. I did it."

Diane wasn't quite sure what she had heard.

"I wanted to get money so I could buy you nice things. I wanted us to have a better life. But it didn't work out. I got very little and I hurt her mum. I think I hurt Alice as well, although I didn't touch her. It was wrong. I was trying to do the right thing."

There was bare truth and raw regret in his eyes.

"I got a bit of money but nothing like what I thought. I was even going to go and give it back and say sorry, but I would have been arrested and that would mean losing you. They would take you away from me. I'd go to prison. But that's the right thing to do. Maybe I should do the right thing."

"No," Diane said, instinctively. "You can't leave me. We only have each other. It might sound like the right thing to confess but it would be wrong. Mum is gone, I can't lose you."

Fear and self-interest drove her to that quick conclusion. No matter what happened she wouldn't tell anyone what he had done. She couldn't. It might be wrong to keep the secret but it was right because she needed her dad. He needed her.

"I did bad, Diane. I did something very wrong."

"We don't need money, Dad. We need each other,

that's all. I hate my phone. I hate it for doing this to us. For making you do what you did."

"I'll never do it again." Tears fell down his cheeks.

"I know you won't." She squeezed his hands hard. "I need you, Dad."

He got up, came round the table and hugged her. He had done a terrible wrong but in that moment, Diane couldn't help but feeling everything was so right. The hug was right. The closeness with her dad was right. The honesty, the openness, the needing of each other, it was all right. How could something so right be wrong?

She realised she may never understand the differences between right and wrong.

But was it worth it? Was everything that had happened – the pain, misunderstanding, robbery and scarred lives that brought them to this moment of perfect love and closeness with her dad – worth it?

She smiled grimly, her heart full of compassion and love.

Yes, it was worth it.

Ghost and Horror

The Good Boy

a short story by Beth Heywood

Donald's fingers delved into his trouser pocket and extracted a filthy red handkerchief. Flapping it open, he drew it slowly across his sweat-soaked brow.

The digging had been hard and worse lay ahead.

As a Virgo, he must always be perfect. His job title, "morgue orderly", didn't make the job easier, any less unpleasant. But he needed it to sustain himself outside the Locked Ward.

Laundering soiled and bloodied hospital bed linen was one thing. Incinerating abortions quite another. Which was why seven foetuses were packed into ice-cream cones lying alongside the seven holes he had dug.

He leaned into his spade. Three feet deep. That was enough.

Always a good boy, he would still carry out the necessities. And if that meant being locked away again, then so be it. But his conscience would be clear.

Taking the ice-cream cones in one hand, his fingers sought out each slimy unit. He placed one into each hole.

A quick shovelful of earth and the Innocents would return to the bosom of the Lord.

Finally done, he turned homewards, unaware that below the surface, seven pairs of tiny hands were frenziedly crawling towards the earth's surface.

Odds Against

a short story by Nick Johns

The snub-nosed, blue steel revolver pointed squarely at Santa. The barrel followed a bead of sweat dripping down his forehead but stopped right between his eyes.

I really thought about sitting this one out.

But I couldn't let it happen.

At that range, the bullet would paint the contents of his skull across the wall like a Jackson Pollock.

And I never liked abstract art.

I pushed off the wall of the alley and summoned forth a Gremlin.

I grabbed it by the scruff of the neck and pointed it at the gun, before it screwed up the streetlights or bollixed whatever else its gaze fell on.

It giggled, springing towards the swarthy, heavy-set guy in the handmade Italian suit and shoes. His Taurus .38 was a reliable piece, but no match for the mischievous power of the scaly imp sitting invisibly on his wrist.

Saint Nick, who by now was about as nervous as a mouse at a cat convention, stared at the hoodlum.

"I don't know how you did it, fat man," a gold tooth sparkled, "but you picked the wrong guy to play for a sucker. Say hello to Jesus." And squeezed the trigger.

The Gremlin chittered and placed its finger between the firing pin and the round.

Click.

I grabbed Santa by his hair and dragged him backwards off his feet. I dropped across his sprawling frame and his breath whooshed from beneath his whiskers like air from a smith's bellows.

The second round slammed into my back, and ricocheted off down the alley.

I jumped to my feet and clipped the gunman just hard

enough to put him out for the rest of the week. I made a mental note to send the Sandman to bring him some nice dreams while he was out; after all, he was the victim here. I looked down again and saw that he might need the Tooth Fairy as well.

I banished the Gremlin, then pulled our grubby absconder to his feet by his flowing beard, ignoring his slightly muffled squeals.

"OK, Nick, first off, leave the money," I said.

He gave me his trademark twinkling smile and murmured, "Money? I'm not sure I understand... "

His excuses stopped with a whoosh and he doubled over as I dug a jab in under his short rib.

"OK, OK," he wheezed once he had caught his breath. He turned his sack inside out and dropped a rain of multicoloured casino chips down on to the unconscious form of his former assailant. "There, no harm done," he whined at me. "Just letting off a little post-Christmas steam."

"By using your ability to know the Christmas wishes of children to read your opponent's minds in a poker game. Yeah, very noble, Santa."

He hung his head and shuffled a foot in a puddle.

"So I guess it's back to Lapland in irons again this year?" He held out his wrists.

"Not until you tell me where you sold the reindeer for your stake money," I replied, slapping on the cuffs.

Benjamin

a short story by Allan Shipham

I can't remember why, but I find myself walking through the greenhouse. As much as I like it, I have to admit it's been a while. I haven't been able to get out much lately. It's uplifting to see the pansies with such beautiful colours: reds, yellows and blues. My marvellous geraniums are also doing well this year. It should be warm enough to put them out soon. Maybe I'll transfer them to the conservatory until I'm sure the frost is finished.

I look through the glass into the garden. The morning sun fills every corner. How lucky I am to live in such a wonderful place. And it's a relief not to have the pressure in my head. Those pain killers I took this morning must have kicked in. So many pills! I must rattle as I shuffle down to the Post Office every Tuesday and the pub every Sunday lunchtime.

I pause to remember my beloved wife, Ethel. I can see her grave and the sunflowers and lavender I left there last week. I hope she saw them. She loved the contrast between the purple and the yellow. I hope she could smell them. She loved lavender. She was always regarded as a bit of an oddity, with her herb recipes and her doll collection. But she was my wife and I loved her.

And now I am in my study. I look at the books in my book case. My! How I've collected a lot. I've worked hard and I've achieved a great deal. On my desk is my favourite book, a leather bound first edition of *Huckleberry Finn*. How many times have I joined Huck and Tom on those adventures? I stroke the leather binding. I love the sensation across my fingers. I smile.

And to my farm. I've not visited for a while now, but it hasn't changed much. They still have the raver fired up. I can see the smoke rising from the chimney. How I loved that old beast. It has fed me and kept me warm most of my life. I look across the bottom field down to the river. I can see the sheep pen, the cherry and the apple trees. I remember Shep, Amber, Whiskey and of course Flash. You never forget a good sheep dog. How can I forget any one of them. I'll see them all soon.

I can hear voices but I can't hear what they are saying. The hearing hasn't been too clever lately.

I remember sitting in a wheelchair this morning beside a statue surrounded by lobelia. I was sitting with Robert, my son, Michelle, my daughter, and Ken, my son-in law. The children were running around the garden enjoying the space, there was a summer house and a swing. I remember Michelle crying – she was quite upset. Robert and Ken looked grim and comforted her. I knew nothing I could say would make things better, sometimes things just are, and you have to get on with it. The children were oblivious and broke the silence with their games. Michelle stopped weeping, looked across at the children and smiled.

"We're losing him now." A voice breaks my meandering. I can now hear the voice. It's not anyone I know.

"Love you, Dad." Michelle's voice is gentle and comforting. "Give Mum our love." I can feel warmth and some pressure from both my hands.

"Thanks Dad... for everything." Robert struggles, but his words mean everything.

Before me I see a tunnel and a bright light, my face feels warm and my energy returns. I know I want to move towards the light.

"It's all been rather lovely."

Lantern

a short story by Beth Heywood

All was silent in the house save for the flickering of the candlelight behind the eyes of the Hallowe'en Lantern. Jane turned over in bed. It was no use. She'd never sleep this way. She had to turn back. She had no choice. Reluctantly she opened her eyes and viewed the lantern. Why couldn't she get out of bed and blow the candle out? She already knew why. She's already tried last year and the year before that. Each year it became more difficult. This year it was impossible. The lantern had a name. Jack. Jack the Insane. She watched as the flame moved as if in a draught, and smoke came through the eye sockets. This was it. She tried to scream but no sound came from between her parched lips. Where was Daddy when she needed him? She already knew where. He was out. With his latest squeeze. The smoke from the lantern curled towards the ceiling, forming a picture in the half-light. Please, Daddy, come home. Soon. Sooner, she prayed, her mind now desperate. The smoke curled upwards and formed a figure. She couldn't help but watch. As she watched, the smoke transformed into a man. Even at her tender age, she could appreciate it was a good body. A body any woman would be proud to know. She watched his head, his shoulders, his chest emerge to become lifelike. Then lower down, his waist, his trouser buckle, his zip. Then, no trousers. Naked, he stood before her, resplendent and proud. She watched as he stiffened and became rigid. She gasped. He was bigger than a man had a right to be. Wouldn't her mother and sisters be jealous? Daddy, don't come home yet. Suddenly she heard the door slam. Damn. Now she would never know the joys of Jack the Insane. She sighed. She would have to wait another year.

One Dark Night

a short story by Allan Shipham

Above the abandoned Abbey, the Angels looked down with sadness and frustration. Tonight was going to be another night of demonic evil. Hope rested on the shoulders of one extraordinary individual. But he had no idea of his worth.

One dark night, Jim, the estate manager, grabbed his coat and opened the door. In no time, Cookie, his dog, was halfway across the field. Cookie was excited about his walks. He loved to chase ravens through the medieval building. He never caught them – he just liked to scare them. It was Hallowe'en, but that mumbo-jumbo never bothered Jim. He lived out of town so was never bothered by trick or treaters, didn't like pumpkin and hated horror films.

He started his patrol around the estate. It took about an hour and a half, but as always there was no rush. The bracing air and the clear starry night provided the best work environment Jim was ever fortunate enough to find. The darkness played its tricks around the decrepit building.

He might not have had any rational fears but he kept noticing unexpected movement in the periphery of his vision.

He dismissed it. You couldn't live on your own in a place like this without occasionally questioning the solitude. He knew it wouldn't be a werewolf or a vampire – they didn't exist – but he'd occasionally wonder if an escaped prisoner was looking for somewhere to lay low.

After some sniffing around in the shrubs and barking at a displaced hedgehog, Cookie walked by his owner's side. Jim dismissed the hedgehog. If only he'd questioned why it was out on such a cold night, he might have realised something wasn't right.

As they headed across what used to be the cloisters, Jim detected a stale smell. He sniffed the air several times but couldn't place it. Cookie whimpered. As they moved into the nave, they were stunned by what they saw.

Jim froze to the spot.

A group of teenagers dressed in dark robes were standing around a large free-standing yellow orb in the middle of the building, chanting a mantra.

Cookie growled. Jim had never seen him so aggressive. It was clear to Jim there was more to this than some wayward intruders.

Jim called out to the youths and asked what they were doing.

They ignored him.

He called again, telling them they'd have to leave.

Cookie barked and slowly approached the circle.

One of the youths turned around. As the youth growled back at Cookie, Jim noticed he had piercing light where his eyes should be.

Cookie yelped, then bolted past Jim and out of the building.

Jim asked the young man who he was and demanded to know what was going on. Then two youths, a male and a female, grabbed him from behind and forced him into the circle. He struggled with the youths, pushing and pulling and shouting for them to release him. But they were possessed by evil and much stronger.

They continued to chant.

As he was pulled closer to the orb, Jim became sick to his belly, he felt dizzy and disorientated. Then he was thrown to the ground and held down by the youths. As he lay pinned down, a bony hand reached out from the lawn and gripped his neck. He was powerless to fight. He feared he was about to die.

Suddenly, Cookie bounded through a doorway. He crashed through the fracas, knocking the orb to the ground smashing it into a thousand pieces, dissolving it into thin streams of wispy steam. The spectral youths and dismembered hand also dematerialised, leaving Jim and Cookie alone.

In silence, Jim looked into the lonely darkness that surrounded them. Cookie lay panting on the ground, his eyes reflecting Jim's torch light, his ears perked up.

He picked himself up and rubbed his neck.

"Good boy!"

The angels looked down with relief and smiled at what had passed. They could sleep peacefully tonight.

The Old Man in Town

a short story by Allan Shipham

I am tired. Youth left me long ago, taking with it my energies and my vigour. Time has not been kind to me, living has been a task and not the pleasure I imagined it would be when I wore smaller clothes.

Every day I slowly cross the street from the Union Workhouse where I live, and I inch along Castle Street. I'd quicken my step but the injury I got working in the Artlenock mines had rendered me lame for the rest of my life. I'd fall over if not for this trusty home-made crutch.

Each step is a painful reminder of the accident. Luckily for me, they say, the collapse was small and I was dragged out a-coughing and a-spluttering. My leg crushed, the Infirmary did the best they could, but the damage was already done. I would work no more. I now spend my days in the market begging and helping myself to throwaways at the end of the day.

I turn left into Midland Road and limp up the hill toward Market Street. The first time, the road was grandly dressed with a parade of trees encouraging me to reach the top but I've seen many changes. Sadly not all have been for the best. Fine buildings turned to ruin, rubbish and waste litter the streets, people talking in languages I've never heard before, trees felled and sawn up. Sometimes I don't recognise the place.

Most people walk straight past me and don't even acknowledge me. I don't know why they ignore me. If they looked at me, maybe they'd pity me, and that's not nice. Maybe they'd feel uncomfortable and obliged to tip me a coin or a morsel of food. I don't want much, sometimes I just want be noticed, that'd be enough.

As I always pass the huge garden on the left, the big dogs rise from their slumber and launch themselves at the brick wall between us. A-raging and a-barking, they've the devil himself inside them. Even the owner ignores me as he chastises them,

"No-one there!" he says.

No-one indeed!

I even frighten the cats when I pass, many a time turning a corner and finding a cat arched with fear, a-spitting and a-hissing. There's no need for all that.

You may have seen me before. You may even have tried to speak with me. I find it hard to engage in conversation. I want to respond, but I feel I won't be heard or understood. Most of the time, I hang my head in shame and embarrassment. I don't like to be a drain on your time or your pocket, but everyone has a right to eat. I used to accept the charity of churches, but I can't taste food now. Maybe my tongue was poisoned, maybe the food's too bland, or maybe there isn't any salt.

It's funny, I remember each step with such clarity, the wind in my face, the noises, but I can't remember where I slept last night or what I did in Market Street yesterday. I know I hate the Workhouse, nobody likes me there, nobody welcomes me and nobody loves me. I hate this life, a-scrounging and a-stealing, but I must make this journey every day, it's all I know.

My simple clothes may be old and worn, but they keep me warm and cover my modesty. They used to be grey. Everyone wore grey, unless of course you had money. Over time they've bleached with the sun and turned almost white.

As I make my way into town, I'm puzzled and confused by things I barely understand, vehicles that move without horses, food that would make me retch, conversations about things I'll never understand... By the stars, what is Twitter?

There are times I get noticed, but they're few and far between. Usually at night as I make my way back. Some woman or child will look at me and stop in their tracks. A few have screamed. A couple have shrieked. There were even a couple who mocked my age and my clothes.

"Oh my God! A ghost!"

But I don't look up. I want to, but I carry on.

I have to be back in the Workhouse by nine or they lock me out.

A ghost indeed! Huh!

The Quality of Darkness

a short story by Deborah Bromley

It felt as if I had been waiting forever, but perhaps it was only a few minutes. When you are nervous, time seems to expand and stretch out. While I was waiting, I noticed the pale neutral tones of the décor. There was a cream leather sofa against the wall opposite. But I didn't feel like sitting. I paced, as quietly as possible, worried I might be disturbing someone in the adjacent room. Another person who needed therapy. Before I had time to gather my thoughts and prepare myself, the door opened a fraction and a warm, friendly voice asked me to step inside.

The interior of the consulting-room was similar to the waiting-room. She motioned me to sit down on another cream leather sofa. She sat on a low chair facing me. A large notepad lay on her lap.

"I'm sorry you had to wait. Are you comfortable there?"

"Yes, quite comfortable, thank you for asking."

"Good. I'm ready to begin if you are?" She paused and glanced in my direction, then continued. "So, in your own time, in your own words. Tell me why you've come."

I settled into the soft leather, wondering how to explain what had drawn me to this place. I had been over the problem time and time again, but now the words in my mind didn't seem to make sense. If I'm honest, I was worried about being asked about my feelings. It's a man-thing, I suppose.

The woman looked tactfully at her hands. I wasn't sure I wanted to have eye contact at this point. I'd have to relax a bit more before I could really explain my worries. But she kept her gaze lowered and waited for me to be ready, which I appreciated.

"I suppose I should start at the beginning?"

"That would be fine," she assured me.

"I can't seem to get over... no, that's not right. What I mean is... I'm having trouble moving on from something that happened. And I haven't told anyone about it. It's traumatic. But I guess you hear all kinds of traumatic things in your work."

"I do." She nodded gently in my direction.

I had a sense, in that moment, that she might be able to understand.

"It all happened about six months ago. October. During that stormy weather we had. I had always loved storms, until... "

"Go on."

"Well, I had to attend a conference. It was about IT risk management for small businesses. I had been booked to give a paper on current trends in disaster recovery. Exciting stuff. But probably only if you are interested in the subject. Anyway, I was going to be there for three days and that included the residential stay. All held at Henley Business School. Have you ever been there?"

"I don't know that area, no."

"Very leafy, lots of nice pubs. I explored a few. I gave my presentation on the morning of the third day. It was well received. I had quite a number of delegates coming to see me afterwards and I gave out lots of business cards. I was looking forward to a bit of a surge in business when I returned home.

"Over lunch I decided it would be sensible to leave early. The weather was filthy. I knew traffic would be bad later that afternoon. Roads are terrible around the M40 during rush hour. I checked out around two o'clock and set off back to Marlow to rejoin the motorway. I'm glad I did because it was already pelting down. It was like night, the sky was absolutely leaden. Black almost."

I could see the scene in my mind as I retold the story. And the same feeling of foreboding weighed heavy in my chest. I paused and took a few deep breaths, then continued.

"It was a good job I knew where to go. Around Marlow,

it was chaos. Shoppers running for cover. Roads awash with surface water. I nearly knocked over a couple of women who dashed out on to a zebra crossing, trying to avoid the downpour. Stupid of them. Getting wet is pretty irrelevant if you end up squashed as flat as a pancake."

I paused again and tried to collect my thoughts. The next part would be harder to explain.

"I took the main A-road to Stokenchurch. It takes you to Junction 5. You'd never know it was an A-road. No white lines, no cat's eyes, just black tarmac. And it meanders around like a drunk. So I kept to forty miles an hour. But the road kept coming and the cars coming towards me were... sort of... aggressive. Bright headlights on full beam. Hogging the road so I had to swerve to avoid them. It was hard to concentrate. People are so inconsiderate these days.

"I came to the set of villages called Lane End and Bolters End. Dead-and-alive sort of places, if you ask me. And that's when I felt it. It may not make sense to you but I felt like an unseen force was *behind me*. Nipping at my heels. Not exactly making my hair stand on end, but I felt compelled to plunge on. I worried that if I stopped to get a coffee or go for a pee, it might catch me. Whatever it was."

"Sounds like you felt spooked. It would be understandable in those circumstances."

"You've got it. I did feel spooked. And an overwhelming desire to get home as quickly as possible. As if some force wanted me gone. Well, the feeling was mutual. And it stayed with me even when I got on to the motorway. I put it down to the weather. And I just kept concentrating on the road ahead of me which was awash with water by then."

"Yes, I've been caught out in those sudden flash storms, I do know what it must have been like."

"We should be used to it by now. Typical British weather. Anyway, soon I saw the signs for my exit. I was still feeling a little spooked, as you called it, by then. But I knew I could be home in forty minutes or less. At least that's what I thought.

"But, as I took my usual route home, I saw the Road Closed signs. I could have kicked myself because I noticed them on the way there. Road closures for major resurfacing. And the diversion would take me right back towards Oxford. Well, I thought, I can find a better way home than that. So I took the next exit off the roundabout and wished, for the umpteenth time, that I hadn't left my Satnav at home."

I paused again. I wasn't sure how much of the next bit was relevant. I'd already owned up to some pretty odd feelings – illogical feelings – and I didn't want to give her the impression I had lost the plot. But as I looked up, I saw she was looking towards me with such kind eyes. I sensed she accepted me; she didn't think I was unhinged or deluded.

"It's hard to explain fear sometimes, isn't it?" I said.

"You can only explain what you felt. It's subjective. So don't concern yourself with whether it sounds logical or believable. Whatever you say is valid because it's what you experienced at the time."

That was all the encouragement I needed.

"So I'm slowing down to about 20 miles an hour and the road is just a narrow single track but I'm sure it's going in the right direction. And all the time this compulsion to press on is eating me up. Even if I wanted to turn back, I had the nagging worry that some malevolent force was waiting for me to falter.

"I studied the signposts and looked for something, some clue, that I recognised. I even toyed with calling the RAC; I'm a member. But I didn't know where I was so how could I direct them? I was annoyed with myself for being so stupid but another part of me was sure I would soon find a major road and get my bearings. And then, suddenly, the road did widen and I felt quite relieved."

"That must have helped."

"No, not really. It wasn't what I thought it was. And the next part is a bit jumbled up. But it seems the road I thought I saw was some local flooding. I didn't notice until I was in it. And there were no hedges at the sides of the road so I could only see blackness. And feel the car shifting under me; it had lost its grip on the road. It was horrible, terrifying. I never want to experience that again. I was moving but I had lost control. Sliding, shifting, pulled by unseen currents. And in the back of my head I'm shouting to myself that I'm stupid. I should have turned back."

"And do you remember what happened next?"

"Barely. Because the engine failed and the lights went out and all I could sense was the drifting of my car on the water and the helplessness of it all. The aloneness. In that moment, I tell you, I knew *despair*. There was nothing to do but accept my fate. But it wasn't a peaceful acceptance. It was more a furious, agonising desolation. I can't even think about it. I don't want to think about it."

"Don't dwell on it, then. We can come back to that memory, if it's necessary, later on. Let's... move forward in time and you can tell me what happened next."

I couldn't speak for a few minutes but she didn't rush me. I latched on to the next solid memory I could conjure up.

"I was walking, drenched and weak and alone, across a field. I had nothing with me except my clothes. No phone, no briefcase, no identification. Then I saw some lights ahead of me. One of the tiny villages in that part of Oxfordshire, I suppose. There were a few houses bunched together around a crossroads.

"I thought I'd find a friendly face and get some help. I thought I could phone home and get my wife to come and pick me up. It took me a few minutes to find a house which was occupied."

"I suppose people might have been prevented from getting home, cut off by the local flooding."

"That's what I thought. There was nobody about, that's for certain. Look, I know I was in shock. I looked a sight. I probably had pondweed dripping from my hair, I don't know. But I found this house with lights on. And inside I could see this man. He was in his living-room eating his tea. I could see the butter dripping off the toast on to his chin, I was that close.

"I banged on his window. I shouted for help. He hardly stirred. He was so wrapped up in his own comfortable existence. He couldn't be bothered to help a fellow human being in need. I was so annoyed with him! If I could, I'd have walked right in on him and given him a piece of my mind but both his doors were locked. I know because I had a good try at breaking in. That would have shocked him out of his selfish *couldn't care less* attitude."

She didn't say anything but I felt her empathising with me, so I carried on.

"Then I found a shop. A little village shop with newspapers and food and drink and it looked so welcoming. The lights were on but, with hindsight, I suppose the weather had caused them to close early. The door handle wouldn't turn and I couldn't get anyone to let me in even though I knocked and shouted as loudly as possible. I think maybe the rain drowned out any racket I could make. I felt pretty despondent at that point. But I didn't give up.

"Rather, like a vagrant, I found a barn to sleep in and wait out the weather and the night. At least I had shelter. But I assure you, I have never, ever, felt so alone, so separate, so inconsequential. It brings it home to you, you know. Something like that. My own personal 'series of unfortunate events'. You really understand how small you are, how irrelevant. Without your family and friends, you really are nobody."

"At least you can talk about it now."

"Yes, hindsight is a wonderful thing."

"Then tell me. What happened in the morning? They say everything looks better by the cold light of day. I assume you made it safely home?"

"I did get back to my home town, yes. My house, my wife, my friends and family."

"And you recovered from your awful experience? Once you were home safely and could get a sense of perspective about it all?"

"Well, no. That's why I'm here. That's why I need your help. The traumatic events of that night have changed something inside me. I'm not sure I can explain it properly."

"Like you don't fit anymore?"

"Like I don't belong anymore. Whether it was that desolate feeling of aloneness that changed me or the fear and panic I suffered. I don't know."

"And your wife, your family?"

"It's not the same. I feel they don't know me anymore."

"And your business? Work can be a great healer."

"I haven't been able to work."

"I see. Yes, I can see now what is wrong."

"Can you? Can you really?"

"Now I have the whole picture, I know how to help you."

"At last. Someone who understands."

"I do understand."

"And can you help me now, today, or... "

"All I need to know is that *you* are ready."

"I am. Now I've told my story to someone who is prepared to listen, a great weight has lifted. So I'm happy to have whatever treatment you think will help me."

"Good. I'm glad. Now just rest and let me take over."

It was a blessed relief to let somebody else do the talking. I did as she asked and I lay down on the comfortable sofa, feeling like I was floating. Soon I was listening entranced to her soft voice guiding me and leading me towards a more relaxed way of feeling. I had been too tense and stressed. She helped me to let go of those feelings. It was a really pleasant experience.

Then she asked me to open my eyes and look towards her. I moved my head and noticed what she was talking about.

"Look into the space behind my head," she said.

Her eyes were glowing. The room seemed to crackle with energy.

"Very soon you'll notice a bright tunnel of light appear behind me. The most warm and comforting sight you have seen in many months. This light will be shining and vibrating with healing energy, designed to make you whole again. You can forget all the trauma and pain. You can use the light to heal you."

It made so much sense. She definitely had a real gift. I felt better already.

"Continue to concentrate on the light. And when you are ready, allow yourself to rise up off the sofa and move towards the light. Soon you will see loved ones, family members who have already passed over. They will come to greet you and take your hand. It is now time to go."

She was right.

Light, love and acceptance. And a feeling of freedom like no other I had ever experienced.

I was going home, after all.

Lost in Steampunk

a short story by Allan Shipham

The writers' group sat down and took out their prepared pieces.

As Allan began to read his contribution, he was interrupted by a loud noise from the reception area of the building.

Mike swapped his reading glasses for his distance glasses and rose to his feet. "We've got a new member tonight. Joanne. I'll go and let her in. Maybe the door's stuck." He left the room.

After a moment, the door slammed abruptly and there was another louder noise.

"Aaaggghhh!"

Mike's distressing cry unnerved everyone.

"What was that?" asked Lizzy.

Nick and Allan went to investigate.

Jason also made his way around the table. "Stay here, everyone. We'll find out what's going on, so we will."

As Jason held the door open, Allan and Nick stepped out into the empty hall. The front door was ajar. Allan looked outside and called for Mike.

"What's that?" asked Nick, looking along the corridor. A crack in the wall had opened up and a pale grey light emerged, suddenly illuminating the room. Another noise sounded like an explosion. Allan and Nick were swept up in a tornado and into the crack.

"What's going on out there?" asked Helen.

"Allan and Nick just disappeared. Don't come – " Unable to finish his sentence, Jason disappeared.

The doors slammed as the air was sucked from the room and several leaflets fluttered around on the noticeboard.

But then everything fell silent.

"Where are we?"

"It's dark, so it is!"

"I can see it's dark. What happened?"

A woman's voice responded from the dark.

"I can't find my glasses!"

"Who are you?"

"This is Joanne," explained Mike. "She's the new member; I met her at the door, then this!"

"Hi, Joanne!"

"Hi!"

"Hi!"

Jason switched on a torch app on his mobile phone. The beam illuminated what appeared to be a brick-lined under-croft in a building. There was a dripping noise and a pungent smell.

"How did we get here?" asked Nick.

"We've been transported somewhere," Allan replied. "But where?"

"It's like a science-fiction story!" added Jason. "Maybe it's one of yours, Allan?"

"Can someone tell me what is happening here?" Joanne enquired.

"This isn't normal!" explained Mike. "In fact, it's never happened before. We usually read out stories."

Nick and Allan started to explore the environment, their feet splashing the shallow water under foot. A door opened.

"Who are you and what are you doing down there?" A gentleman in a long coat and top hat stood in the doorway, casting a shadow across them all.

"We were brought here, but we don't know how," replied Nick. "Where are we?"

"You're in the Jamaica Street experimental warehouse of Mr Sherlock Holmes."

"That's funny," said Jason. "And who are you? Dr Watson?"

"I'm Inspector Gregory Lestrade – "

Everyone gasped.

" – and you'd be careful to pay me a little more respect, young man," he added, staring at Jason.

Once they were outside, they could see they were in Victorian London. The warehouse was close to the Thames and everyone could see and hear a steam contraption inside the ground floor of the building.

The inspector coughed. "I was just talking with Mr Holmes when his experiment seemed to become possessed by a banshee and bedlam occurred, so to speak." The Inspector observed everyone's clothing with disdain. "Thrown to the floor I was, in the explosion. I woke when I heard a blast in the basement."

"That was us arriving!" explained Allan.

"The real Inspector Lestrade?" remarked Mike. "I have so many questions!"

"Get real, Mike. Lestrade is fiction! Holmes is fiction!" stated Nick.

"Conan Doyle had to get his inspiration from somewhere," Mike replied, smiling at the inspector.

"I want to go home!" said Joanne. "You're all mad!"

"And how do you know Mr Conan Doyle?" asked Lestrade.

"Where is Mr Holmes right now?" enquired Mike, looking around.

"We don't have time for this!" said Allan. "Whatever brought us here has taken Holmes somewhere else."

There was a flash of light inside the warehouse.

"What the – " asked Joanne.

"It's still running," stated Nick.

They made their way to Holmes' experiment.

"It's probably best not to touch anything," said Lestrade.

Big belts raced away into the space above their head, driving cogs that in turn drove other cogs and wheels.

"This is a nightmare!" exclaimed Nick.

Allan, Joanne and Jason reached the steam engine controls and tried to make sense of them.

"The engine is clearly creating some kind of kinetic

energy!" explained Jason, pointing to the drive belts over their heads. "Could it be electricity?"

"Maybe it's sending it to that cage over there?" suggested Joanne.

"Okay, everyone, I think I've worked it out!" exclaimed Allan. "Holmes must've been using electricity to create a tachyon energy field around that Faraday cage." He looked around to see where everyone was. "He must've used it to transport himself through time and space. An accident pulled us back through."

"Important question. Can we get back home?" asked Joanne.

"I'm working on it," Allan replied re-setting dials and tapping pressure gauges. "I'm quite sure we can activate it again, but we'll need everyone inside that cage. Lestrade is going to have to destroy it after we've gone!"

"Destroy it?" said Lestrade.

"You can't risk ripping others from history and pulling them into Victorian London. Your next visitor might be a dinosaur."

"What is Victorian London?" puzzled Lestrade.

A large hairy leg searched for a purchase on the floor from behind some packing cases. Its appearance went unnoticed. A second, much larger hairy leg struck the floor twice and came to rest next to the first one. Within a microsecond, the menacing and frightening face of a giant spider came into view. Its presence drew everyone's attention.

"Into the cage!" shouted Jason. He reached up for a rope and pulled himself up and over the engine to avoid the spider's clutches.

"Escape!" screamed Allan.

The spider headed toward Mike, but jumped on Joanne at the last moment. It dragged her to the floor and sank its fangs deep into her chest. Her screams were cut short as blood spurted from her open wounds and the spider garrotted her chest cavity.

"Lestrade! Your gun!" shouted Allan.

Lestrade threw his pistol across the room. Hanging on the rope, Jason grabbed it out of the air and tossed to Allan. He caught it, jumped on the spider's back and collapsed it to the floor.

Bang! Bang!

As Allan fired off two shots into the spider's head, it was despatched.

"She's dead!" Mike said, staring at Joanne.

Nick helped Mike into the dome.

"Allan, will Holmes return when you disappear?" asked Lestrade.

"I've no idea! I don't even know if we'll get home."

He passed the gun back to its owner.

"What'll we do without Mr Holmes?"

Allan thought for a moment and then addressed Lestrade. "Tell Mr Conan Doyle to write the stories anyway. Tell him... to let people think Holmes is fiction."

"What stories?"

"He'll know."

"Allan!" shouted Jason, pointing at a large steam gauge in the red pressure zone.

As Allan climbed inside the dome, there was a deafening explosion.

All four found themselves on the floor of the meeting hall.

"My head hurts," said Jason.

"And mine!" said Nick. "Allan, I didn't know you could shoot a gun."

"Neither did I!"

"Mike, what about Joanne? We can't do anything for her now."

All four looked at each other grimly.

"No-one saw her arrive tonight," Mike said. "No-one needs to know where she ended up."

"Suppose we'd better take a break," said Pat peering around the door. "Shall I put the kettle on?"

"The real Inspector Lestrade!" said Mike shaking his head slowly.

Marriage is a Compromise

a short story by Deborah Bromley

John

Barbara is an opera buff. She is a friend of English National Opera. We get free wine and nibbles when we attend the preview evenings. I tolerate this obsession of hers and accompany her to performances from time to time. I pat myself on the back for sitting through all that wailing and we usually have a nice dinner in London afterwards. I attempt to make meaningful comments about opera-related matters while we eat and drink, which pleases Barbara. Marital harmony is important. It's all about give and take. Going to the opera without complaining is just one of the ways we balance the necessary ebb and flow of marriage.

Of course, I do my best to keep her away from the golf club. I know that all golf clubs now have to admit women members; even St Andrew's had to cave in. But I keep away from female golfers. They're a different breed, really. My golf is my time away from female influence. Barbara respects that. I have my suspicions she is glad to be rid of me and get me out of the house. She can crack on with the laundry and so on. Give the glassware a buff and polish.

Every now and again she has a little dig about the cost of my club membership. And the bar account, of course. I can deflect the crossfire by mentioning how much ENO are in debt, despite the exorbitant subscription she pays to be a friend and the elitist cost of tickets. That's without the extra truckloads of cash from ordinary taxpayers. I don't press my point too hard. That would be cruel. Keep your powder dry, I say. And then slip in how much you are looking forward to the new production of *Carmen* set in an opium factory in Afghanistan, sung entirely in the native tongue. It's subsidised, of course, by the Arts Council. Barbara then simpers in my direction and the subject of my golf club membership is shelved.

It was, therefore, with a rather high-minded sense of generosity that I agreed to accompany her to Glyndebourne this year. I congratulated myself on my noble sacrifice. We were to be the guests of Robert Michaels OBE and his wife Selina. Barbara and Selina are old school chums and I gathered my dear wife had been angling for an invitation for some years. Included in our invitation was the dinner, held between the second and third acts. How civilised, I thought.

All we had to do was organise some overnight accommodation. You would think that was well within Barbara's capabilities, wouldn't you? Well, I certainly thought so or I wouldn't have let the silly woman choose the hotel. And if I had not been laid low with a nasty cold I might have remembered to check with her that she had booked something appropriate. Because, for all the woman's charming qualities, she's sometimes rather forgetful about my likes and dislikes.

Barbara

For a man who is dependably conservative in his views, John is being ridiculous. He's got this idiotic notion into his head that he is susceptible to seeing ghosts and things that go bump in the night. What nonsense. There is no such thing. I blame his mother. She was the kind of person who would jump at her own shadow and, with John being an only child, she obviously had too much influence on him.

To my way of thinking, this Glyndebourne trip would be a chance to stay in a local place with some atmosphere. I wanted to choose a hotel with history, somewhere with connections to important events from the past. It would fire up my imagination and make the whole trip really memorable. Goodness knows, we don't get away enough.

John is so wedded to the golf club and his regular schedule. It bores me rigid listening to him go on and on about it.

I don't understand people who aren't interested in the glorious past of this country, even if it's sometimes a little blood-curdling. I like that kind of history the best. I will concede to a certain apprehension when I discovered the hotel had served as an assizes for the witch hunts of the Cromwell era and that the victims of that barbaric practice were burned at the stake in the town square, a little way from the hotel. But I put that nervousness down to the inevitable row when John eventually found out where we were going to stay.

To me the argument was simple. Why would you book into an anonymous Travelodge when you could soak up history and absorb all that fascinating background about the past in an historic hotel? I decided to go for broke because you can actually stay in the rooms where the events took place.

I chose carefully. I had done my homework and decided to book The Red Room. It's the most haunted room in the place! By a stroke of luck, the room was vacant. I booked it like a shot. I had in my mind that I would exorcise this foolish belief from my husband's psyche and prove him wrong. He is such a stubborn and opinionated man. If we have a peaceful night's sleep, he'll have to admit I am right and he is wrong.

But obviously I didn't tell him until a few days before our trip. I didn't want to give him too much time to get all worked up. We had a nasty row about it, despite my patient explanation that we would enjoy ourselves more by staying in an atmospheric coaching inn than in a stuffy air-conditioned room in an impersonal chain hotel. I know my plan will work.

Of course, when we arrived it was exactly as I'd anticipated. The Red Room was gloomy and mysterious with a quaint low sloping ceiling and a dark oak floor that undulated alarmingly. The huge bay window had a velvet covered settle where you could sit and watch the street below, imagining the scenes from bygone days. If I leaned out, I could even see the square where the witches were burned. I was in my element. John was annoyed. He is still sulking.

John

It all came to a head when we were packing.

"Are you seriously expecting me to stay the night in a haunted coaching inn?" I asked. I was trying to be reasonable.

"It's too late to do anything about it now, John. And anyway, you'll like it, I know you will."

"That merely goes to show how little you know me, Barbara, or you wouldn't put me in this position."

"Oh, John, do try to look at things logically. What can happen? Nothing. It's all in your mind."

"Logic doesn't come into it. And if you had ever experienced... "

"Come on, you're a grown adult. Vice-Captain of the golf club senior team."

It was a low blow, I thought, to remind me of that. It scuppered my argument for a while. But, even as I was weighing up how embarrassing it would feel to be outed as a lily-livered ghost avoider, the gnawing anxiety slithered back into my body. I was stuck between a rock and a hard place. With nowhere else to go. So I gritted my teeth and made up my mind to go along with it.

I stomped out of the bedroom as angrily as I could and sat in the car drumming my fingers on the steering wheel. I know that really gets on Barbara's nerves. She flounced out of the house a good while later, acting as if nothing had happened. It's going to be a long night.

The journey was uneventful. The roads were quiet for a Friday afternoon. I had ample time to think about my predicament.

I left Barbara unpacking and went to have a quiet word

with the manager. Surely they would have a spare room in the modern annexe for us? I didn't even mind if I had to sleep there alone. Barbara could spend all night being haunted in the Red Room for all I cared! Unfortunately for me, the Glyndebourne Festival attracts so many visitors, all the rooms in our hotel were booked up.

The manager even searched on the internet for me, to find out if there were any vacancies in other hotels. It was very kind of him. By this point, my stress levels were going through the roof. As the manager searched hotel booking sites, I prayed for one local hotel to have a room. One little room, just for me, with no supernatural visitors. But it was not to be.

The manager took me to the bar and poured me a stiff whisky. "I understand how you feel," he said. "I'm only sorry I can't help you."

"Really?"

"Being haunted isn't everyone's idea of fun."

"Quite agree, old chap. But my wife seems to be positively looking forward to it. Although she's not the one who'll be clutching the bedclothes at three o'clock in the morning, terrified witless," I joked, beginning to feel a better.

"Well, when you work here, you do get used to it," the manager laughed. But when I looked at his face I saw fear. He lowered his voice. "Most of the staff live out, you know. I have to sleep in, alternate weeks."

"So you see things and hear things?" I asked, half-hoping he would reassure me that my anxiety was unfounded.

"Like I said, you get used to it. It depends how it affects you. Not everyone is sensitive."

"Yes, yes, that's me. I'm sensitive. And my stupid wife thinks I'm exaggerating."

"Sorry, I can't promise she will see and hear anything ghostly, but there is every chance. This place is alive with... " He paused.

"With what? Come on, you'd better tell me now you've

started."

"Well. Let me put it in context for you. We get a lot of ghost hunters coming to stay," he said. "Generally they are a bunch of thick-skinned idiots, hell-bent on proving ghosts don't exist. They have their fancy equipment and insist on clogging up the public rooms with their stuff, braying loudly about their special investigations to anyone who'll listen. Unfortunately, it's good business or we would ban them. I would say that nine times out of ten they get nothing, stay up all night for nothing and their recording devices are blank. We don't give refunds but they often request one."

"But the other times?"

"The various spirits and spectres give them a show they won't forget in a hurry."

"I don't like the odds."

"But remember, those guys are asking for it. And our ghosts oblige, but not all the time. It's as if they want to be unpredictable. I can only tell you about my own experiences in this hotel. I think it works like this. If you happen to be in the wrong place at the wrong time, you witness a ghost simply going about its normal business. Walking through a wall or having a bit of a wail about something. Throwing a glass on the floor... nothing very dramatic."

"But what you don't understand is the terrible fear that I get. It's uncontrollable. I might only think I've seen something and my imagination goes into overdrive!"

The manager poured more drinks. He looked me straight in the eye and lowered his tone. "I do understand, believe me. My advice would be to enjoy your evening at the opera, have a nightcap when you return and, with luck, you'll sleep until morning. I'll make sure your mini-bar is well stocked. I'll get Housekeeping to put some ear-plugs in with the bathroom toiletries."

I nodded, sensing he wanted to end the conversation. I would do as he suggested. But, as I thought more about the night ahead, I realised I might have another option.

Barbara

Carmen was breathtaking. The performance was the best I've ever heard. The wonderful arias from the lead contralto were so moving. I loved the atmosphere. And Glyndebourne is magnificent. Everyone was dressed in their finery. You don't get that in London these days; people wear jeans and hoodies to the opera. No dress code – quite disgraceful. But tonight I was able to experience what it must have been like in the glorious past, when attending a performance was considered a treat worthy of looking your best.

The dinner was perfect, not too heavy. I was able to catch up with Selina. How well they have done for themselves! I didn't realise her husband is now considered the top lawyer for mergers and acquisitions. Not that I understand much about business. But John seemed impressed. He was chatting happily enough with Robert. I think John had rather a lot to drink but it didn't matter. He held his own and he's getting ready for bed in the bathroom. I think I hear him humming.

John

Barbara is asleep. I can hear her little snores and grunts. I'm warm and fuzzy and full of dinner and whisky. I'm hoping to be asleep any moment but only if my heart slows down and my mind stops thinking about what might happen. I've got my back-up plan, though, and that's helping me to relax.

Barbara

I congratulate myself on a blissful night's sleep as I stretch before turning to wake John up and see about making some early morning tea. His side of the bed is empty. Rumpled but empty. I had planned on teasing him about his ridiculous fears but, clearly, he hasn't had a good night and he's gone off. How rude of him! Now I have to find the silly man. I'll have to skip breakfast. How very annoying.

It takes much longer than anticipated because I can't find him anywhere. I have to check and recheck all the public rooms, the lounges and bars and all the many corridors and odd little side rooms that don't seem to lead anywhere. I can't find him indoors. He must have gone for a walk. I check my phone to see if he has left a text message, but there's nothing. There's not even much signal so I don't know if he has tried to let me know what's happened.

I wait for the manager to be free and ask if he has any information about my missing husband. What an odd conversation! It seems John and he talked about me yesterday. I feel quite... insulted. And I'm not sure he is being very helpful. He tells me I shouldn't have been so dismissive about my husband's worries. How rude! It's none of his business. But he can't help me anyway. He can't locate a person who doesn't want to be found. I realise that now.

John

My plan didn't work out. I thought I would give Barbara a good fright by faking a disappearance. I'd get my own back by making her feel some of that anxiety she has put me through. I woke up, as I knew I would, around three o'clock in the morning. I don't know if I did hear something but I didn't wait to find out.

I had my overnight case ready and I picked up a pillow and a couple of spare blankets from the cupboard and crept out of the room. Barbara didn't stir. I braced myself and walked along the dark passages, hoping that nothing would leap out to terrify me. I clicked the latch on the main hotel door and stepped out into the cold night air.

I had parked the car as far away from the hotel as I could. It was way over in the corner by a tall stone wall.

Sleeping in the car was my preferred option so I kept my eyes firmly on my destination and potential safety. But the lighting was dim and the scene seemed to shift as I walked over the cobbles, aiming for the far walls of the car park boundary. And, although I was striding along, I didn't seem to be getting any closer.

John – later

She's arguing with the manager who shrugs and shakes his head. I can't hear the words but the effect on her face is clear. First annoyance, then disbelief, then... something else. It might be concern for me. Not that I care much about that now. Everything that happened before is unimportant. As I observe her, she appears defeated. Her head drops and her arms slump down by her sides.

I wonder what she will do now. She has searched the room and noticed my missing case. Perhaps she'll try looking inside the car. Maybe she'll find something, I don't know how these things work. I've tried to comprehend this, believe me, I would do something if I could. I would explain if I knew how.

She just walked straight through me! I don't understand how she could do that without any glimmer of recognition. It is exactly as the manager explained to me last night. Some people can see and hear and feel and some can't. I now realise how hard it will be to reach her.

I try brushing my fingertips against her cheek but she is unmoved by my touch. I shout in her ear but she is so engrossed in her own world, she barely registers my presence. It's futile. I slip through the wall and stand beside the manager who is still talking to her. But there is nothing I can do to catch her attention.

It's too late. The clamour is growing around me. Voices calling out for truth and reckoning. The scene inside the hotel fades to grey and I am drawn backwards with an ever-increasing intensity. I come to a halt standing outside under a bright blue sky with the sun on my back.

The square has been prepared. I notice the crowd hushes respectfully as I make my inspection of the carefully built pyres. Four daemon-worshipping hags for burning. A goodly crop that will make a righteous spectacle for the assembled townsfolk. I note their slumped bodies, arms tied tightly to the stump, shoulders bent where joints have been racked for confessions. Only with sufficient penitence can they be assured of mercy from our Lord God. Dressed in their filthy soiled rags with their limbs twisted and bodies broken, they dare not meet my eye. They whimper instead to the baying crowd.

I pause to ensure all are focussed on my next act. Any doubts in the minds of the crowd must be dispelled before I begin. My certainty will become their clarity. I must not flinch. As I reach for my burning torch, I am full of life and strength and power. As I light each pyre, I breathe in a burst of fresh smoke. The first shriek of a witch is said to be the daemon leaving the body. The fire cleanses all her sins as she burns.

I pause until I am satisfied with each blaze, until the scent of burning hair and skin and flesh reaches my nostrils. I have a reputation for being thorough in my work.

Three are burning merrily and there is but one left to set ablaze. As I light the tallow-soaked faggots by the feet of the final witch, I notice that her face is turned towards me. She wears a defiant stare that I recognise, but then all these hags are defiant until the pain of the fire humbles them. One witch is much like another, in truth. Yet, a vision tugs at my memory. Perhaps this face is from another time or another place. I struggle to recall the details. Memory can play tricks. I know that I have never associated with any of Satan's followers. I only do the work of the Lord. I am his dutiful servant. I step back to enjoy the blazing spectacle.

History and Myth

The Lisbon Connection

a short story by Allan Shipham

Rufino slowly stirred a dull metal teaspoon in his coffee. He'd already blended the finest Brazilian coffee and the sweetest sugar cane, but it made him feel better and passed the time. Across from the café, an old fish merchant opening his shop in the morning sunshine broke his concentration. He made a clatter as he folded the shutters and tied them back.

He envied the fishmonger. He didn't know him but imagined how much simpler his daily routine was, compared to his own life. As he watched, the fishmonger slopped water over his threshold and brushed it out into the street.

Rufino sipped his coffee. Today was a big day. He needed his wits about him.

The young, handsome, Special Services soldier discreetly opened an orange folder, revealing the secret file he'd diligently accumulated. *Trapp Projeto: Hans Friedrich Karl Franz Kammler*. He wanted to remind himself of the evidence once more, before shadowing his suspect one last time. The other customers were oblivious to his actions.

He turned over the pages and skim-read the data. He recalled how surprised he was when he first found out about "Trapp Projeto", a secret sting programme to track down and catch Nazi war criminals. Many were caught and tried, but some of the worst offenders escaped and were scattered around the world. The page before him flopped back revealing key details and early images of his target.

Hans, or as he was known, "Heinz", was a German civil engineer who was said to have led the work on the V2 Missile. While it was commonly thought that he was buried in Germany in May 1945, Rufino had discovered the misplaced assumption had arisen from a dubious statement gathered by an inexperienced Nazi-hunter. Kammler had left a different trail which Rufino had been able to follow. The deathbed confession of a German priest, a story about a boat trip during the exodus, technical developments across international borders, and Portugal's efforts to rejoin post-war Europe and escape its fascist history. An eye-witness tip-off presented a suspect. Rufino already had his name and was on the case.

He heard the rumbling of the carriage and the screech of the tracks as the trolley car approached the adjacent terminus. He closed his folder, stowed it away in his leather satchel and finished his coffee. Portuguese, his local accent and knowledge gave him the cover he needed to help him observe his suspect in more detail and report back to Santos Carlos, Portugal's Special Services recruiter and his superior. Rufino joined the other passengers in the queue and climbed aboard.

He knew Kammler would embark at the second stop, as he did every day. The old man worked at a jewellery shop in the town. According to his investigation, Heinz – or "Herminio" as he was now called – let it be known to neighbours and customers that he was Jewish, although it was never talked about. Herminio ticked many of Rufino's boxes, he had no family, no notable friends and he fitted the profile. Rufino had an up-to-date photograph that had been folded several times across the suspect's face, but he could still make out his features.

The bell rang out its warning and the trolley moved off. Rufino had ridden the tram before, but not shadowing a suspected murderer. The bus jerked away from its stop and trundled along the track. A faint smell of electrical sparks and wheel grease filled the interior, but there was no noise, everyone travelled in silence.

The old man was waiting as expected at the next stop leaning forward on a walking-stick. Herminio reached out with his hand to catch the handlebar as it approached, it coasted into his open hand. He quickly launched himself up on the bus and shuffled along the carriage to a seat. He fell backwards into a seat, facing others. He looked toward the front of the bus as most passengers did before settling in.

Rufino lifted his satchel from the floor and then threw back the front flap, reached in and took out the aged, faded photograph and raised it discreetly to compare profiles. Sure enough, his face was very similar. There was a mark in the picture that he couldn't see on the old man's face, but he wasn't sure if it was a real feature or damage to the photo.

The trolley bus moved downhill, occasionally stopping.

A woman and a small girl sat next to Rufino, directly opposite the old man. The girl had a doll and, as she played with its hair, she asked the woman about their excursion. Most of the bus overheard the conversation and several smiled at the girl when it was clear they were visiting a sick relative in hospital and she didn't want to go.

The old man saw Rufino glancing in his direction. "Can I help you?" he asked in fluent Portuguese.

Rufino didn't detect a German accent. "You look like a friend of my father's," he said. "I'm sorry."

"This is not a problem," he replied. "Lisbon, 'the city that never stops', they say."

"Yes."

"Lucky for us, this bus does," he smiled.

Rufino cringed at being dragged in an impromptu conversation with his mark. He hoped he had given nothing away in his responses.

Across from Rufino, an elderly lady sneezed.

The old man looked up and politely responded. "Gesundheit!"

The woman wiped her nose with a tissue and nodded toward the suspect in gratitude.

Several people took a curious second look at the old man, Rufino wondering if they had also noticed the old man had spoken German. Rufino took the opportunity to pack away the photo, and re-checked his revolver was stowed in the satchel in case he needed it.

Placing his satchel back on the floor, Rufino drew the old man's attention again. The old man frowned, looked down at the girl, at her doll, at the woman and then back at Rufino.

Rufino could sense something dangerous was about to happen. He worried the old man might even take the little girl hostage. Most Nazis had suicide pills, but some had gone down fighting when they were close to getting caught. If something was about to go down, there might not be enough time to alert the local police.

With a screech of brakes, the bus came to an abrupt stop, throwing everyone forward. The little girl laughed nervously, in excitement. Again, the warning bell sounded and tram set off with another jerk as the brakes released, throwing everyone backwards. This time, the passengers were taken by surprise and the girl dropped her doll on the floor. As the tram moved away, the old man immediately knocked it close to his feet with his cane.

Rufino prepared to get up from his seat and to intercept the Nazi suspect before he made his move. He was sure, now more than ever, that he had his man.

In a moment of stillness and silence for Rufino, the old man reached down to pick up the doll. As he reached out, his coat sleeve and long-sleeved shirt slid up his arm, revealing part of a numerical tattoo.

Rufino gasped and pressed back into his seat. How could he be so suspicious of this brave man? How could he be so wrong?

The old man handed the doll to the little girl. She thanked him. He noticed the exposed tattoo and quickly pulled down his sleeve. In the cool morning air, he flushed as he looked about the tram.

His eyes met with Rufino.

Rufino looked toward the front of the tram and sank back in relief. His pulse slowed, he took a deep breath. There was no need to question the old man.

He was not Hans Friedrich Karl Franz Kammler.

The Path

a short story by Elizabeth Parikh

The boy wiped the contents of his stomach from his cheek when the island came into view. Constant arching and falling of the boat had left him feeling badly unloved and more poorly than he had ever known. He thought of holding bread on a fork over the fireplace at home, the flames burning his face, and his sister trying to shove him aside to toast her piece nearer to the fire before nanny took the toast away to be buttered.

He pulled the stenched, useless blanket back around his shoulders and sat back down on the floor of the open wooden vessel. He heard another tear in his tatty throw and glanced up at Thrabale, a thin man who had been rowing silently for hours. Thrabale looked back with no comment, the boy looked for just a hint of a heart and tried his best smile again. It took no effect. The man simply looked at his boy-cargo like a sack of potatoes.

He gave up and tried to warm himself further by folding his legs up to his belly, trying to cover as much flesh as he could from the soft drops of rain that persisted to soak every possible inch of his body. He felt new drops now running down his neck on to his chest, and heard his father's voice "You will go, you will learn, and so will return a man, ready for this kingdom."

The boy didn't want to be a man. If this was "being a man", he'd stay a boy and toast bread all day and catch butterflies in the summer.

With this journey's end not too far, he began to dread what was still to come. Would he be welcomed with open arms, a warm bed and a hot plate of food – or would he wish he were back on this wooden crate on the seas of some hell?

The old man angrily pulled on the bendy, stubborn

branches that the mistletoe had taken hold of. The creaking oak would not give way, he knew he'd tried to pull out far too much at once but his patience was now gone and the tree was left to show him what strength was.

He straightened up and placed his hand on the underarm of the branch. "Once again, you remind me. I am behaving weakly. I know. I have a boy-scholar arriving. Another request from Cornwall and yet will they remember us when the time is here?"

From behind, the old man heard a small cough. The small scholar had already arrived and was approaching with Thrabale, fresh from the seas. Looking back at his steadfast branches, he continued in his pursuits and when he next looked up some minutes later the boy was standing alone. His frozen spine and shivering skin made his back tall and straight, he looked like he could have been wrung out.

"Go start the fire, you'll find all you need. My house. It's back there," indicating behind himself.

The boy looked beyond but could see nothing but a small stone structure no bigger than himself. He looked back to see him still struggling to release any mistletoe from the tree and didn't know what to do for the best.

The man stopped and looked again at the boy, who stood as still and as rooted as the oak, his thoughts and fears wrapped around him as the mistletoe. He stopped and looked, right at the boy's eyes. One flashed green, the other, dark.

He came down from the tree to take a closer view. The boy gasped as he approached, the long beard and scowling eyes now in full view.

He looked down at the boy who looked ahead not daring to move his neck should it snap and crack from the cold winds and rain. He gently lifted the boy's chin to look into those eyes now pinched shut.

"Name, boy."

The boy opened them slowly and peered out. He saw a face with millions of lines of years, like the bark of the oak, he sensed both stubbornness and kindness.

Pulling apart the lips that had now flaked and stuck together, the boy replied, "Arthur."

Sow the Wind...

by Nick Johns

I did tell one person.

God help me.

During desperate times, I borrowed money.

From a Jew.

Despite my military pension, I couldn't repay it.

After all, the Republic was drowning in inflation.

Bitterly, I ranted at my neighbour, "These rich parasites are destroying this country. Something must be done."

The little Austrian corporal nodded.

A Walk on The Wild Side

by Nick Johns

"Don't look back. Run, quick sticks, and hide in the woods with Missy. No, don't stop. I'll come find you."

I hoped I would, anyway.

His hand was a dead weight on my shoulder. The bridge boards creaked beneath his weight.

Red-rimmed eyes peered from a thicket of beard and wild hair. His breath rattled and bubbled like a broken down old steam engine. I wrinkled my nose as he leaned closer. He was one of the bad ones. Seeping sores scattered his sweatshirt with red and yellow patches. One bloody, weeping toe peeked through his ripped tennis shoe.

"Now then, sweetheart, I kept my word, let the little ones go. Now it's your turn."

His grin was a ruined castle of broken teeth, and he smelled like the cesspit after Daddy got too sick to empty it.

He bent down. A filthy, nail bitten finger raised my chin.

"Hell, you're pretty! How come you didn't get the sickness?"

I clenched my muscles, tried breathing through my mouth. It didn't help.

How long had it been? Had Missy and Laura reached the woods yet? I tried to sneak a peek across the bridge but the finger stopped my head turning.

"No, honey, it's you and me now. What you got for me?"

I tried to smile at him. Like I'd seen Momma look at Daddy before they got sick.

"I'll show you."

I untied the front of my coat - and showed him.

The roar of the sawn-off twenty gauge made my ears ring, but the finger was gone, and the smell was now of gunpowder.

He reeled back, toppling from the bridge.

I sprinted for the woods.

"Girls! Let's play hide and seek! We must be quiet as mice."

The gunshot would attract more of them, I knew.

Excerpt from The Malford Chronicles by Horace of Christian Malford c 690AD

a short story by Allan Shipham

"Wake, boy!"

Young Owain was woken by a rattling wooden spoon in a bronze cooking pan. The pan was nearly worn along one edge, but it still boiled water and woke those who slept through daybreak. Owain helped his uncle tend to his animals, there were not many, but it was enough to keep the small family alive with the occasional wild animal feast when fortune favoured them. He had moved in with his uncle and aunt after his mother died from the bad weather and his father died after they had a poor harvest. It was some winters before, but Owain always remembered the river had frozen over soon after; it had been difficult to break the ice to get to the fish.

Uncle Uther often woke him at daybreak so they could go hunting, not that they always caught anything. The wild boars that lived in the woods were easily distracted in the early morning, nuzzling around in the undergrowth looking for truffles. Owain was in training to be a man; this day he would learn how to trap and kill a squealer. He had been looking forward to it for several weeks. He rubbed his eyes and looked across to the hut doorway. The skins were tied back to the doorjamb and he could see the sunlight creeping into the hut. It illuminated the smouldering, unburned shards of wood on the fire. The wood was damp from the rains, but the steam and the hissing made the late night storytelling more interesting.

"Be swift... For the beast will have their fill and retire, finding him and killing him will be harder."

Owain stirred from his half-sleep and rose to his feet. He stepped outside and relieved himself in the open latrine behind the hut. Owain's aunt Deuteria called out his name. He knew this meant he would have to go to the stream to collect some fresh water for cooking and washing.

"Uncle?" asked the boy, as he gathered several pots.

"Yes."

"Why is it that we don't eat the goose or the rabbit? They are plentiful and look like they carry meat for two, maybe three meals."

"Ah, that is a good question for a hunter," Uther smiled. "Legends are told that this land was once occupied by barbarians who worshiped stronger gods than ours. We believe if we kill a goose or a rabbit it will anger their gods, and the Barbarians will return to haunt us. They are likely to drop us back to ashes."

"Who are our gods? Won't they defend us?"

"Some Druids believe in the harmony of nature, peace and caring love." He paused. "Our people believe in many gods and goddesses, our lives revolve around worshipping and praising them. Mere mortals, we do not expect our gods to come down to earth to help us, we must find our own way and that is why today we hunt squealer. Now fill those pots with haste."

They set out toward the hunting grounds, near the floodplains. The valley of trees scented the air when the wind blew in the right direction. Today was one of those days. Sunlight glistened off the pools of swampy water from the south that peppered the floodplains, chasing the river down to the sea. A fine day, they bagged two pheasants and a squealer. Uther let Owain butcher the meat so his aunt could salt and cook it later. He liked to excavate the gizzards from its torso and watch the feral dogs steal them away, pulling each other as they fought over the same length of gut. Sometimes he had to stop slicing and sharpen his blade on a sharpening stone. Owain liked that it made him feel grown up.

They tied up the meat on a sapling tree after Owain had stripped the branches. They carried it between them as they set off back to the hut dropping by the sweet water well on the way. As they drew within feet of the well, they were surprised to see other countrymen nearby. The group came down the valley from the north scattering the crows as their horses gasped and neighed and their hoofs thundered their arrival. Owain could see several warriors on horses dressed in garish colours of green, orange and purple. They wore masks on their heads and, for protection, they carried large wooden shields and long metal swords.

Owain and his uncle crouched down in the dry wild grass at the side of the track way.

"Purple is the colour of the king," Uther said in a hushed voice.

"King Arthur Pendragon?"

"Last I heard."

They listened for the dialect of the warriors. Uther understood what they were saying, rose to his feet and approached the well. He knelt before the knight in purple colours; this was beyond a doubt the king.

"My Lord! Welcome, drink and share our beast."

Owain also knelt and looked up bewildered as the king thanked them both.

The king glanced down at Owain and said loudly, "Look! My god has sent me a toy for my lion beast."

His companions laughed and chortled.

"We muse with you, young man."

He steered his horse and stooped its neck closer to Owain. "I will need a fine young man like you to do my bidding, when these bones are old and weary." He smiled and winked at Owain.

Owain nodded, in confusion and fear at what he was agreeing to. The king's party dismounted and made camp.

All were interrupted after a while by another group arriving from the south-west. They were fewer in numbers and on foot. They had donkeys laden with goods. They appeared to be traders – dark in complexion and dressed in long gowns, they spoke broken English laced with Latin, a shared language with other cultures.

119

"My Lord!" exclaimed the trader who led the group. "I am looking for My Lord Arthur Pendragon."

"I am he. Speak your business."

"I am Joseph of Arimathea. This is my nephew and these are my companions. We have travelled some distance by boat to trade tin and deliver these scripts to the monks at Glastonbury. May we ask alms of you?"

The king nodded in agreement and embraced Joseph the leader.

"You are most welcome, sir, to join our company. We would be interested in your stories and would be pleased to share some of our own."

Owain quickly made friends with the trader's nephew as they were of the same age. The two of then took off to some rocky outcrops nearby that were known to Owain for exploration and adventure. They climbed large oak trees, bouldered some of the rocks and even discovered a nest with some eggs in it to help with the feast.

They got to find out about each other's lives as they walked back to camp.

"My father also died, and I too live and travel with my uncle," explained the boy.

"It is sad for us both."

"No, we must rejoice!" replied Owain's new friend. "We still belong and we have a reason. You must trust there is a place for you, and you must work hard."

"You are right, and I will."

Uther and the knights had set up a campfire and cooked off a lot of the meat. Joseph and his companions had gathered wild fruit, berries and tree bark. Fortunately, the knights were able to share ale they had brought with them. Everyone had a hearty feast and enjoyed each other's company. Joseph told stories of deserts and good deeds to the poor, the king spoke of mythical dragons and a crazy alchemist. Uther and Owain were pleased they had made new friends.

Afterwards, Uther explained they had to go home, and they prepared to leave.

"I hope to see you again," Owain said to his friend.

"I am to study for a while at Glastonbury," he replied. "I will try. Maybe you can visit me at Glastonbury."

"That is a great idea. I will also try. What is your name?"

"I am Jesus," he replied. "Remember my name and go in peace."

Soul Music

a short story by Nick Johns

At first they thought the child had a spring fever.

They were wrong.

Eventually, secretly, ignoring their priests, they called for me.

I knew it for what it was.

I studied it through the bars.

Seeing me, the child snarled and flew at the door. The weathered oak shook as if struck by a battering ram, giving final confirmation of my suspicion.

He fell to the floor, stunned and peaceful for a moment. Then I saw the feral glint return to his eyes. Crawling away, he crooned under his breath, his body rocking from side to side. Fingernails ripped crimson channels in his forearms, drops staining the floor as he sat, head on one side, regarding me with cold hatred.

Our eyes locked. He knew me.

I drew out my chosen weapon for this task and, taking a deep steadying breath, searched for a tune.

At the sound of the first note, his rocking stopped abruptly. A laugh began inside him, forcing its way out through pale red lips in single sounds, like bubbles from hot mud.

I changed to a different melody. A slow, halting lament, mirroring the rhythm.

The laugh rose in pace and pitch, daring me to follow. I moved to a sailors' jig, rising up the scale.

His mouth pursed then relaxed to emit a ragged giggle.

He stared, not blinking now, no movement in him, a wailing gargoyle. Faster he cackled. My jig became a frenzied tarantella, fingers flying across the stops.

He threw back his head and let out a throat-searing shriek. A single note, a demented torment to dogs and bats

– and me.

With sweating hands, I gripped the suddenly treacherous pipe, lest it squirm from my grasp and damn me. I gasped to wring the terminal note from its wooden guts and, a ringing noise rising in my ears and lights dancing before my eyes, found it.

It soared from the pipe, thin as the last failing breath that propelled it, pure as a morning echo across a winter lake. It called with a magical summons not to be denied in this world or the next. A hook and line cast into the netherworld.

The note shook, a ghostly vibrato and returned to me, its ethereal catch snagged, wriggling but helpless. It sank deep into the now cracked wooden flute and lay silent.

The child lay still, life betrayed only by an almost imperceptible movement of the chest, features now smooth once more in innocent rest. I leaned against the door, pale and sweating, legs shaking and called for my payment.

As footsteps approached in the passage outside, I snapped the tainted instrument between my shaking hands and ground the splintered shards underfoot.

They came but would not approach me or meet my eye. I thrust their grateful guilty gold deep into my pockets, brushed aside their nervous thanks and insincere offers of lodging and asked for directions to Hamelin.

The last piece

a short story by Pat Aitcheson

The stranger looked the type who didn't stay in one place too long. While I served the other customers, I watched him drink his pint of dark ale and silently brood. He wasn't local. We don't get much passing trade.

Dark hair escaped from his dark green knitted hat and curled over the collar of a very shabby leather jacket. The rest of his clothes were an odd assortment; ripped jeans, well-worn boots with Cuban heels that he must have got from a charity shop somewhere, and a spotless open-necked cream shirt. He had brought a couple of messenger bags with him and kept them at his feet.

I found him fascinating, and the symbols tattooed on his hands only added to the mystery. I obviously wasn't subtle enough, because the other barmaid Sam started to tease me about him.

"Watching the customers again. Or maybe just Mr Mysterious over there, eh?" She nudged me while handing change over the counter.

"Oh, stop it. Why should customers interest me tonight, or any night for that matter?" I kept my eyes on the half-poured Guinness in front of me, watching patterns swirl as it settled.

"He looks like he's always passing through somewhere, for sure. Want him to pass your way, maybe? I'll ask him for you." Sam stacked glasses as she talked.

"You will not." I topped up the Guinness and handed it over the bar to the customer. "Bet he won't be back tomorrow."

* * * * *

But the stranger did return, every night for nearly two

124

weeks. I served him perhaps three times, but he didn't really speak to me until the night I was wiping the table next to him.

He startled me. "Excuse me, but am I upsetting you? You have been watching me these nights."

My heart almost stopped, then hammered in my chest like a mad thing. "Sorry, no, of course not." I raised my head and found myself staring into clear grey eyes. He wasn't aggressive or drunk. All the same, I was wary.

"Is that no, I don't upset you, or no, you haven't been watching me?" The ghost of a smile played on his lips, and I might have found him attractive if I wasn't so flustered.

I pasted on my professional smile. "Enjoy your drink." I went back to the bar with my head held high and avoided him for the rest of the night.

* * * * *

Three shifts went by without seeing him. In quieter moments, I found myself wondering where he had gone. I had almost convinced myself that he had moved on, as Sam had said, when he came in early the next evening. There were no other customers at that hour. He wore the two messenger bags crossed over his body. They seemed heavy, but not enough to weigh him down.

This time he came directly to me at the bar. "Good evening, Laura. I hope you would not mind me asking, but would you care to talk sometime, over tea perhaps?"

My mouth fell open. I closed it again, relieved that Sam had the later shift and would not witness this exchange. I took a deep breath and looked into his eyes. I saw no threat there, yet I hesitated. Working in a pub meant I saw the worst of people, but he seemed different.

"Of course, I quite understand if you would rather not. Please forgive my impertinence. Good – "

"How do you know my name?"

"We are given two ears and one mouth. I use mine accordingly. I apologise for the intrusion." He turned to go, and I decided there and then that my boring life could use some novelty.

"No need to apologise. And you are?"

"I have quite forgotten my manners. Gavin North. Pleased to meet you." He held out his hand, revealing a gold signet ring and rather cleaner fingernails than I expected.

I shook it, feeling a little awkward. "Laura Bevan. We could go to the coffee shop on the high street. There's only the one, you can't miss it. Would tomorrow at three suit you?"

"Marvellous. I shall look forward to seeing you then." He still held my hand, and for one crazy moment I thought he might kiss it. Instead he nodded and left, just as the first regulars arrived.

I scolded myself silently for taking a chance on a stranger, even a cute one with grey eyes. Then again, there was nothing else in my calendar. At the very least, I'd get a story out of it to share with Sam.

* * * * *

I set out early the next day, but he was still earlier. He waited outside the coffee shop with his bags, a dark green hat pulled over his ears.

"I am so glad you came," he said with a smile. "Shall we go inside? It's a little fresh out here in the wind." He opened the door for me to go inside first. We ordered, Earl Grey tea for him and hot chocolate for me.

"I wonder why you chose to accept my invitation, Laura. Although naturally I am delighted that you did."

"No reason, except you look like you have a story to tell. We don't get many travellers here, being off the beaten track. Apart from a few tourists looking for the end of the rainbow."

He raised his eyebrows. "Really? I thought everyone knew that to be a complete myth."

"Well, it's said the rainbow touched the ground near

126

here three times, and opened a gateway to the fairy realm. And of course the fairies buried gold nearby to distract anyone who got close. They don't want humans troubling them. But no-one has ever found a door or any gold. And why would they? It's just a yarn told to attract tourists. There's nothing else going on around here."

"Do you believe any of that?" He sipped tea, but his eyes never left my face.

"Oh, I loved all those stories when I was a girl. I wished I could be taken away by the wee folk. My dad used to tell me some really tall tales at bedtime. When he could."

I looked away from Gavin's intense gaze and studied my mug. I didn't want to remember the nights when drink stole Pa's stories and unleashed his temper on Mam and me. Life was hard. Stories became my escape. I was grateful when Gavin spoke, his tone gentle and impossible to place.

"Bedtime stories are the best kind. Some of them are even true. What would you say if I told you that my life is a kind of story, a search for something most do not believe in and have never seen?"

I sat up. "I would say, tell me more."

"I found the end of the rainbow." He glanced at me and went on. "It happened many years ago. I was a poor farmer's son then. I thought I saw it touch down in the next field, brilliant and about a yard wide. I dropped my tools and ran, but to my horror there was another man running for the same thing. He was weighed down by saddlebags, but he got there first."

Gavin's tale had my complete attention and I nodded at him, fascinated. "And what happened next?"

"I was prepared to fight him for the gold, but to my surprise he dumped the saddlebags as soon as he reached the rainbow. Gold spilled all over the grass. I thought he was crazy. I ran faster than I ever had in my life. As I drew closer, I saw his hair was turning white. He aged in front of me, becoming bent and wrinkled, but continued to

127

smile. The yellow band of the rainbow widened and grew bright like sunlight. He stepped into it and vanished.

"Well, all I cared about was the gold, as you can imagine, and I scrabbled around gathering every last coin." He stopped and stared out of the window. A light rain was falling, and he stirred his cooling tea absently, his eyes fixed on some distant spot.

"I paid my family's debts, and I found a girl, and we married. We spent a lot of the money on a house and land, but we never had a family. Then Catherine was taken by the smallpox."

I looked at him, confused for a moment. Smallpox was some old-time disease, wasn't it? "When was that, Gavin?"

Silence stretched between us, and when he raised his head, a tear ran down his cheek.

"I made the wrong choice, Laura. I only looked at the short term, and I was blinded by greed. In turn, I was cursed to stay young, to watch those I loved come and go. Now, I want to make the right choice. I have all the gold save one piece, and this is the best place to return it. I should know." He laughed bitterly. "I have wandered these many years in search."

I reached over and touched his hand, the soft hand of a man who had never laboured for a living, who was clothed in an old-fashioned shirt of fine linen.

"I am so sorry." I thought of my Pa's tales, and the pendant he had left me in his will. There was nothing to keep me in this forgotten town.

"Why have you told this story, why me, why now?" I kept my voice down, though the café was empty.

"Something compelled me, from the first time I saw you. I cannot fully explain it. This is my burden to bear, and I have no right to foist it on you." He produced a white handkerchief from his inside pocket and dabbed at his eyes.

I decided that a fresh drink would help, and excused myself. He had regained his composure by the time I brought tea and hot chocolate back to the table.

"Gavin North, you may have your wish. I have a proposition for you." I pulled my pendant out of my shirt, and watched his eyes widen. Silently he took a single gold coin from one of the bags, the twin of my own. A little spark passed from one to the other. Both coins glittered. Our eyes met.

"My father found this coin in a field, before I was born. He had it made into this pendant for my twelfth birthday." I closed my fingers around its familiar shape, felt the warmth where it had lain against my skin.

"It was the only thing he left me, but somehow I could never sell it, even when times were really hard. He told me stories about it. I know where and when we can make our dreams come true."

Expressions chased across his unlined face, finally settling on hope and relief. There was something ancient about his grey eyes, and his smile was beautiful to see.

"I knew it. I left this place more than once, but something always drew me back. I hardly dared hope, but... you mean it? Do not trifle with me, Laura. I am so tired. All I want is to rest."

I gripped his hand. "I want time and you have had all you want. We return the gold, you pass through, and I will have all the lives I need." Excitement bubbled in my chest as the sun peeped through rain clouds. "Let's go, right now."

Gavin kissed my hand, and shouldered his weighty bags. Together we stepped outside, into sunshine and rain that promised the futures we both dreamed of. As the rainbow showed pale in the sky, he took my arm and guided me to his motorbike parked nearby.

"Horses are not much in vogue nowadays," he said with a wink.

"Very true," I replied. "Head west, out of town. It's getting brighter every minute." Although I'd never been on a motorbike before, I climbed aboard without hesitation. I settled and put my hands on his waist.

Then we were off, watery sunlight glinting off wet roads, the wind in my hair and hedgerows flashing past us in a green blur. At my direction, he rode through a gap in the hedge and into a field. The rainbow glowed above us, and Gavin slowed down. He came to a halt a few yards from where it rested on the grass, shimmering and beautiful.

"I have to leave the gold here, and then it is all yours." He dropped the messenger bags on the ground, and took my hands in his. His curls were already turning silver, his cheeks sagging and lined, but his smile still lit up his face.

"I am so glad to have known you, Laura Bevan. If only for such a brief time. You remind me of her, and now perhaps I will be with my Catherine again. Thank you, my dear, and good luck. Don't stay too long. Only until the world is a burden on you. Remember life is nothing without love." His voice wavered, the words of an old man.

I supported him the few steps to the band of yellow light, which expanded as we approached. "I will never forget you, Gavin North. Rest well." I kissed his hand, now gnarled and liver spotted, and watched his hunched figure vanish.

The rainbow sparkled for an instant, then vanished with a distinct pop.

The bags really were heavy. It took some effort to hang them on the bike. I couldn't ride it. Not yet. But my house, the place where I grew up, was only two fields away. That was no distance to push a bike, not when it carried your whole future.

Excitement bloomed in my chest and I laughed, exultant, giddy with possibility. Clouds chased across the blue sky and a thought came to me.

Even several lifetimes will not be enough for all my adventures.

The Dying of the Light

a panegyric by Nick Johns

My Lord, here are your guardsmen. Each is worthy of your trust and love. Every man here bears a champion's name and tales are told of their great renown. Families across the land have welcomed them and feasted them on the hero's portion. Our enemy's men tremble and their women frighten children with the mere mention of their names.

Here is Einon ap Geraint, justly called the Anvil. He stood against their vanguard in the first rush of their charge. They swarmed and swooped numerous as starlings roosting on a summer evening, but they broke against him as waves against a rocky shore.

Here is Brynmor ap Idris, the Mountain. He slew the enemy's champion, Grimm the Kinslayer, who boasted that his spear was a gift from their Gods. In that mighty struggle, Brynmor took the first thrust from the spear in order to lay hands upon the warrior. With arms rippling like oaken boughs in a winter storm, Brynmor lifted the enemy high above his head, then threw him down, breaking Grimm's back. The very earth trembled and shook with the impact. He cut off the Kinslayer's head and broke the spear across his knee.

Here is your captain, Cadfan, the Battle Raven. In the heat of the fight, his flame shone and dazzled like the setting Sun. He carved a path of blood to their Prince and none could stand against him. Alone at last, he faced the royal guard, who fell to his terrible sword like ripe corn falls before a scythe, and great was the slaughter of his passing and worthy of song.

The last man here is best known to you. Maldwyn, named Brave Friend, whose butchered body we found shielding yours, broken sword in hand, faithful even to his last breath.

These warriors are the brightest and the best of our people. Each of these mighty men, sworn to defend you, and oath breakers none, now travels with you, in death as they did in life, as you begin your next journey.

The wood of your pyre burns fitfully, gathered at night from land still wet with the blood of your enemies. Broken weapons surround you, Arthmael, last Lord of the Cymru, but your hand still holds your royal sword.

Your people have dire need of you, and your champions, against an enemy that lays waste to our homes and families. May your return be as swift as the next Sun's rising. The smoke bearing your spirit rises and turns toward the setting Sun. So, until come again, we will sing our songs and look to the West.

Cowboy's Lament

a short story by Michael J Richards

"All I'm saying, Bob Hargrove," he says, "is I'm a hero waiting for his hour to come. What's wrong with that?"

"What's wrong with that," I say, "is that you're speaking too loud and too often for anyone to take serious anything you say. You gotta be careful, Joe, I'm telling ya, ya gotta be careful. You don't know who's listening, do ya, and one of these days – "

But Joe Grant ain't listening. That's 'cos he don't listen to no-one. He don't even listen to himself.

He's a great big bulk of a bear, leaning up against the bar, his belly hair bursting out of his shirt. The top button's missing 'cos he's two sizes too big to wear a shirt two sizes too small and so you can see hair sprouting out the top as well. And his arms, the size and elegance of prickly pear cactuses, are covered in black hairs the strength of the wire they use to link up corral posts.

His beard, untrained and uncombed, has bits of brown meat or soup entwined in its whiskers. And his hair hasn't been washed for days – no, weeks. It's untamed, straggled and hanging wherever it lands.

Sad thing is, in the early '70s, some eight or ten years ago, he was smart, good and sober. He was an honest wrangler who put in a good day's work for Mr Lucien Maxwell and then, after he died in '75, for his son, Pete. But for some reason, he went off the rails. Some say he got himself hitched up with a Navajo woman and he treated her bad so she went back to her people. Some say he got in with a gambling crowd who fleeced him for every dollar he had.

Nobody knows, 'cos Joe don't speak of it – which don't make him no unacclaimed hero. He's a drunk, a fat slob of a lazy, thieving drunk. And he's leaning over my bar, once

133

again drinking himself into forgetfulness. But he's one of my best customers, so I'm good to him so he buys my alcohol.

"You see," Joe pipes up, "before the day is out, everyone will know my name 'cos I'm gonna be a hero."

But I'm no longer interested in false tales of foolish bravado. I got a saloon to run. Up the corner, the brown-hatted Chisum brothers are in a poker game with two Mexicans and I can see even from here the Chisums ain't gonna win. They twitch too much and whoop when they get dealt winning hands. They ain't never heard the words "poker face".

And Ella, the chantoosy, leans against the joanna, listening to Clark, my dim-witted sap of a brother, picking out some tune or other. No idea what it is. I ain't gotta head for knowing tunes. As far as I can make out, it's just a noise. But customers like tunes so tunes is what they get. And it keeps Clark in work. It's the only thing he's any good at. Which is just as well, 'cos I need a piano-player in my saloon.

Ella breaks into "Cowboy's Lament", which she always says is her favourite song. I recognise it from the words, not from her charmless singing – and certainly not from my brother's clumsy-fisted playing:

"I see by your outfit, that you are a cowboy.
These words he did say as I slowly walked by.
Come sit down beside me and hear my sad story,
For I'm shot in the chest, and today I must die."

Watching Ella, Joe pushes his glass towards me for a re-fill. When she finishes, he throws his hands in the air and claps loudly. "Yah, yah, yah!" he shouts. "Ain't that the greatest song you ever heard?" he hollers over to the poker players. "Ain't she the prettiest singing bird? Say, Miss Ella, let me buy you a drink."

"No, thanks, Joe," she says, turning her back to him, so she faces Clark, who breaks out into some dirge or other.

Well, it sounds like a dirge to me.

A man I ain't seen before pushes through the batwing doors. He's young, maybe early twenties, smooth and clean-shaven, about my height – that's five eight – he comes up to Joe's shoulders – with the stillest, bluest eyes you ever did see. As he passes the poker-game, he nods to the Chisum brothers.

They wave to him. Maybe they know him. Maybe they don't. Maybe they're being friendly. Maybe they're trying their darnedest to distract the grinning Mexicans.

And he sure is neatly dressed, like when he leaves here, he's gonna have his wedding picture took. Grey pants, grey vest with a silver watch-chain, white shirt and a sleek black coat. He's wearing a black sombrero which, when he takes it off and rests on the bar, lets his blond mophead fall about his ears. A holster on his right side carries a Colt Thunderer, which having a 41 Long Colt double action, is a nice piece.

"What can I get ya?" I say.

"A bottle of Ayer's Sarsaparilla, if you please," he says quietly, as if speaking to a preacher man.

"And can I get you a smoke?" I say.

"No, thank you, sir," the young man says. "I don't use the stuff."

I pour him the drink. He gives me a dollar piece.

Joe laughs. "That ain't no drink for a man," he says – again, loudly so everyone can hear.

"Well, sir," says the young man directly at him, "I ain't never had the pox. And that's 'cos I take Ayer's Sarsaparilla. So you laugh all you like, my friend, and as you laugh, I remain in good health."

Joe turns and looks at the young fella. The young fella doesn't move. Suddenly, Joe bursts into raucous laughing. The young fella smiles and toasts Joe with his sarsaparilla. Joe steps forward and slaps the young fella on the back.

"That sure is right," Joe shouts to everyone. "That sure is right." His whinnying horse-like laugh echoes around the room. "Let me buy you another."

"That's mighty kind of you, sir," he replies. "My name's McCarty. Glad to make your acquaintance."

They shake hands. The newcomer pulls out a silk handkerchief from his pants' pocket and wipes his palms.

"And I'm Joe Grant," Joe says. "Bob," he says, turning to me, not noticing the young man's insult, "let's get some more drinks here. And a sassprilla for Mr McCarty, my new friend who's standing here full of good health and not the pox."

As they laugh again, I pour out the bourbon for Joe and another herbal remedy for McCarty. Joe hands me the coins.

"So," Joe says, "what's your business here?"

"Just passing through," he says. "Thought I'd get some refreshment. And you, sir, what's your business?"

"Me?" Joe snorts through his drink. "Oh, I don't do nuttin' much in partic'lar. Just hang about. Looking for – Well, when I rose this morning, I kinda decided I'd make myself a hero before this day is over."

"Oh, give that up, Joe," I say, cleaning some glasses 'til they gleam.

"Oh?" McCarty says, studying his refreshment. "Why would you wanna do that?"

"Well, it's like I figure. It's the only way to get on these days. Working for a living is for numbskull critters and those who ain't got two brains to rub together. Me, I'm smart. I'm gonna walk up Easy Street. Gonna get myself a name for some deed or other and then live off the proceeds for the rest o' ma life. I'm gonna shoot me a known killer or maybe capture a desperado on the run. Then collect the reward and get in all the newspapers. Charge hundreds o' dollars for interviews and sell my story. Like that. Yes, Mr McCarty, sir, that's my plan."

"And you gonna do all that by sunset today?" McCarty says.

"Yes, sir. I am."

"And who's you planning to capture?"

"Oh, jeez, I don't know," Joe says, leaning forward

over the bar, starting to slump down. "I thought maybe Jesse James. Or Johnny Ringo, Billy the Kid, Ike Clanton. Someone like that. It don't matter who. As long as they're famous and carry a price I can collect."

"That calls for courage, my friend," McCarty says, looking about the saloon. "Have you got that sort o' courage?"

I too survey the scene. The poker game has stopped. The four men at the table have put down their cards, the stakes momentarily forgotten, as they study the two men's discussion. Joe puts his elbows on the bar and rests his chin in his cupped hands.

"I reckon so," he slurs.

"Then," McCarty says, "you'll be a hero."

Ella leans against the piano, a glass of water in her hand.

"Yes, sir," says an increasingly befuddled Joe. "That is my intention."

Clark's sitting with his back to them but slowly turns so he can see.

"Everyone loves a hero," Joe says.

I'm standing, hands resting on the bar, tensing up, ready for sudden movements.

"They sure do," says McCarty, swirling his half-drunk sarsaparilla around in its glass. "I know the feeling well."

"You do?" Joe says. "You see," he whispers so only McCarty and I can hear, "I ain't never had anyone look up to me. J'unnerstan'? Nobody has – ever – ever – told me it was worth my while breathing on this God's earth. That's all I want. Someone to tell me I'm worth the trouble. That ain't much to ask of a man, is it?"

The young man leans forward and gently pulls Joe up. "No, course it ain't," he says. "Course it ain't." He looks at me. "Another drink for my friend here. Anyway," he sighs, "being a hero ain't all good. Always on show, always having to be ready to perform. And you ain't allowed no weaknesses." He holds up his empty glass and hands it to me for another drink. "Everyone thinks they know who you are," he adds, "and they don't."

Joe wipes his brow. "I'd kinda like that," he says, as I pour him another shot of bourbon.

"No, you wouldn't."

"You seem to know a lot about it, my friend."

"No, sir," McCarty replies. "Can't say I do. Just passing comment on what I've observed."

I give him another Ayer's and take his coins. I breathe a little more freely as a brief crisis rides outa town. The others obviously sense the same. The men go back to their cards. Clark plonks out some ditty on the upright. Ella strolls into the back room.

"Anyway," McCarty says, "how are you intending to carry out this heroic deed?"

Joe stands tall, his belly sticking out more than usual. "My weapon is my companion and my ally," he announces, producing his pistol. "It ain't never let me down yet," he says, "and I ain't planning on it letting me down this time, neither."

McCarty leans over to take a look. "That's a mighty fine weapon you got there," he says. "Mind if I take a look? Is that – is that handle mother of pearl?"

"No, sir," says Joe, swaying somewhat as he tries to stand, 'though whether he's intoxicated through the drink or because someone is interested in him, I can't say. "It's genuine ivory. Here, take it. Hold it. Ain't it grand?"

McCarty takes it and wraps his right hand around it. "Yes, sir," he says. "It's grand all right." Joe has slumped again on the bar. McCarty puts his index finger on the trigger and, trying it for size, waves the piece about.

He glances down at Joe, who is staring into another empty bourbon glass. He frees the weapon from his hand, opens the cylinder and gives it a turn. He's counting the bullets. The normal five in a six-barrel chamber. Greenhorns who don't know what they're doing fill a six-cylinder chamber with six bullets. Those who know their weapon-handling fill only five chambers and keep the sixth resting on the hammer. Then the weapon don't accidentally fire and injure someone.

McCarty turns the cylinder so the empty chamber rests against the hammer. He takes hold of the barrel and, gripping the panel, offers Joe the weapon. Joe's nearly asleep, so McCarty places the weapon back in his holster and smiles at me. Out of the corner of my eye, I see Ella come back to the piano.

"Some hero," McCarty says.

"Yeah," I say, "more like zero."

He laughs. "Where's your latrine?"

"Through that door there, mister," I tell him. "Turn left."

He saunters off, his right hand clutching his Colt.

When he's left the room, Ella shouts across to me over Clark's playing, "He's grown a swagger since he first came in."

"Seems like he has," I shout back.

"Yeah, well," Jim Chisum shouts from the poker table, "maybe he's got something to swagger over."

"What's that mean?" Ella shouts back as she slaps Clark on the head for him to stop playing while we shout around the saloon. But Clark takes this as a signal to play louder and faster.

"Clark!" she hollers. "Stop that, will ya!" And she slams the piano-lid on his knuckles. He don't cry out. He's used to it. She does that at least twice a day. His knuckles must be made from boulder-rock. He gets up and goes out the same way McCarty did.

"Well, for his sake, I hope he gets back here before Clark reaches him," Ella spits out as she walks over to me for another glass of water.

"I think he can look after himself," I say. "Maybe he likes a bit of latrine action."

"He sure is a pretty boy," she says as she takes the glass from me. "I wouldn't mind a bit of action with him myself."

By now, Joe is coming to. "Gimme another drink," he slurs, pushing his glass to me.

"Ain't you had enough for one day?" I say.

"C'm' on, Joe," Ella says, putting her arm around him. "Time to go home, eh?"

McCarty comes in from the way he went out. "So, Joe," he says as he approaches the bar, "you made yourself a hero yet?"

"I'm gonna shoot Billy the Kid," Joe announces, standing up, suddenly wide awake and sober.

"Joe – " I say.

"Oh, leave the old fool," Ella snaps and walks over to the poker game to chat with the Chisum boys and the sharp-eyed Mexicans.

"No, Joe," I say again. "Listen – " 'Cos now, I'm sure of the feeling that's been growing in me for a while now. Something about McCarty ain't right and I don't much like what I'm fearing.

"You see, Joe," McCarty says, "your problem is, you don't know what Billy the Kid looks like so how're you shoot him?"

The black-bearded giant looks down at the blond young man. "I'll know," he booms. "The Lord will guide me."

McCarty looks around the room, at the quiet poker players who now realise what's going on. At Ella, who latched on a few seconds ago. At me, who worked it out when Ella remarked on McCarty's swagger as he went to the outhouse.

"Well, Joe," McCarty says, "this is your other problem. I told you my name is McCarty. William Henry McCarty. Mean anything to ya?"

Joe shakes his head. "Not a damned thing," he drawls.

"These days," he adds, "I go by the name of William Bonney."

He shakes his head again. "No, sir, don't mean a damned thing, either."

"Jesus H Christ, Joe!" Ella shouts across from the poker game. "Don't be such a fool. Don't you know nothing? He's Billy the Kid!"

Joe's lower jaw drops. His tongue falls out his mouth

and hangs like a pair of on-duty whore's knickers.

"Now's your chance, Joe Grant," John Chisum yells. "You can be the hero you've bin sayin' you're gonna be."

Billy picks up his hat and puts it on. Smiling, he turns towards Ella and doffs his hat. "Ma'am, it's been nice to have met you."

He waves at the Chisums. "You ain't gonna win that game, boys," he calls. "That Mexican's got a full house. Three aces, two kings. And he's got another ace up his sleeve." As Ella backs away, the Chisum brothers stand and reach for their weapons.

Billy turns to face me. "And thank you, Mr Hargrove, for your hospitality. This sure is a fine saloon for a hero to rest at."

He puts his hat on and turns towards the exit. His back to Joe, he raises his left arm and waves. "'Bye, Joe," he says, walking away.

Like in slow motion, Joe pulls his pistol from its holster, levels it up and pulls the trigger. An empty click echoes around the room.

Billy turns and fires, hitting Joe on the chin. As he lurches backwards, Billy fires another two shots into his heart and chest. His body falls to the floor, blood and inside body stuff spilling everywhere.

Billy stands there, replaces his weapon and looks at me. He says, "It was a game for two, and I got there first," and with that same swagger, leaves my saloon.

Clark runs in from the back, pulling up his pants. "What happened?" he shouts. "What did I miss?"

But it's either too late or too early to explain.

"Don't matter," I tell him, as the Chisum boys put their weapons away, sit down and pick up their cards as if nothing's happened. "Go get the sheriff and the undertaker, there's a good boy. And then get me the bucket and mop."

Humour and Whimsy

Why do I write?

a poem by Allan Shipham

I want to tell you I'm a literary expert,
books, stories, poems and an occasional excerpt.
But alas, I'm green, unnoticed,
hoping one day I will get noticed.

I write songs people like to sing,
like: I'm a puppet on a string[1].
I write humour which appeals to me,
It's an ex-parrot, it has ceased to be[2].

For moral guidance, like monks medieval,
Yea, though I walk... I will fear no evil[3].
Romance creeps in but it's not in my plan,
Frankly, my dear, I don't give a damn[4].

I write a story to make you freeze with fright,
like: Listen to them, children of the night[5].
Science fiction reaps its payloads,
Roads? Where we're going, we don't need roads[6].

Drama can make your hair go curled,
like: She burned too bright for this world[7].
But I like a challenge, if truth be told,
imagine a poem that begins: In days of old...

To answer the question was rather tough,
I always ask have I done enough?
Other times, hours done fatiguing,
to make the stories more intriguing.

So why I write is a complex thing,
some may read and others may sing.
I have to say it's for my enjoyment,
in hope one day it leads to employment.

[1] "Puppet on a String", song by Bill Martin and Phil Coulter, 1967

[2] "Dead Parrot Sketch", John Cleese and Graham Chapman, 1969

[3] from Psalm 23, *The Bible,* Authorised King James Version, 1611

[4] from *Gone with the Wind*, film directed by Victor Fleming, 1939

[5] from *Dracula*, film directed by Tod Browning, 1931

[6] from *Back to the Future*, film directed by Robert Zemeckis, 1985

[7] from *Wuthering* Heights, Emily Bronte, 1847

Tell me a story

a prose poem by Pat Aitcheson

Tell me a story. Give me tales of a thousand nights, warm scented breeze in my hair, sand in my shoes. Take me to the farthest pole, blue-green fire dancing in the sky, every breath clouding in crisp night air.

Tell me a story. Let me taste salt sea tang while scorching sun beats down on wooden decks. Show me dolphins, flying fish, great whales breaching white-topped waves. Let me glimpse bright eyed merpeople watching deep under the surface, waiting.

Tell me a story. Carry me on red and silver rockets to vast silent space stations where the brilliant stars never go out. Show me galaxies born from cosmic dust. Bring whispers from strange aliens and even stranger, once-human creatures.

Tell me a story. Lead me up the tallest mountain, rocks skittering away under exhausted feet, lungs screaming for oxygen. Describe that joyful promised land seen only from the summit. Inspire my belief. Take me there on wings of faith.

Expand my horizons. Play my emotions. Cloak mindless chatter, soothe unthinking wounds, only with words. Let me shed this skin, be someone else, somewhere else, sometime else. Let me be lost and found. Give me distance, just for a while.

Tell me a story.

Kissing Tarmac

a short story by Allan Shipham

I remember exactly how it all started. I was dreaming about a car crash. I have no idea how I came to be in the car crash, but there I was.

For some reason, I was driving my sister's car in the middle of the night down some road. I hate her guts, and I've absolutely no idea why she'd let me drive the damn thing, but there you are.

During this crash, I was thrown out of the car and I bounced along the tarmac until I hit the plastic road cones. They slowed me down to a stop and it all went dark.

Next thing I remember was waking up with a banging head. I found it hard to focus my eyes and I could smell this awful smell, like burnt cola. I tried to find out where I was and I realised I was still in the middle of the road. I thought my life was in danger, so I tried to run to the side of the road as I could hear cars coming.

I couldn't move, not one bit. I looked around to see why and all I could see was orange! On my life! Orange!

It may be hard to understand but somehow I was changed into a road cone! I was stuck to the middle of the road for hours, lots of cars tore past splashing cold wet mud all over me. A bus even ran over my foot 'cos the driver was weaving and skidding all over the place.

I cried and I shouted for help, but no one came. I was powerless. Do you know how scary that can be? Do you have any idea?

Well, eventually about five hours later, this lorry comes close and some guy picks me up and stacks me with other road cones on the back of this lorry. I could feel their weight on top of me and all around me. It was hard to breathe. I couldn't see anything or hardly hear anything.

I remember while we were moving along, the driver of

the lorry drove around a corner too fast and the stack I was in fell over. Then I was on my left side for a long time which was a whole lot worse. It was like being tied to a conga line and then thrown over in the back of a lorry. I felt sick, and my headache got worse.

We pulls up and they starts throwing the cones along this path. There was no care or consideration and one of the bastards even kicked me. There was a lot of flashing lights and sirens, I've no idea what was going on, I couldn't see.

When it was all over, this policeman takes a pee all over me, it was disgusting. I never expected that. It stank and was hot, it scalded. I cried again for about two hours, but no one could hear me. As luck would have it, it started raining about then and most of the piss washed off. Never thought I'd be so grateful for the rain.

The rain was welcome when it started, but after several hours and with a bit of wind, it stings! I couldn't believe how draining it was to be abandoned in the rain and the wind. I was knackered. I was cold, and I was wet. I really couldn't see where it was all going to end.

I'd given up shouting for help at this stage, I hadn't any tears left to cry. I actually believed that this was my lot! I could feel the day was nearing its end as the light started to fade; dark cold, wet and with the worse headache ever. It felt like I had a hole in my head!

Just my luck! Some teenage kids then decides to have a kick-about with me. Kicking me between each other and then tossing me in the air like a badminton shuttle. I think they were drinking alcohol and smoking weed because they became louder and more abusive. Then several of them left the game.

One lad sat on me as they sat in a circle passing the joint around. He kept farting on me, the smelly little shit bag. I think he'd eaten a curry the night before and had a few beers. It was disgusting! I know they were smoking weed as one of them puked up all over me and this fat kid kicked me into the canal. I was half-in, half-out of the canal half-covered in puke and I couldn't lose that smell of piss.

Around midnight it went dark again and I woke up in my own bed with all my arms and feet again.

It was some kinda curse I tell ya! Some kinda curse!"

* * * * *

That's all very well, Mr Crowman, but it doesn't explain how you came to be found with the stolen laptop and its carry case. This is a stolen goods investigation and you are in a police station. Now, I haven't interrupted you, will you now answer my questions?

I just called to say

a short story by Elizabeth Parikh

Dials on phone. Waits.

– Hi, Jonathan? It's Jenni Eccles.
– Hiiii!
– Yeah! It's been, what, at least two years! How are you? How've you been?
– Married!
– And children!
– And a house! Wow! You've really packed it in!
– And a six-figure salary! Stop! You're making me jealous!
– And what does she do?
– A supermodel?!
– A brain surgeon. Right, right. Listen you might have been better with a urologist.
– Me? Yeah, I'm great! Fantastic! Yeah I've just been out shopping, and erm, now I'm back. In my house, flat, studio apartment. Yeah, it's a really great space. Got everything I want. In the one room. Anyway, I just called to say that I've er, got Chlamydia and you might want to get tested too just in case. Er, and that's it.

Knocks on table.

– All right, I'm gonna have to go. That's the door.
– Yep, that's the wood on the door being knocked.
– Okay. 'Bye, now. 'Bye.

Hangs up. Dials on phone. Waits.

– Hi, is that Mrs Parker? It's Jenni Eccles here.
– I'm fine, thank you. How are you, Mrs Parker?

– Well, yes, you can trust Hoskins Homeware. Sorry to interrupt, Mrs Parker, but is Terry there?

– Siberia? Well, it's a bit delicate, Mrs Parker. Terry and I loved each other very much, for a fortnight, and we had coitus and I've got Chlamydia and I need to let him know, so he can get tested.

– No. I don't think it will have gotten on your sofa.
– Well, I'm not sure, Mrs Parker. You could give it a steam clean if you're concerned but, as I said, I don't think it works that way.

– Well, Hoskins might stock a steam clean range. You'd have to give them a call.
– I better go, Mrs Parker, but lovely speaking to you. 'Bye now.

Hangs up. Dials on phone. Waits.

– Hmm, answer phone.
– Bonjour, Didier, je m'appelle Jenni Eccles et je suis met you on a ski trip a while ago, et nous had sex and now je suis got Chlamydia. Vous might want to get tested. Je suis désolée! Au revoir.

Hangs up. Dials on phone. Waits.

– Dave! It's Jenni Eccles. How are you?
– Right.
– Dust mites.
– Trillions of bacteria, I see.
– Yeah.
– So basically there's nothing wrong with you.
– Okay, but before you tell me about *down there* I need to tell you that, er, I am fighting fit, really great, apart from one thing. I've got Chlamydia. Now, please don't freak out. It's fine. You just need to get tested. There's

152

no hygiene element. You don't need to clean everything.

– Yes, I've heard those steam cleaners are good but it won't make any difference. You just need to get tested.

– I think you can get them from Hoskins, but you'd need to give them a call.
– No, I will not contribute to the cost!
– Even if they are on offer!

Hangs up. Phone rings. Answers.

– Hello?
– Yes, this is Miss Eccles.
– No, I have not been recommending that your steam cleaners will get rid of Chlamydia.
– I honestly did not.
– Yes, I understand Hoskins does not dispense sexual health-related contraptions.
– Actually, while I've got you on the phone, are they on offer?
– Buy one get one free? Interesting. I'll have to call you back.

Hangs up. Dials on phone. Waits.

– Dave. It's Jenni. I'm still angry with you but the steam cleaners are on buy one get one free at Hoskins and Terry Parker's mum wants one too. So give her a call. 'Bye.

Hangs up. Dials on phone. Waits.

– Hi. Ronnie?
– It's Jenni Eccles. Remember me?
– Curly hair?
– You left me in your flat.

– For three days?
– I looked after five of your kids?
– While you went on a bender with my dad?
– And your brother visited from the Highlands?
– And I took my tea weak?
– Yeah! You do remember! Well I just wanted to let you know I've got Chlamydia.
– No. It's not an achievement. It's a sexually transmitted disease.
– You mean you gave it to me? And you never called!
– Not being able to pronounce it is no excuse! I could be infertile because of your gutless actions. Shame on you! And your selfishness! Have you no moral compass?

– I should think so too. Is your brother there? Well, just pass on the message to him as well. 'Bye.

Hangs up. Phone rings. Answers.

– Hello?
– Yes, this is she.
– A mix up?
– I don't have Chlamydia?
– I've never had Chlamydia?
– But I've got flat feet.
– Yeah. Thanks for that. Not.

Hangs up.

A day in the life of an Animal

a song by Allan Shipham

I woke late this morning, my head was thick,
Dr Teeth was yawning, gold sparkles and sick!
Floyd was still snoring, some chick on his arm,
she looked like Miss Piggy, fresh from the farm.

Big Bird came a-knocking, is it a he or a she?
I couldn't be doing, I needed a pee.
Waldorf and Statler burst in through the door,
"Bah, I hated that party!" "Gee, I wanted it more!"

Kermit stirred groggy, "Guys! Show starts at two!"
"Fat chance of that!" scoffed Doctor Honeydew,
"I'll try my new joke," said Fozzie Bear. "Knock
Knock, at the door"
"Shit!" Rizzo growled, nasty. "Answer it and you're
sore."

Now Gonzo was sober, he tried not to drink,
but Beaker had spiked him, that dude could not blink.
I started a drum roll, Ralph tinkled the keys,
a fanfare in B flat was just what they needs.

Now, if you like puppets, that ain't got no strings,
then you love the Muppets, they dances, they sings.
But after a party, still drunk and abused,
Mahna Mahna, is all you're likely to hear.

Mahna Mahna…

Life's a Drag!

a comedy sketch by Allan Shipham

CHARACTERS

in order of appearance

LADY-ROSE FLOWERS, an experienced drag queen

MISS BIANCA DEVINE, an inexperienced drag queen

A SMALL, SQUALID DRESSING-ROOM OF THE BLUE ANCHOR THEATRE AND ENTERTAINMENT BAR.

Drag queen LADY-ROSE FLOWERS comes in, furiously looks back out on to the stage, then sits in front of an elaborate dressing table mirror, illuminated by small light bulbs and adorned with feather boa.

As he removes his outrageous wig and places it on a mannequin head, a second, smaller drag queen, MISS BIANCA DEVINE comes into the room from the stage.

MISS BIANCA DEVINE
What?

LADY-ROSE FLOWERS
Don't you what me! I gave you a start today, I gave you a show! No con'drag'ulations for you!

LADY-ROSE FLOWERS rises to his feet and paces across the room.

LADY-ROSE FLOWERS
You were supposed to be 'serving x' out there!

In silence, MISS BIANCA DEVINE sits down at a smaller table. LADY-ROSE FLOWERS returns to his table. They both start removing eyelashes and beauty spots.

MISS BIANCA DEVINE
'Serving x?' What do you mean? You know I am new at this! If you use drag-lingo, explain what it means.

LADY-ROSE FLOWERS

Darling, 'Serving x!' You know! Serving fish!
Presenting as a female to my audience! And squirrel
hides his nuts, you were supposed to squirrel before
you came on stage, not halfway through my
performance of "I Will Survive"! And oh! Do you
even know the words? The wheel was spinning, but
the hamster died!

MISS BIANCA DEVINE

You prima bitch! How dare you! I practised for
hours learning those words. *(He composes himself
and draws a breath.)* Do you want some cheese and
crackers to go with that whine?

LADY-ROSE FLOWERS

Face it, sweetie! You were crap! Dancing, singing,
make-up, you were crap at it all! Crap! Crap! Crap!

MISS BIANCA DEVINE

You two-faced cow... You were no better! I'm
young and it's my first night. At least I have an
excuse.

LADY-ROSE FLOWERS

Young! That twinkle in your eyes is actually the sun
shining between your ears! Please breathe the other
way. You're bleaching my hair.

MISS BIANCA DEVINE

What old queen insult book did you get that one out
of ? I'm actually blonde!

LADY-ROSE FLOWERS

Blonde! What colour is the sky in your little make-
believe world? Anyway, you piece of discount fruit,
that's my hair piece; you haven't paid for it yet.

MISS BIANCA DEVINE
I'll bet your mother had a loud bark!

LADY-ROSE FLOWERS
(smiling at himself in the mirror, pursing his lips)
It's about talent, sweetie! Don't feel bad. Lots of
people haven't got talent. It's like working with a
spayed cat when you sing. Honey, a guy with your
IQ should also have a low voice as well!

MISS BIANCA DEVINE
(admiring his make-up before removing it) Anyway,
at least the make-up was good. I look great. Look
here in this mirror. My eyes and cheekbones are
excellent. I look quite beautiful as a woman.

LADY-ROSE FLOWERS
Oh, honey! I heard those two shifty guys on that
table near the bar, talking about you. One said, "That
lady-boy has a nice butter face!"

MISS BIANCA DEVINE
(removing his extravagant dress) See!

LADY-ROSE FLOWERS
The other said, "Yes, she looks pretty, *but her face!*"
and they laughed. He said he thought you put your
make-up on using a rear view mirror.

MISS BIANCA DEVINE
You got that from your book or you made that up,
you cow! You're so ugly they used to put roast beef
in your lap so the dog would play with you!

LADY-ROSE FLOWERS
Honey, if I wanted to hear from an ass-hole, I
would've farted!

LADY-ROSE FLOWERS makes his way to the open door, looking for any loiterers looking for autographs. He looks out to the stage again.

> ## LADY-ROSE FLOWERS
> That audience – they loved me. They were gagging when I stepped out *on* the stage.

> ## MISS BIANCA DEVINE
> There you *go* again, "gagging"? You have to tell me what you mean. I can't understand all this jingo, bitch.

> ## LADY-ROSE FLOWERS
> "Gagging" means I was so pretty some of them came close to vomiting. Baby, they clapped. No! They applauded me, as the curtain rose.

> ## MISS BIANCA DEVINE
> Clapped? They were putting their hands over their eyes and ears.

> ## LADY-ROSE FLOWERS
> You must have got up on the wrong side of the cage this morning. *People* pay money to see me perform. Remember that!

> ## MISS BIANCA DEVINE
> You old *troll*, people only follow you out of morbid curiosity. You're so old your blood group is obsolete.
>
> Well, I also heard those guys by the bar as well. They were talking about you! *One* said the song would be better if you weren't eating a banana while you were singing it.

LADY-ROSE FLOWERS

Who's been researching insults on the internet now then, sweetie-pie? I've only got one nerve left and you're getting on it. You don't know the meaning of the word "showbiz", but then again you don't know the meaning of most words!

MISS BIANCA DEVINE

Please!

LADY-ROSE FLOWERS

(*solemnly returning to his chair again*) No, duckie, it didn't work tonight. I've got an idea! Maybe we should do a pantomime together. We could be the horse. I'll be the head and you can be yourself.

MISS BIANCA DEVINE

So, a thought crossed your self-centred little mind? That must have been a long and lonely journey!

MISS BIANCA DEVINE has removed his make-up. He stands up and faces LADY-ROSE FLOWERS.

MISS BIANCA DEVINE

We were supposed to put on a show tonight! It was my first *chance*! That bickering on stage was awful. It felt like a cat fight. It ruined my chance of ever getting noticed singing "I Am What I Am". I don't know what makes you so stupid – but it really works!

MISS BIANCA DEVINE starts to put on his male street clothes.

LADY-ROSE FLOWERS

Yeah, well, you ruined my show tonight. You could have warned me you got hit *by* a parked car today. Look at the damage it did to your face!

MISS BIANCA DEVINE
My face is fine. There're several people in this
world I find obnoxious, and you're all of them. I
don't know why I thought this would work. Your
mouth is dirtier than a wicker toilet seat! Thank you
for letting me try out.

LADY-ROSE FLOWERS
Don't thank me for insulting you. It was all my
pleasure.

MISS BIANCA DEVINE
Well, I'm not sure we can work together any more.
There's nothing more to say.

LADY-ROSE FLOWERS *(coldly)*
Close the door on the way out.

MISS BIANCA DEVINE pauses at the door and spins
around.

MISS BIANCA DEVINE
Are we having Chinese or Indian tonight?

LADY-ROSE FLOWERS
I thought Indian. I've got a voucher. Two for one.

MISS BIANCA DEVINE
Indian it is. No 24, 45 and two garlic naan?

LADY-ROSE FLOWERS
Yes, thank you. Easy on the curry sauce. Gotta
watch my waist. We both have a show to put on
tomorrow – again.

THE END

The pros and cons of organ donations from trauma patients

an essay by Michael J Richards

It is established that music "has helped with communication and socialization of children with autistic disorders, tinnitus, relief of acute, chronic, and cancer pain, decreasing aggressiveness and inappropriate behaviors in elderly patients with dementia, improving quality of life in terminally ill patients, and even relief of chemotherapy-related nausea and vomiting,"[1].

However, the Trauma Department of the General Hospital at Much-Bandage-on-the-Arm, Dermishire, has been unable to identify recommended methods of music transmission to support this necessary therapy.

This paper outlines trials on the essential question of transmission, as carried out by Dr Simon Mandible and the Trauma Team[2].

First, it was decided to run twelve-hour daily broadcasts of the three main national music radio stations, each for a week, this part of the trial therefore lasting three continuous weeks. Each station was aired in the hospital's main trauma ward.

Patients included a 34-year-old female with acute

---

[1] "Music Therapy: The Art of Healing", Chelsey Forbess MD, NYU Langone Online Journal of Medicine, 2013

[2] The Trauma Team, led by Dr Mandible, comprised Consulting Surgeon Robin Femur, Registrar Candice Tibia, Sister Fenella Lymphona, Staff Nurse Wanda Mucus, Nurse Melvyn Pancreas, Nurse Hannah Cartilage and Student Nurse Jeremy Metatarsal. The team is indebted to Shantala Hegde for her guidance, particularly "Music-Based Cognitive Remediation Therapy for Patients with Traumatic Brain Injury", US National Library of Medicine, National Institutes of Health, 2014

tinnitus; a 48-year-old male suffering from chemotherapy-related nausea and vomiting; three elderly patients, one male, with dementia; a sixteen-year-old male and a seventeen-year-old female, both with mild brain injuries.[3]

BBC Radio 1 proved too upsetting for patients.

Its constant stream of chatter, jingles and pop music without, according to them, discernible melodies and what one patient called "bubble-gum pounding" left them sleepless and disoriented.

Tracks such as "Get Ur Freak On" (Missy Elliot), "Bump & Grind" (N-Dubs feat Lady Saw) and "They Reminisce Over You (T.R.O.Y)" (Pete Rock and C L Smooth) confused rather than helped anyone.

BBC Radio 2 was more calming but the dementia patients were confused by the lack of differentiation between messages of love and family and news of war, murder and famine.

Matters reached a head one Sunday afternoon when a bulletin describing Middle Eastern terrorist attacks was immediately juxtaposed with a recording of "There's No Business Like Show Business". Several patients were observed to cry uncontrollably.

Potentially, BBC Radio 3 offered more with its blend of considered music and sedate commentary.

However, a playing of Brahms's *Requiem*, an eighty-minute choral piece honouring the dead, was inappropriate to patients' mental welfare. The UNO's Symphonic Wind Ensemble's recording of a piece for three vacuum cleaners and a floor polisher[4] did not improve things – especially when the ward's cleaners joined in with variations of their own.

Research moved to pre-recorded music – CDs brought in by staff and patients' friends and family. While the

---

[3] At this time, the policy of the hospital was to maintain mixed sex wards. The policy was later discontinued.
[4] available on YouTube at https://www.youtube.com/watch?v=TxaEIizTNTU.

theory of this approach remains good, its practice was discouraging. Younger patients wanted to listen to Justin Bieber, Wiz Khalifa (feat Charlie Puth) and Sam Smith. Those in their 30s and 40s preferred Florence + The Machine, Gorillaz and Kaiser Chiefs. Those dementia patients able to express their wishes opted for The Carpenters, Peter Skellern and Gladys Knight and the Pips. Staff Nurse Mucus preferred 1940s jazz band music.

This trial was closed early when, one afternoon, four CDs were simultaneously played in different corners of the ward. The cacophonous confrontation between "Drag Me Down" (One Direction), "You're Beautiful" (James Blunt), "Under the Moon of Love" (Showaddywaddy) and "The Peanut Vendor" (Stan Kenton) led Consulting Surgeon Femur to withdraw from the ward with a severe migraine.

The following day, as Nurse Cartilage was emptying bed pans, she spontaneously sang "You Are My Sunshine". Before long, all the staff and patients had joined in. This led to an improvised thirty-minute singalong[5]. Noticeably, patient tranquility and medical stabilisation measurably lasted for 36 hours afterwards.

It was decided to investigate this happy discovery in more depth.

A local school band[6] was invited to give a concert. While they did their best, Handel's *Water Music* played by first-year students of stringed instruments did nothing to improve patients' difficulties with incontinence.

Another concert was arranged, this time by the Much-Bandage-on-the-Arm Ladies' Singing Group[7].

Unfortunately, renditions of "I Don't Like Mondays",

---

[5] Songs included "All You Need is Love", "We'll Meet Again", "Hey Jude", "Somewhere over the Rainbow", "It's a Wonderful World" and "Ev'rytime We Say Goodbye". Interestingly, everyone knew all the words to all of the songs.
[6] Year 11's Music Band, St Bladder's Academy, Much-Bandage-in-the-Arm, under the direction of Ms Astrid Fallopian.
[7] Directed and conducted by Mr Arthur Pituitary.

"Alone Again (Naturally)" and "Suicide is Painless" in church chorale style resulted in three patients requesting overdosages of secobarbital and pentobarbital.

It was concluded that these versions of live music had not "helped with communication and socialization".[8]

A last-ditch, third attempt at live music was reluctantly agreed.

Wilhelmina Hippocampus and Her Singing Banjolele, accompanied by Georgiou Ossicles and his Yamaha PSR 275, proved successful. Their songs included "Get Me to the Church on Time", "Everything's Coming Up Roses", "Don't Rain on my Parade" and "Hello, Dolly", leaving everyone requesting frequent return visits by the talented duo.

Sadly, six days later, Mr Ossicles was involved in a road accident between a Dermishire Dairy Company milk float and the Dermishire Fresh Snail Company delivery van, resulting in his registration to the Trauma Department of the General Hospital at Much-Bandage-on-the-Arm. The prognosis, borne out by surgery, was that Mr Ossicles would not play keyboard again, his manual dexterity completely lost.

Consequently, Mr Ossicles very generously gave his Yamaha PSR 275 to the Trauma Department in support of its research into methods of transmitting musical therapy.

The local newspaper[9] featured a story about the gift, which encouraged two other trauma patients to gift a Hammond SK-2 Twin 61 Key Stage Keyboard and a Wurlitzer 300 Digital Music System.

Whether the donations of the keyboards should be accepted raised practical questions.

Against was the view that, without players, the organs were redundant. Storage was thought to be a difficulty but the staff cleaners found space to accommodate the

---

[8] Forbess, ibid.
[9] See "Local Musician Donates Livelihood to Hospital", *The Dermishire Chronicle*, 14 September 2015.

instruments when not in use. Care and maintenance of the instruments was an issue but, after discussion, not thought to be difficult.

In favour of accepting them was information that staff members from other hospital departments were enthusiastic to lend their musical and keyboard knowledge. Volunteers from within and outside the hospital became plentiful, to the extent that a waiting-list and rota system have had to be devised.

Therefore, after a meeting to discuss the pros and cons of organ donation from trauma patients, it was decided to accept the Yamaha, Hammond and Wurlitzer instruments.

The research team is in the process of collecting and analysing data arising from studying the effect live music therapy is having on patients and hopes to provide comprehensive details in a year's time.

Dr Simon Mandible and Trauma Team
Trauma Department
General Hospital
Much-Bandage-on-the-Arm
Dermishire
August 2016.

Science Fiction

A Lesson in Ancient History

a short story by Gordon Adams

"Ancient people had some very strange ways of trying to cure illness," explained the teacher. "In Pre-Historic times, a practice known as trepanning was common. This involved using an animal's bone to knock a hole into the human skull. The Ancients believed this would release evil spirits. Of course, this was a slightly messy procedure, as you can imagine."

Ugh!

Jonah was only five years old, but he hated the thought of blood.

The whole class recoiled at this gruesome thought.

"Several thousand years later, applying leeches – small worms – to the skin of an afflicted person, to suck their blood, was thought to cure all kinds of illness."

How foolish, how stupid, how primitive, muttered the classmates.

"In the 19th and 20th centuries, surgeons would cut open the bodies of their patients, using sharp knives, to remove diseased organs; they would cut and mend. Sometimes they would even insert artificial organs, made of plastic or metal."

Jonah didn't much like the sound of sharp knives.

"Then, in the 21st century, keyhole surgery was developed, allowing a surgeon to damage a patient's body only slightly (or so they thought at the time) when conducting surgery. This was believed by people then to be High Science indeed," observed the teacher.

How foolish, how stupid, how primitive, muttered the classmates.

But when did they realise the human body could heal itself? asked Jonah. *That all you need to do is ask it to?*

"Not until the current millennium, Jonah," replied his

teacher. "Our ancestors really were quite primitive creatures. They even moved their bodies around from place to place in small boxes called cars, rather than simply travelling everywhere with their minds. But that's a subject for another day. It's time to end our class now."

Ah, must we? complained Jonah.

"Disengage your telepathic link now, everyone," instructed the teacher.

And from three thousand points around the universe, the classmates disconnected.

I do love Ancient History, thought Jonah to his mother.

Who's There?

a short story by Nick Johns

I always suspected that the other people in the world weren't entirely human. There was just something off about them. I noticed it early but couldn't put my finger on it. As a child, I considered that it was me that was not human. I abandoned that explanation as illogical. I knew it wasn't me. It was them.

My whole life has been a struggle between me and them. As I developed a new tactic to find the truth, they adapted their methods to frustrate me. After all they've done to me, it's difficult to think.

Where to start?

* * * * *

Years ago, I noticed that they there were a finite number. I saw that they used the same model more than once, usually in minor roles. I call them reproductions, or repros. I must assume that they are manufactured and stored somewhere when they're not around me.

I would see one in the park who had been on TV the week before. Obviously they tried to make changes, make them more difficult to spot, but once I was old enough to have seen a lot of them, there was no doubt. I was able to watch for the signs. They tried not to use the same one to play important parts in my life. I mean, my repro uncle never became the local taxi driver. But even when they were careful, I would catch a glimpse of one I recognised turning away from me at the bus station, trying to stay out of sight. There were lots of them, but not seven billion different individuals like they told me. Even young, I was more observant than they thought.

It gave me some problems. I was forced to avoid

groups as I became consumed with identifying previous versions of repros they had used before. That made it difficult for me to concentrate on the biggest puzzle – what did they want from me?

My avoidance of crowds could have been my subconscious suggesting a way of finding out what I needed to know. My subconscious was very helpful like that. I paid attention and remembered things that would prove important. No answers but some really useful questions. Not great scientific or philosophical questions. I found these made no sense to me, anyway. Complicated fictions to tie up my mind, fill it with white noise.

I knew that I was unique, that things existed because I was there. But the repros controlled my environment. The facts they fed me about the world were false. I could only rely on what I could prove myself and what I could work out from that. I became more systematic looking for evidence. Things were not as they seemed.

I didn't laugh. It's one of the differences between me and them. They laughed all the time. Laughed at what I did, what I said. And told jokes. They pretended they were trivial, just fun. I knew different. Science was nonsense; jokes were important. They were questions for me to consider, not only things to bray at like they did.

"Knock Knock!"

"Who's there?"

That question formed the start of much of my early research. In the real world – my real world – I could never know the answer until I looked. Behind every knock on every door lay a huge number of possibilities that were not resolved until I answered. It was more complex than the simple alive or dead of Schrödinger's Cat. Who's there? And why?

I tried opening the door before the knock came, challenging the first repro I recognised. I would call it by the first name I knew it by.

"Hello, Mr Davies!"

"Hello," it'd say with a smile, but then it would furrow

its brow, remembering who it was supposed to be and say something like -

"What did you call me? You must be mistaken young man. My name is Iain. Iain Wilson."

Of course, soon they changed the programming, or whatever repros have, so it didn't work every time. But by then it was too late. I knew that I was right. It was the same repro used again. Why were they watching me?

Despite all my theories and questions, I had one really serious problem. I didn't know how or even if they die. I had attacked some when I was younger, but they were stronger than me or worked together in groups. I trapped animals and so on, to experiment on, but that proved nothing – they were not repros.

When I tried with the baby sister repro, they found me and that was when they sent me to the hostel. They watched me even more closely after that. As I grew, they produced ever larger repros to follow me, innocently loitering nearby, providing security for the smaller ones.

Due to their constant surveillance, I had to direct my attention to other aspects of the problem. I began to wonder about the physical environment around me. At first, I had thought that the major physical laws were OK. I mean, gravity worked the way it was supposed to; but later I adopted a more scientific approach. Gravity worked in my immediate vicinity and when I was awake. I could not judge what happened when I was not there or was asleep. They must be doing this for a reason. I needed to find a way to discover what it was.

"What does an occasional table do the rest of the time?"

This gave me a good deal to think about. I began looking behind things and underneath them, trying to see behind the facade they were presenting for me. I knew I must be on to something when they began to stop me doing this. If I ever managed to slip away and get somewhere interesting, like under a bridge, and waited to see what would happen to it, they would send repros to find me and bring me back to the hostel where they had better control over the scenery. I was making progress.

"If a tree falls in a forest and there is no-one there to hear it, does it make a sound?"

It was while I was researching the answer to this question, having escaped and gone into the national park to chop down some trees at various times of day and in different ways, that they finally decided to stop the pretence.

They sent some police repros for me. I recognised all three of them straight away; they were easy, three of their biggest repros, Pete's Dad, Ivan the blacksmith from that country show and Mr Nichols the butcher in the village where I grew up.

They were better trained now, of course, they did not react when I called them by their names but I could see in their eyes that they realised that they were not deceiving me anymore.

Was I close to a breakthrough?

They must have been getting worried then as they changed tactics and locked me up in the clinic.

* * * * *

In here, they observe me even more closely than the hostel. They control my movements better. They try to lull me by using repros they think I haven't noticed before.

I have given great thought to what to do next. I pretend to go along with whatever they want, even when they try to confuse my thinking with drugs or shock treatment, but this is my biggest chance. Believing me cornered, and confined behind locked doors, they will not build scenery outside my immediate location. I just need to get out of here unobserved to prove that I am right once and for all.

They think they're so clever, watch me so closely, know all about me. They don't. When I was in the forest, unobserved, I trapped a young repro. I now know they die easily.

Tonight is the dark of the moon, the worst time for them to observe me. I know where the keys are kept, know when there is only one staff member on duty. Tonight it's Iain. You know, used to be the milkman.

A repro is always slow, because it's reacting, not planning like a real person. I'll catch it unawares, like I used to with the name calling experiment. I have a broken metal bed tie, sharpened quietly and patiently against the wall.

I can hear its footsteps near my door now.

Quiet! I must attract its attention.

"Knock Knock."

Death of the Moon

a short story by Gordon Adams

Commander Baljinder Kaur looks around. She is the first to enter the city following decontamination and surveys the ruins with great sadness. India's war with China over mining rights is over. A grim stalemate. Lunar City, the first man-made Wonder of the Solar System, is now no more. Only a ruin remains.

"Twelve minutes."

The G-reader's monotone voice speaks harshly in the ear of her spacesuit. She will have to be quick. Despite decontamination, radiation levels are still very high. It isn't safe to linger here.

First port of call is the former site of Focal Point. The missile strikes hit here first, killing the occupants of the science block. The structure is a twisted mess of metal. It won't win any sculpture awards now! But the Daljabi Diamond is still in place. Baljinder only needs to climb a short distance to reach it.

"Ten minutes," says the harsh voice.

Baljunder takes the extraction tool from her holster and stretches out towards the jewel. The claw hooks on effortlessly. A quick twist and she has the first of the items she has come for. She wraps it in a protective case and stashes it in her pocket.

Suddenly, there a loud crash behind her.

She turns to see a metal support has crashed to the ground, just a few metres away. (That was close! She will have to be more careful).

Now to Eagle Square.

She walks up the ruined street, once known as South Promenade. Rubble is strewn across the former walkway. Only a brief glint of silver tells of its former glory. As she looks over the ruins, she remembers how many of her people lost their lives in this war. She grimaces, realising the dust at her feet contains those human remains. She must not allow herself to indulge in such thoughts now! She has a job to do.

The Golden Globe stands before her, resting improbably still on its marble plinth. To think that this precious gift from the citizens of Earth once proudly marked the first development at Lunar City. The plinth leans alarmingly towards her. Even the smallest of touches could make it topple.

"Eight minutes," says the voice loudly.

Strange that a machine sounds so stern. She doesn't want to risk a radiation overdose: she must press on.

Taking the laser cutter, Baljinder slices the Golden Globe from the plinth. She cradles it in her hands.

It is still improbably beautiful, this exact replica of the Earth, although a gash now runs across its face from top to bottom.

Unable to help herself, she spends a few moments gazing at its intricate design. When she returns to the landing jet, she will have to seal it in the transmission pod. It will return to Earth. She will never see it again. It is so mesmerisingly beautiful! She will have to remember this moment. She places it lovingly in her backpack.

"Six minutes," says the voice in her ear.

Six minutes only! Baljinder is running short of time. Her heartrate increases. She hurries. Twisting round, she trips and almost falls. Something large is buried in the dust. Puzzled, she picks it up. A plaque of some kind? She dusts it off and reads the inscription.

Here Man from Planet Earth first set foot on the Moon. July 1969, AD.

She rubs again. A large crack breaks the next sentence in half.

We came...

... in peace for all Mankind.

The naïve fools!

The tears well up.

"Five minutes."

She casts the plaque back into the dust and rushes on to the landing jet with her precious haul.

Out of time

a short story by Pat Aitcheson

Shortdays, they whispered behind her back, when they thought she couldn't hear them. Wanda grew up knowing that her days were numbered, just like everyone else. The lifemark was imprinted on her left wrist when she was born. The Birthing Sister attended every delivery, interpreted the complex system of wavy lines and dots, and recorded the result on the birth certificate. If the Birthing Sister was unsure, she immediately sought confirmation from Mother Mortimer. And Mother Mortimer was always right.

* * * * *

Wanda's limbs felt pleasantly heavy, her eyelids even more so. She couldn't remember if she had been dreaming, but her mouth felt a little dry. She would get up in a minute, but first she wanted to stretch and turn over. The covers were over her face and she tried to pull them away, but her hands felt stiff where they were crossed over her chest. The edge of the sheet was out of reach. Her eyelids fluttered open but all she saw was black. A faint scent of flowers wafted around her from a posy in her left hand.

Her breathing quickened and she tried to sit up, but there was no room. She lay flat in an enclosed space, and try as she might, she could not remove the linen covering her face and nose. There were walls all around her. She felt panic rising with her pulse, the sweetly cloying scent of flowers adding to her nausea.

She couldn't call out. Her throat closed up, her tongue thick and useless in her parched mouth. She wriggled and tried to bang on the wall and roof of her prison with elbows and fists. Each shaky breath drew cloth into her

181

mouth and she gagged. Hot tears ran down the sides of her face and into her ears, and still she made no sound.

She tried to remember, her brain moving slowly in contrast to her racing heart.

How did I get here?

Fog filled her head. She fought to control her breathing, and memories started to float behind her closed lids.

* * * * *

Wanda did not understand at first why her grandmother cried when she saw her, or why her father did not wish her to attend school after her eleventh birthday.

"You don't need school now. You can write your name and count and tell time. Stay home with your mother."

"But I like school, Papa. I can see my friends there and besides, Peter is still going and he's older than me."

Her father frowned. "Peter needs his education. He will have responsibilities later. Don't argue with me and go and help your mother."

Wanda watched him turn away from her and go into his bedroom, and went to find her mother.

Mama looked up from her weeding as Wanda approached.

"Hello, have you come to help? See these plants with the light green leaves, they will become beans. The dark green ones with hairs on are the weeds, they're the ones we pull out."

"Pull out the weeds, okay." Wanda returned her mother's smile and knelt beside her, and they worked together in silence.

After a while her mother said, "You're quiet today, Wanda."

"Papa says I have to stop school, but I like it and Peter still goes, so why can't I?"

Mama stopped weeding and sat back on her heels.

"I won't see my friends," Wanda continued. "It's not fair, I'm one of the best in my class."

"Well, your father is doing what he thinks is best."

"I want to go. It's not fair." Wanda dropped the weed and her tears splashed on the pile of dying plants. "Peter is thirteen, and he still goes. Everyone else goes until they're big. I always try hard. Have I done something wrong?"

Mama put down her trowel and turned to her daughter. She took Wanda's hand and said softly, "No, you haven't done anything wrong." She sighed. "I will talk to Papa if you like."

At Wanda's mute nod, Mother put an arm around her, stroking her daughter's black curls with the other hand.

"That's enough for today, I think. Let's go and get a drink."

* * * * *

Later that night Wanda heard raised voices in the room next to hers.

"Andrew, please. What harm will it do? Let her learn."

"What good will it do, filling her head with facts when - when it won't matter in the end? She should be outside enjoying the world, while she can."

"There might be a mistake."

"Florence, stop deluding yourself! There is no mistake, there never was, and you need to accept the truth. It is written on her skin, she was born with shortdays, and that's all there is to say." He slammed the door behind him on his way out of the house, and then there was quiet.

Wanda listened, but heard nothing more. When she risked looking out of her window, she saw her father standing with his back to the house, gripping the gate, his shoulders moving up and down.

Wanda lay down and clutched the blankets tight around her neck. She didn't want them to fight about her. She stared at the wall until she fell asleep, dozing until dawn.

* * * * *

At breakfast she toyed with her porridge while everyone ate in silence.

Peter got up to gather his schoolbag.

"Come on, Wanda, or we'll be late." He sat on the floor and laced his boots.

"I'm not going." She fought to control the tremble in her lip.

"Don't make stupid jokes. Tell her, Mama."

"You get going, Peter and don't worry about her, she'll be fine." Papa stared at his son, while Mother was silent.

"But, Papa – "

"Don't argue with me, boy. Get yourself off to school now." Papa pushed back his chair and stood up, anger radiating from his broad frame. The chair legs scraped harshly across the wooden floor, cutting through the silence that hung over the table.

"Why does she get to stay home? It's not fair!" Peter shouted.

Two long strides took his father from the table to Peter's side. Papa grabbed the schoolbag and thrust it at Peter. "School, Peter. Now."

Peter shot one last angry look at his sister before leaving. Wanda listened as he closed the front door, and then slammed the gate. She choked back a sob and rushed from the room. She threw herself on the bed and bawled. She did not understand how she had upset her father so. She did not know why she was being punished.

* * * * *

All the colour went out of Wanda's life after that. Her friends called on her at first, but she could not join in the discussions of schooldays and schoolwork. Soon they whispered that she was stupid, she couldn't even do algebra, and they stopped inviting her out. She spent her days in the garden, helping to cook and clean, ignoring Peter's jibes.

Wanda thought about her lifemark constantly. When

the chores were done, she closeted herself in her bedroom. She traced the black pattern on her wrist with her right forefinger, willing it to change. She knew it never would, but still she prayed to the Divine and hoped for a miracle, a sign that would give her more time. Every day she bore the disappointment of her unchanging fate.

* * * * *

One cloudy afternoon soon after her twelfth birthday, Wanda stared out of her window, her head heavy from lack of sleep. Mama waited at the gate, and when Papa returned from work she placed one hand on his arm. They remained there talking. The conversation became more heated and they started shouting.

Wanda couldn't hear the words but she saw them face each other, Mama waving her arms while Papa stood rigid. Finally she ran from him towards the house, and he seemed to come to life. He rushed after her and grabbed her arm, spun her round and gathered her up tight. They clung together as if they dared not let go, heedless of the first drops of rain that fell on them.

Her mother's tears upset her, but Papa scared her. Wanda could not fathom what could bring such a strong man to weeping. She slid down on to her bed, scrunched her eyes shut and put her hands over her ears. Her world crumpled and shrank tight around her until she could barely breathe.

* * * * *

Memories flashed across her shuttered eyelids as she lay confined, willing herself to lay still, to be calm, to think her way out of the situation she was in. She tried to slow her breathing but it came in quick gasps. Tears still stung her eyes and dripped from the shell of her ear, sweat plastered the linen to her forehead. She held her breath and listened, but the only sound was her own blood racing.

How much time had passed? She couldn't tell.

* * * * *

Wanda and her mother fell into a new routine, and Papa seemed to relax. Sometimes Wanda caught him watching her with a look she could not decipher. He would smile, but it did not reach his eyes. Sometimes while Peter wrestled with his books at night, Papa would take her outside and point out the constellations. He answered her questions, but if she asked about her mark he shook his head and walked away from her. During sleepless nights, Wanda thought of nothing but the lifemark. She resolved to ask her mother about it.

One warm day, Wanda worked in the garden with her mother, making sure to be extra willing with the chores. She wanted her mother to be in a good mood.

"There, we've finished, and you've been so helpful, thank you." Mama smiled, pushing a stray lock of dark hair out of her eyes. "We'll be picking beans in no time."

"Why don't we talk about my mark?" Wanda hated watching the smile fade until only sadness remained on her mother's face. She had done that to Mama.

Mama dropped the Dutch hoe and rushed over to Wanda. She held her daughter close and kissed the top of her head. "It's just we love you so, so much," she whispered.

"Even Papa? He won't look at it. He won't tell me."

"Especially Papa." Mama said. "He doesn't want you to Pass so soon. You have shortdays, and we have to accept your time is less than ours. But we pray to the Divine, and we will meet again, when we go beyond."

"Does… does it hurt?"

Mama stifled a sob. "It's like going to sleep, darling. It doesn't hurt, and we will be with you, always."

They wrapped around each other and wept. Wanda promised herself she would never make her mother cry again.

186

That night she kissed her father goodnight and hugged him. He relaxed into her embrace and stepped away after a moment, wiping his eyes and saying nothing. She went to bed early, and for once sleep came easily.

* * * * *

Mama spent hours brushing Wanda's long hair until it shone. Mama told stories of adventurers who sailed the seas, looking for treasures and eluding capture. Wanda looked forward to these times alone with her mother, weaving tales of exciting lives, survival and escape. She took in every detail of what to eat in each season, how to tell time by the sun, how to make camp and sleep under the stars.

Mama made up for Wanda's lack of book-learning by telling her stories, and in the end Wanda preferred it to school lessons. She was resigned to her fate, and more than a little afraid of Passing. But it could not be avoided.

* * * * *

The Passing ceremony drew ever closer. Everyone had been casting pitying glances at her for weeks. Even Peter stopped tormenting her and treated her kindly. She was measured for her white dress. At the final fitting she almost smiled, for the first time in months.

The dress had a high neck decorated with fabric roses, the waist was pulled in by a narrow belt whose long tails swung with more roses. Its wide skirt fell to her ankles. Her mother unfastened her braid, letting her hair tumble over her shoulders. She hardly heard her mother whisper in her ear how beautiful she looked.

Wanda clutched her mother's hand, looked at their reflection in the mirror, and wept again.

On the allotted morning, Wanda lay in bed, her stomach churning with dread. Dawn light stole through the curtains and painted patterns on the wall. After a night with barely any sleep, she certainly couldn't eat breakfast. She stayed under the shower while the minutes ticked past, wishing the water would wash her completely away down the drain. Then she would not have to face the day.

No-one came to bang on the door and accuse her of hogging all the hot water, and after a while she got out and wrapped herself in a warm towel. When she went back to her room, she found her mother already waiting, clutching a mug.

"My darling girl. I'm here to help you get dressed and do your hair. I brought you a drink, I don't suppose you feel like eating. It's always the same on a big day. I remember the day of my wedding... I felt so sick and faint, I'd hardly eaten for days before, and my mother... well, she said..." Mama trailed off, a brittle smile on her face and her eyes fever-bright.

"It's okay. I'm okay." Wanda took one sip from the mug. "Hot chocolate is always good." Holding her towel with one hand, she sat on the bed and looked up at the white dress hanging on the back of the door.

Mama wrung her hands. "Please drink, you'll feel better, I promise."

"It's still quite hot." As Wanda drank carefully, she felt her tension ease, warmth spreading from her stomach into every vein. She drained the mug and said, "I enjoyed that. I want my hair down at the sides, and maybe in a coiled braid at the back. Can you do that for me?"

"Yes, I can." Her mother seemed calmer too. "I can do any style you want." She pulled the chair forward and motioned Wanda to sit, then picked up the brush.

Wanda relaxed into her seat, soothed by the rhythm of firm brush strokes, and her mother humming a lullaby. She hardly felt her mother's hands, deftly braiding and curling her hair, so she jumped at the warm pressure on her shoulders.

"You're nearly asleep. But wake up now and put on your dress. Then we'll see how you look."

Obediently Wanda rose and dropped the towel without

hesitation, holding up her arms like a little girl while her mother pulled the fine petticoat over her head. She stepped into her knickers and sat to pull on her stockings. She watched her mother take the cover off her Passing dress and smooth out imaginary creases. It was all so perfect, it was going to be a good day, and she felt her spirit loosen and expand into a cloud around her. Nothing could hurt her today.

When she was dressed, her mother put an arm round her shoulders and guided her to the full-length mirror in the hallway.

"Look, Wanda. Look how beautiful you are." Her mother stepped aside for Wanda to see herself, a vision of white with hair falling in tendrils around her neck and many tiny braids from the front joining in a large coil at her nape. She fingered the roses on the ends of her belt and twirled, smiling at the skirt billowing round her ankles.

It seemed as though a golden haze surrounded her and she felt absolutely safe. Even her mother's tears sparkled with gold lights.

"I'm beautiful, Mama, look at me!" She clapped her hands, full of wonder. "Can I have another hot chocolate? Please, please?"

Her mother wiped her eyes, and didn't smile. "I think maybe one is enough for today."

Wanda stamped her foot. "But I want one and it's my day and I can have whatever I want!"

"How about we find your new satin slippers?" Mother took Wanda's hand in both of hers. "You love new shoes, don't you, I think they're in the bottom of your wardrobe."

Wanda clapped her hands again. "Yes, let's go get my slippers." She forgot her irritation and let herself be led away. It was a good day. She felt wonderful.

When Wanda arrived at the Repository of Souls, she looked around with detached interest at the imposing building with its white spires topped with gold stars that glittered in the sunlight. They walked through the tall arched door gilded with astronomical symbols and into a

189

large hall, with tiered seating and white benches on ground level for the aspirants. At the front of the hall, under jewelled lights cast by a stained glass window, candles flickered over rows of white couches. Between the couches and the benches stood a high lectern, studded with sparkling gems of blue and white.

Everywhere, people of all ages, dressed in white, smiled benignly while their families sat rigidly around them, some openly weeping. A young woman carrying a baby sobbed behind her black veil as her partner supported her around the waist. She stepped inside the great doorway but froze. Unable to go forward, she swayed with the baby clutched to her breast. A warden brought a wheelchair, and once her partner wheeled her down to the front, the queue of people moved forward again.

"Look, Papa, that woman is crying. You're not meant to cry, this is a happy day. I feel happy."

"I know, Wanda. Don't point. It's rude." Papa sounded gruff. Wanda glanced at Peter, finding him white-faced and silent.

Wanda sat between her parents and smoothed her skirt over her knees. She loved this dress so much.

A loud chime signalled the start of the ceremony, and by the tenth and final chime the entire crowd had fallen silent.

Wanda heard the choir before she saw them walk down the centre of the hall in deep blue robes. They filed into place around the couches, and the assembly joined in. She had never heard anything so beautiful. Her parents had not brought her to a Passing before, and she wondered why. It was all so lovely.

Bringing up the rear of the procession, the Birthing Sisters added their voices to the song. Wanda had glimpsed one when their neighbour had her baby, and she watched them with fascination. Their robes were not the usual brown, but myriad pastel shades, each with a red cord round her waist.

Last of all came Mother Mortimer. A young boy and

girl preceded her, each carrying a large Book of Days bound in black leather and tooled in gold. Mother Mortimer wore a white robe, the hood embroidered with gold constellations. She leant on a staff topped with a diamond as big as a quail's egg. Wanda was awestruck and turned to her mother to whisper a question. Before she could speak, her mother put a finger to her lips. Wanda fell quiet.

The song ended as Mother Mortimer reached the lectern. Her pages sat on the floor either side, with the Book open on their laps. She stepped up behind the lectern and placed the staff in a holder at the side. The diamond caught the light and sent rainbow flashes darting to every corner of the great hall. There was a collective gasp, then silence.

Her voice rang out, clear and soft, yet carrying to everyone present.

"Welcome to you all. Welcome to our aspirants, their families, and those of our congregation who come to bear witness. As the seed, the leaf, the flower and the fruit has its season, so do we. As they return to the earth to begin anew, so do we. And as our days are written, so does each one of us pass from the human realm into the Great Beyond."

Mother Mortimer threw back her hood, revealing short, steel grey hair. Wanda made out her strong nose and black eyes like those of a bird, her face tanned and lined. There was more talking, and more singing, and Wanda's eyes grew heavy. A golden cloud surrounded her like a cocoon.

Her parents each took a hand and she floated between them, down the hall to the white benches while more songs were sung. Then her name was called, and it was time to take her place on the couch. She was dimly aware of other people being helped on to the couches around her, and the anxious faces of her family hovered above, bathed in soft candlelight and just beyond reach. She blinked slowly.

"And now we bid farewell to our aspirants, our family members, on this day foretold at the moment of their birth.

Our days are numbered, and for this we are grateful. We live fully in that knowledge, and our Passing is no time for regret. We give thanks for the time we are given.

"Time is the ultimate measure of the universe, for it cannot be made, broken, taken nor given. It is the sole gift of the Divine, and we honour the Divine when we give back our lives that were loaned to us."

Mother Mortimer's words stole into Wanda's ears as her parents bent and tearfully embraced her, and Peter crushed her hand in his. Her heart beat lazily and through half-open eyes she saw her family turn and walk away from her side. A veil was lowered around the couches, hiding them from the congregation's view.

"May the tide of time carry you onward."

Wanda closed her eyes and breathed out.

* * * * *

The next thing Wanda knew, she was lying in her prison. There seemed no way out. She lay still, and forced her racing brain to think. Was this the Beyond? It didn't seem like it. Wasn't she supposed to be free? Her mind played tricks on her and she thought she heard her name, whispered somewhere close. She tensed, breathing lightly to avoid the cloth filling her nostrils.

And then there was a tap on the outside of her prison. She would have screamed, but her mouth still would not work.

"Wanda. Wanda, wake up. Please tell me you're alive." Her mother sounded upset.

Wanda managed to hit the side with her elbow, and there was an answering tap.

"Hold still, and keep quiet."

I'm not dead. But I don't know what's going on.

Then she felt cool air on her side and a tearing sound, and her mother's hand gripped hers.

"Divine be praised. I'm going to cut the rest of the shroud, don't move. Nearly there."

Strong arms slid under her neck and knees and pulled her sideways, and she half fell to the ground. Her mother instantly scooped her up and held her tight, which was just as well because her knees gave way and she felt sick. Mother cried into her hair.

"I knew, all this time I knew. And now I'm here to get you out, but we have little time. Here, off with that dress and into these." She reached into a bag and brought out a shirt, leggings, woollen sweater and boots. "Quickly, sweetheart."

Wanda stripped and redressed, swallowing but unable to speak, her limbs refusing to work at first. Then her mother handed her a bottle, and she drained the cool water inside in one thirsty swallow. No drink had ever tasted better.

"Mama? What's happening?" Her voice was scratchy and hoarse.

"We must get away before they come to check the aspirants. Explain later, hurry." Mother thrust another flask at Wanda, who drank greedily, surprised to find hot chocolate. She didn't feel the golden haze this time, just sweetness that warmed her stomach. There was no time to ask why it was different, because a coat was thrust at her and a hat jammed on her head.

"Follow me."

They crept out past rows of numbered pine boxes slotted into spaces in the walls. The light was dim, and Wanda was glad of the extra layers of clothing. Shivering and wobbly, she kept close to her mother, who stopped at the end of a passageway. Putting a finger to her mouth for quiet, Mother took a glance round the corner. She grabbed Wanda's hand and pulled her along to a steep staircase. Mother climbed with a speed Wanda would not have expected, and she urged her heavy legs to work.

They had not met anyone so far, but they halted as they heard voices raised ahead of them.

"Escaped? Impossible." The tone was imperious, angry.

"I – I'm sorry, Mother Mortimer. I made the normal

check of the fresh storage areas – there was a broken case. A discarded dress. It should not be possible."

"You will speak to no-one of this blasphemy, understand? Not a single word. Unless you wish to live out your span in a cell underground. Now stop crossing yourself like an imbecile. Make sure all the exit doors are barred and bolted."

"Yes, Mother Mortimer."

Rapid footsteps moved away from them.

Mama cursed under her breath, then whispered, "We have to go back. There's always another way."

"Back? But—"

"No buts. We can't afford to meet Mortimer, she will stop at nothing to hide the truth." Mother took off, running down the stairs and back the way they came. But when she reached the passage where they hid before, she went straight on instead of turning right, and soon they were even deeper in the warren of catacombs. The air grew stale and sourness filled Wanda's lungs but her mother's pace never faltered, and she had no breath to do any more than try to keep up.

Eventually they came to a door that seemed to be a dead end. Wanda's mother reached into her pocket and brought out an old key. The key turned with difficulty, and the hinges protested, but the door opened and there was fresher air on the other side. The two women squeezed into a small brick-lined space and listened. They heard distant voices and Wanda's mother shoved the door shut and locked it.

Wanda looked up at the clear night sky dotted with stars, and took a lungful of fresh air. Tears spilled down her cheeks, but her mother nudged her.

"Nearly there, you've done so well. Climb, you'll see the footholds. Climb now."

Wanda's eyes adjusted until she saw rusted iron hoops beside small recesses set into the walls of the circular shaft. She followed her mother and just when she thought her arms would give way, her mother disappeared from view. She leaned over the edge of the well and hauled her daughter out.

They stood for a moment, gasping and sweating in the dark. They had emerged from the shaft behind large shrubs at the edge of woods. The Repository's spires gleamed in the moonlight half a mile away, and Wanda pointed to it.

"Did we come from there?"

Her mother said, "Help me with this."

She gripped a slab of iron that lay at her feet, and Wanda took the other side. Soon she realised that it was hinged, and together they heaved until it fell into place with a dull thud. Mother locked it and took off into the woods without another word. Wanda, now completely alert, ran after her.

They jogged along the path for several minutes until they reached a clearing. Mother sat on a fallen log and motioned for her daughter to sit next to her. She embraced Wanda again, kissed her forehead and took her hand.

"There are things I need to tell you so please, just listen. They'll be here soon. You were born with shortdays, but that isn't the whole story. Your lifemark means far more, and that's why I had to get you out."

She traced Wanda's wrist tattoo as she spoke.

"Not many have your mark, but Mortimer sees to it that they are recorded as short in the Book of Days. She wants the secret of travelling in time, so she can control it herself."

"What? What do you mean?"

Wanda felt panic again, but her mother cut in.

"Hush. We're taught that time is beyond our control. That we are carried in time, like boats on a river until we pass. But some people can stand outside of time. They can move through time at will. People like you, when you learn, when you grow into your power. It will be so exciting, my darling, this is why I had to save you, but it's time to go."

"No! I don't want to go, I just found you again. I want to go home to Papa and Peter!"

195

"Sweetheart, you can't come home to us." Mother wiped Wanda's tears with a trembling finger. "Remember the stories I told you? Everything you need is there. And I am always with you, here."

She pointed to Wanda's heart, then pressed the old key into her hand. "Take this, and if you ever want to return, you will know where to come."

"Mama, no." Wanda felt helpless. Why had she had escaped death, only to say goodbye again?

Her mother took off her pack and placed it in front of her daughter, then stood and held out both hands. There were no words to express the pain and fear of separation, and they clung to each other, eyes closed, heedless of time passing. When Mama finally pulled away Wanda jumped, startled by two hooded figures standing a few paces away.

The nearer of the two approached. "You brought her, Florence. Is she ready?"

"I have prepared her as best I could, but there is never enough time. And I have to go back, they will be checking back at the house when they realise she is gone."

"You should have left me there! Why are you sending me away?" Wanda shouted, kicking the pack aside.

"You are alive," the woman said. "The tattoo never lies, there cannot be any mistake. If you survive Passing, they make sure you never emerge from behind the veil. But Mortimer needed you, and you slipped through her fingers. You will be safe with us. Come now."

Wanda glanced from her mother to the two people. They pushed back their hoods, revealing themselves as a man and woman of similar height, both with black curly hair like her own but darker skin. They held out their wrists and showed their marks. Wanda pulled up her sleeve, and gasped when she recognised tattoos identical to hers.

"See, they are the same," the man said. "We are kin, even if you don't know it yet."

Wanda picked up the pack and slung it over her shoulders. "I really have to leave you and go with them?"

Her mother sighed. "We'll be all right, as long as I'm back in my bed before they make the dawn visit. They say it's to comfort the family, but we know better. Goodbye for now, my darling. Visit me when you can."

"I don't know how." Wanda's eyes filled with fresh tears and her throat closed up. Why was this so hard, when Passing had seemed so easy and natural?

"You will. My dreams await you." Florence hugged her daughter tight, kissed her cheek once, and with a stifled sob hurried away. Soon she disappeared among the dark trees.

Wanda turned to her new companions.

"So, where are we going?" she said. She felt abandoned, too sad to be truly afraid, and she had no more tears left.

The pair replaced their hoods, and each took one of her hands.

"Not where," the woman said, "but when."

Wanda had no time to reply. The stars glowed impossibly bright and she was pulled into a tunnel of light.

A Time for Dancing

a short story by Gordon Adams

It was a little early for me to be laughing, I know. It was only a few hours after I'd heard the news. You wouldn't expect a man who has just learned he had a few hours to live to be laughing. Or dancing. Not dancing in the street with all his neighbours. Dancing like there was no tomorrow.

I'd told my two grandchildren first. That's what is left of my family these days. I wake early, about 6am, so had sent a brief thought alert to them on the etherlink. We'd had a tearful exchange of emotions, but no-one had much to give. Our brains were numb with the news – it was still sinking in. Of course, we knew in our hearts that there was nothing that could be done.

In the street, the PC Max was blaring out rock and roll. Gloria from No 4 was dancing with Edwin from No 28, whooping and shaking her hips like she was whirling a hula hula hoop. You know, I'd always thought those two would get together! They make a good couple. The young divorcee with the bob from No 7 looked like she was entertaining the three Arts students from the end of the road single-handedly. This was going to be a party like no other.

Even Graham and Bob were talking animatedly, cans of lager in their hands. They'd had a row over the positioning of a fence twelve years ago and hadn't spoken a word since. Before today, that is. I guess that was all forgotten now. Well, who cares about such trivial things anymore?

Old Mrs Clarke leaned her head out of her bedroom window, with the strangest look on her face. "Turn that music… UP!" she cried, "I'm coming down to join you!"

I was feeling almost delirious. This was bizarre. It was awful and yet wonderful at the same time. We knew we had only a few hours to live and we'd decided to go out dancing.

"They've announced a New World Government," yelled Ellie, the neighbourhood gossip.

I wasn't really interested – what did it matter?

"The New Distribution Order has seized control at the World Assembly! And Rui-Shan has definitely gone. Nobody knows where for sure."

She had one of those Googleplex watches relaying information to her directly into her mindpiece. No-one seemed to listen to her, though. We were all too busy living it up – enjoying the experience of life while we still had it.

I wondered briefly how quickly the end would be, after the meteor struck. They said it was ten thousand times the size of the meteor that had wiped out the dinosaurs and it was heading straight for us. The chance of a strike like that on the Earth was very small indeed.

Oh, lucky us!

It would hit the world with the force of a million atomic bombs. I couldn't even begin to picture a million bombs simultaneously exploding. There was no hope, it seemed.

The media message from the scientists gathered at the Emergency International Symposium had been brief and bleak.

'We regret that there is no scientific response that can avert this disaster. Even if we had years to prepare for it, we would be powerless to stop it. People of Earth should therefore prepare for the worst. This impact will inevitably wipe out not just all human life but all life on Earth. We are sorry to be the bearers of such tragic news.'

I kissed Sheila from No 13. We gave each other a big hug.

"I didn't know you cared," I joked.

"I don't," she replied, with a broad smile and we embraced again, for even longer this time.

The sonic boom we heard next could probably be heard in the next town and perhaps across the border too. We looked skywards to see a plume of smoke following a rocket, which had just emerged from Spaceport 77.

"What's that?" I asked, but knew the answer before the words were out of my mouth.

"Rats deserting a sinking ship," muttered Ellie. "There have been hundreds of launches today from Spaceports. They'll be trying to head for the Lunar Bases, though, God knows, there won't be room up there for all of them. And with no supplies of food from Earth… "

Anyone who did escape from Earth would probably just have a slow death rather than a quick one.

Crazy!

The Earth had probably lost half of its world leaders and billionaires in the mass exodus today. No doubt everyone with power and money and the capacity to make a run for it was on their way already. They wouldn't get far though: the Moon bases were the only places they could realistically head and those bases weren't self-sufficient. They never could be.

"Nice that they decided to stick it out in solidarity with their people," I muttered. "Isn't the captain meant to go down with his ship? But, to be honest, I think we're better off without them. Who wants to be listening to announcements from Rui-Shan in their last moments?"

On the other side of the street, Ellie was ecstatically punching the air.

"The New Distribution Order has announced the seizure of the assets of the billionaires," she yelled breathlessly. "And universal ownership of the technology companies!"

She'd always been a bit of a revolutionary. I bet she never dreamed she'd live to see the day when GoogleMax, Apple-Xcel and Excalibur would be taken into public ownership. Shame it would be our last day.

I filled my glass. I'd been saving the thirty-year-old malt for a special occasion. Well, you don't get more special than the end of the world, do you?

"Cheers to us all!" I shouted, "I love you all, you

lovely, lovely people!"

That's the last thing I remember.

* * * * *

I'm in bed. My head hurts. The world is eerily quiet.

But it's still here. The world is still here!

My PC Max is still working, broadcasting the same message over and over.

There was no meteorite. It was all a test of loyalty from the New World Order (as they are now to be known). The New World Order is now in full control and we should be calm. Our world has lost 116 of its leaders and these deserters will not be allowed to return. The world has also lost 38 billionaires who between them had controlled half of its wealth. They are leeches who had been draining the world of its lifeblood. They too will not be allowed to return.

Welcome to the New World. It's time to start again!

And All Our Yesterdays Have Lighted Fools...

by Nick Johns

I had thought they had all been hunted down following the scourge.

The electric light said different.

I crept in. Dangers lurked here.

There! A cough!

I entered the damned light, the stone floor clean and cold against my torn, dirty feet.

He sat in a chair with wheels – and an engine!

Sightless, milky eyes followed me from within a grey sweating face.

"I knew you'd come if you saw the light."

"Extinguish it, or you shall surely die!"

"Too late. I'm already almost there. I'm using the last of my battery power. You'll light my way."

"No! 'I am the way, the truth and the light'."

"Not in here. *I'm* the light, or rather the wind generator is. Not enough juice for my chair any more. Damn lithium batteries." He coughed wetly and dabbed his mouth with a red flecked cloth.

"Blasphemy! 'Shun the evils of the machine.' " I intoned.

"Oh, save me the 'technology brought the scourge' sermon! It was a viral pandemic. Bad, sure, but we'd have recovered eventually – but for you idiots."

"Sinner!"

"Yeah. I'm a sinner." He closed his eyes and dipped his head. "Come on, boy, I'm ready. Do what you came to do."

"For the wages of sin is death... "

I raised my club.

Love and Romance

Buy the ticket, take the ride

a poem by Pat Aitcheson

I'm sorry I kissed you
Because in my quiet life
I said I was happy
I called it okay.

I'm sorry I kissed you
Because I preferred stories
Imaginary worlds where
Everything works out.

I'm sorry I kissed you
Because in my small world
All was known
And everything made safe.

But your lips pulled me away
To the edge of the diving-board
The brink of the cliff
The top of the ride.

Now I must choose
Shall I buy the ticket
Take this newly fragile heart
And jump and fall?

And I am afraid
And I cannot turn back
You broke down my walls
With your smiling embrace.

Deep deep breath
Don't look down
Drown in your eyes
Don't look back.

I'm sorry I kissed you.

Secrets*

a song by Allan Shipham

She was a teen

he'd done it again. You know

My mind was wild
not more than a child. You know

She needed to talk
we went for a walk
Her story she told
and my heart went cold. You know. You know

From inside my head
the words that I said. You know

On that night
I saved a life. You know

The tears that she cried
so painful inside
She would have died
if I hadn't tried. You know. You know

I told her, to live her life with grace
I told her, bad with good replace
Friends will love you till you die
Friends support you when you cry. You know.
You know

Everyone can be brave. You know
Everyone will be alright. You know

She moved on
and lived her life
A soul safe
my secret for life. You know

You Know. You Know. You Know.

* *adapted from the song, "Tonight", Bowie/Pop*

Stand By Your Woman

a short story by Elizabeth Parikh

I haven't written anything for today. This just comes from the heart. To my beautiful, new wife, Kelly.

I first visited Kelly in prison over four years ago. She was sitting at her bench, scratching her name on the table with her fingernail and I knew then and there that she was the one for me. So I proposed, I didn't have a ring, I got down on both knees and asked for her hand in marriage in front of all the other visitors. She said yes, everyone applauded and said congratulations.

And then Kelly was returned to her cell after trying to borrow the warden's wedding ring. I know now why he wouldn't take it off. 'Cause that's how I feel, I don't ever want to take this ring off. Even if a fairly sizable woman with a sharpened biro came at me. I would not take it off for the world.

The next day Kate Middleton came round Kelly's prison on an official Royal visit and Kelly got to meet her. I say meet. She was in isolation at this point so I think Kelly shouted in her general direction but I'm sure Kate heard. Kelly told her that she'd just got engaged and that she'd let the palace know the details. Well, we've not seen her yet but we've put a plate aside in case she shows. But we've no Spotted Dick left, she'll have to go without.

Kelly is a wonderful person, a fairly good mum and very good at DIY, always getting her hands dirty. On the second drugs raid on my house, sorry, our house, the police took ages to find anything. That was when Kelly did a runner to your cousin's, the hairdresser, for a bit. She did Kelly's roots while she was there. The police, they came back day after day, a whole load of them searching. I ended up giving them a shelf in the fridge. When they did pull up all that cocaine under the floorboards, they took the time to admire Kelly's workmanship which I found quite moving given the circumstances. I thought, what a woman!

I've always been a shy man and, well, Kelly, you've brought out the best that there is in me. You've never once taken my love for granted. You have tried so hard to change your ways and you even took that job at the local Morrison's two months ago – which went well for a few weeks. And I do think the judge was a bit hard on you for stealing that cereal, I know you probably shouldn't have driven the whole truck away, and had it dismantled and sold for profit. But, I reckon on that morning, you must have had *your* Weetabix!

Joking aside, thank you for being my wife. I'm so sorry you couldn't be here for all of today but we did it! We've married. You looked simply beautiful in your dress, my heart honestly skipped a beat when I saw you walking down the aisle. Dad on one side, prison guard cuffed to you on the other. She did well to walk sideways all that way. You looked so fantastic, I doubt anyone really noticed.

Finally, from here on in, it's just you and me, babe. I hope you get to see this video soon and everyone wishes you were here now. I'm going to do our first dance. For us. I've chosen something a bit tongue in cheek – When Will I See You Again by The Three Degrees. And we already know the answer to that. In four months with good behaviour. So please, *do* remember that. Don't ever think to yourself 'Does he really love me?' because you know what, babe? I really do.

See you soon. I miss you.

A Winter's Tale

a poem by Allan Shipham

Do you remember the winter snow?
It was late in the season the sun was still low.
I crossed fields and mountains,
frozen rivers and fountains.
I was young and my love I wanted to show.

Remember the old tree that was covered in ice?
The frost in the air, it was hard to look twice.
No foliage on show, it looked close to death,
but only asleep, it captured my breath.
I dreamed of your warmth and I dreamed of spice.

The winter sun's rays crept across the cold sky.
Through branches it peeked just like a spy.
They made me want you and need you,
they made me feel blue.
I wanted to scream and I started to cry.

I will never forget the day I hiked up that hill.
I caught that cough and nearly died of that chill.
I wanted to see you in all of your glory,
so I could write down and tell this story.
You were already with me and that is my thrill.

I know it was worth it, the snow and the gale.
I trudged like a mountaineer through the hail.
My footprints encrusted,
in no time were dusted.
Looking back it was only a winter's tale.

Crossroads

a short story by Nick Johns

Her eyes flashed in the darkness.

There was huge energy in the place tonight. I swung the microphone above my head.

Daltrey never did it better.

I felt her watching me, judging me, driving me on. But the energy came with a sullen and dangerous undercurrent. Spilled drinks might mean spilled blood and a clumsy push might be met with a glassed face.

But, God, I was on fire!

By the final set of the evening, the walls ran with sweat and the people surged like a rowdy, restless storm tide against the stage. I stepped up a pace or two, towards the front, oblivious to hands grasping at my ankles. I sang with new ferocity, feeding on their emotion. My harp licks were sharp and breathless, prodding and driving the crowd ever higher as my voice soared across the songs.

Davie moved in close and prodded me with his bass, eyes searching for what had got into me. I short armed him back and he slid on the beer slick floor, almost losing the beat along with his footing.

In the pause before the final number, I basked in the warm swell of raucous noise.

Instead of the familiar strains of my only minor radio hit, I stamped and clapped a quick, high tempo intro and launched into an edgy, rock version of an old folk song that I hadn't done on stage for years, beckoning the band to follow me.

As they fell in with the frantic, unfamiliar rhythm, I saw her drift to the front, right below me, staring up at me. The footlights' glare framed her glowing eyes and wild grin in a red henna halo, writhing snakes biting at her face as she bounced and swung her head to the beat, one hand on the air.

I goaded the crowd now, conducting them in repeated, ever louder chants of the chorus, before finally dropping my hand to end the song like flicking a master switch. The sudden silence stunned them and they stopped for a second before erupting in a final, frenzied, feral roar.

I jumped the footlights, grabbed her hand and fished her from the swirling maelstrom, hauling her up, weightless, to stand triumphant beside me. She grabbed me by the neck, wrenching me around to face her and I felt her tongue probing for the roots of my songs. Tiny mirrored images of me danced, reflected in her jade green eyes, and I clung to her, like a drowning sailor to a spar. I reeled back when flashing lights from lack of air dappled my vision.

Still clutching my hand, she dragged me urgently from the stage and toward the street.

The clammy heat of the gig steamed from our clothes and hair as we ran, headlong, towards the sodium oases scattered among the buildings by the few, still working street lights.

She pulled me on, hair flicking at my face as I tried to match her wanton energy. At last she stopped near the shadowed doorway of a boarded up brownstone and I doubled over as the midnight chill stole my breath away, and my ears rang with the unamplified silence.

A china white finger under my chin forced my head up and I stood with it, still gasping, marvelling at her pale, shining composure.

"Did you feel it?" she asked. "Did you feel the power?"

"Yeah, it was a good gig, sure... "

"Good? It was your best – ever... " She stepped back, regarding me, her face now a porcelain mask. "... and I can give you that, and more. You can have great. But it will cost you."

Another backward step into the doorway left only her beckoning hand in the light. She hooked a finger in a slow, hypnotic rhythm.

I peered for her in the gloom.

Her voice slipped sinuously into my ears and tugged at my soul. "Do you want it? You know what you need to do. Come and get it... "

I paused, but then, my treacherous foot moved towards her.

Her eyes flashed in the darkness.

And she laughed.

When I met him one day last summer

a short story by Beth Heywood

When I met him one day last summer, he told me his name was Earl-y. I was fourteen years old and hitchhiking from Manchester to London in search of a better life. I was wearing my favourite red dress, high heels, and make-up and was carrying a small pink back-pack. In the distance behind me, I could hear the drone of a pick-up truck and, as it slowed down, my heart beat faster. The truck finally stopped and the driver wound down the passenger window.

"Hey, little lady, want a lift?"

I look at his face. He had blond curly hair, piercing blue eyes and the most beautiful smile I'd ever seen. I didn't have to think about my answer. I smiled back.

He leaned across the passenger seat, opened the door and in I jumped.

Conversation was slow at first with Earl-y asking how far I was travelling, then if I was in a hurry to get there. The weather was clear and fine with a warm breeze, so I said I was in no hurry. That seemed to please him. Therefore, I, too, was pleased. Then Earl-y asked me how old I was.

I lied. "Eighteen."

And he nodded and smiled again.

Again, I was pleased. It seemed to me that all I wanted to do with the rest of my life was please Earl-y. It was then that I knew I was falling in love.

That night we pulled up at a truck stop and went into the café where we each had a burger and milkshake, and played pinball a while.

"Let's go back to the truck," said Earl-y. "I've got some good stuff back there."

We climbed into the bed of the truck, reclined on a

large mattress and rested on some old pillows. From a blue cooler by his side, Earl-y extracted two bottles of rum and coke.

"Have this for starters, babe," he said, opening one with his teeth and handing it over. He took another for himself, opened it, and let the contents slide down his throat. Then he belched loudly. "Come on, drink up!"

I drank up. I don't know how many I had. Finally, when my head was woozy, Earl-y reached into his jacket and pulled out two reefers. He lit them and handed me one. "Come on, baby, suck it up, suck it up."

So I sucked and sucked until I got the giggles fit to burst. Nothing would stop them.

I don't remember too much of what happened next except that I seemed to be rolling round on the mattress a lot and in the morning I felt like I'd been riding an unbroken stallion all night.

Silently, we drove to London. Earl-y told me he would find me a room to rent and then go on his way.

"But I thought we were an item," I cried.

He pulled up and dried my eyes. "I'll be back in six months. You stay here and wait for me."

So I waited.

And I waited.

And I put on weight.

Of course, I realised too late what had happened. But one day, into my ninth month, there came a knock at the door. I opened it and there stood Earl-y.

I was so delighted to see him I threw my arms around his neck. "You came back!"

Earl-y picked me up and twirled me round, then set me on to the floor. He frowned. His face darkened. "What's this?" he said, pointing at my bump.

"Oh, Earl-y, we're having a baby. Just imagine!" I said, expecting him to be delighted.

He was certainly emotional, but not in the way I had expected. He blacked both my eyes and broke four of my ribs.

Later, when he had finished shouting and my pains started, he took me to the hospital and waited until our little girl was born.

Then he said, "Hey, babe, wanna come on the road with me again?"

I was overjoyed. We would be a proper family.

The baby started to cry and Earl-y took her while I went to pack our bags and we got into the car.

After about an hour's worth of driving, I noticed the baby was very quiet.

"Where's the baby?"

"I put it in the trash, didn't I?"

I never even gave my little daughter a name and I don't know what became of her.

I'm no longer with Earl-y.

Is there any forgiveness for what I did?

Darkness on the Edge of Town

a short story by Nick Johns

I am dreaming about Becky when a hand falls on my shoulder.

I turn slowly, instantly alert, the open mic night sounds fade into the background.

"I been hearing tales 'bout what you been doin'. I'm here to tell you how it's going to be for you from here on in... " he slurs.

"Do yourself a favour, Billy. It's not your business what I do."

"'Cept if it's with my girl, City Boy, then it's my business."

"Becky's not your girl, Billy."

The whistle of the cut-off pool cue cuts through the bar room drone. I jerk my head back. It just catches me across the shoulder instead of full in the face, and smashes a bottle on the bar. A girl behind me screams. I kick the bar stool away and back up, flexing my arm. Not bad, just a bruise. I feel dry boards under my feet, some clear floor space, and stop.

"Last chance, Billy. Walk away now."

Billy's face is red as his ball cap. He's breathing hard, shoulders bunched, pool cue held in two hands now, out in front, weaving it from side to side. I ignore it. Watch his eyes, his feet. He's flat on his heels.

"Or what? This here's my town, you ain't got no business here, City Boy. And in here... " he gestures, " ...no kin, no buddies, no-one to help you... "

The hubbub dies away – that tense, hold your breath quiet that always foreshadows the start of a fight.

I still have options. I can leave now or... but my mouth makes the decision for me – like always.

"You think I need help? Against some flyspeck town

football player? A shrivel dick steroid queen? A loudmouth, drunken redneck and his pansy pals?"

Billy's eyes widen. "Redneck? Why, you – "

He swings the cue back. A full, home run wind up, veins in his neck pumping, biceps straining at his tee shirt.

I'd warned him.

I step inside the swing, kick the outside of his right knee, landing my foot behind him. I throw my left arm up to stop the cue, striking hard with my forearm, cracking his elbow, and hit him full in the gut with a straight right. Six inches, no more. He whooshes like a broken steam pipe and, as he jack-knifes towards me, I butt him full in the face. As he reels back, I whip my leg back from behind his knee and he falls away, toppling slowly at first, like a dynamited building, before landing hard on his back, head lolling to one side. Blood from his broken nose paints a crimson river delta across his slack face.

Out of the corner of my eye, I catch a shape scrambling towards me. I hit the bar tender's wrist with a bottle, grabbing up the blackjack he drops, then elbow him in the face, sending him reeling back the way he came, crashing into the mirror behind the bar.

I look for my guitar case, but think better of it. I guess I have about a minute before the stunned silence breaks, so stride to the back door. I throw the blackjack into the weeds and jump in the truck, offering a silent prayer to the God of broken down pickups as I turn the key. The engine coughs one, twice, three times then, deciding it had scared me enough, rumbles into life. As I reverse out, my headlights light up some local boys, including a few of Billy's team mates, bursting through the bar room door, like wasps from a dropped nest.

I swing the wheel around and spray them with parking lot gravel as I head for the highway.

The night air through the open window of the truck is clean after the bar room's close, stale atmosphere. Even the temperature had fallen a little from the tar-melting daytime high.

The adrenaline shakes hit me and I grip the slippery wheel tighter, staring at the road, thinking about how I had managed to screw up again.

I should have known better. I was meant to be keeping a low profile. Great work, genius.

A woman again.

* * * * *

I had only stopped to listen to her play her guitar. She was good. Sweet, pure voice with a twang, flowery dress and a real pretty smile. She saw the guitar case in the back of the truck and waved me over. I sat on the grass, sang some harmonies, played some counterpoint. It was fun. I gave her a flower, held her hand, talked about my life up north. Well, the parts that wouldn't identify me, anyway.

We arranged to meet again.

I lowered my guard, forgot who I was, what I was. I just wanted a moment of normality, of peace. After a few days, I even started to dream about staying here, with Becky. She calmed me and I made her laugh.

I mean, who would think to look for me out here in the boondocks? I could play guitar in the bars, do some farm work.

* * * * *

I mean, farm work? Me? Really?

No. If it hadn't been Billy, it would have been something else. I'm a trouble magnet, you see, just like my mother always used to say.

The dawning sun drives the night time shadows away and a whole country beckons to me, one road at a time.

What about Florida? The Cubans keep it pretty tight down there. I reckon I'll find something more in my line.

So long, Becky, it was great while it lasted.

Romancing Sophie

a short story by Allan Shipham

The birds began their morning song and the summer breeze breathed across the fallow field. Wild flowers danced in the warm air and the grass waved toward the crimson sky. The smell of the salty sea nearby filled the air, cooling the skin of anyone who rested in the field.

Laurence woke and looked around, yesterday had been a day like any other day, except he'd met that special person and his life had changed. They'd spent the day and evening together chatting and making friends. It was clear she liked him a great deal. He wasn't that experienced with girls so being romantic was a struggle, but it must have worked.

They ate out and had walked for ages, finding themselves eventually in a large, open unattended field near the coast. They lay beneath the stars and talked for hours about everything they valued about life and everything they wanted for the future. The sound of the waves relaxed them and they were in awe of the marvellous creation before them. Something magical happened; it was hard to imagine what had contributed the most.

He looked across at his new belle, she was everything you could ever want and everything you could dream about. They'd nuzzled noses and embraced, and they had teased each other, and they had made love. Somehow, he just knew what to do and, somehow, she just knew what to expect. He reflected that it probably wouldn't have been his best performance, but, now he was adult, he knew he'd have other chances to perform.

She stirred and looked around at the hedges, scanning for the birds.

"Bloody birds!" she said.

"Sleep alright?"

221

"No! It was all rocky, I hate that."

"You should have said, we could have moved."

"I couldn't wake you! You were snoring so loud I was surprised you didn't wake yourself."

"I don't snore. "

"You do, believe me!"

He licked his lips; they were dry with the salt air. "I fancy a drink, you with me?"

"Drink! All you can say is drink."

"Sophie, what's up, darling?"

"Don't you darling me!" she rose to her feet and brushed herself down. "Mother said you'd be like this!"

"Mother?" he gasped. "What's any of this got to do with her?"

They hardly spoke as they walked down to a freshwater stream that ran along the side of the field.

"I'm not drinking out of that cesspit." She stomped around. "That's got cows' pee and all sorts floating around in it."

Laurence took a drink, "You can't taste anything like that."

"I know it's in there, everyone does. I want to go home."

"If you want. Just not sure why you are being funny with me." Laurence was confused and starting to regret what happened the night before.

His mouth refreshed, he started to make his way back where they came.

"Don't forget me!" she whined.

"I am leading the way back," he said. "Come on."

"Just like mum said," she said. "Oh God! What if I'm pregnant?"

"Pregnant!" He stopped in his tracks. "Why would you be pregnant?"

"I'm not on any protection and I know you didn't use any."

"You'll be fine. Unlikely. It's our first time."

"Only need once."

Laurence found the hole in the hedge where they'd entered the field and they found themselves in the lane.

They made their way back to her home. He'd drop her off first, then go home himself before anyone noticed they were missing.

As they walked down the lane, they could hear a dog barking excitedly in the distance.

"Oh no, it's that damned dog!" Laurence said. "I knew it was going to bite me last time it was out."

"And you know that awful farmer won't be far behind. Miserable bastard."

They continued down the lane.

They heard footsteps approaching and looked around for a gap in the hedge where they could hide. As they made their way towards the hedge, they were confronted by Shep the dog. He was barking.

"Well done, Shep," called the farmer. "Where is she?"

The dog barked some more and the farmer drew close. He paused as he caught his breath.

"That damned ram from Manor Farm!"

Laurence looked around.

"What have you been up to with Sophie?" he asked. "I've been saving her for Zac."

Laurence wasn't sure which way to run. He needed to get away. Sophie was frozen to the spot, hypnotised by Shep.

The farmer drew close and grabbed Sophie by her horns. "Come on, girl, back to the pen. I don't even know how you got out!"

Shep barked and charged at Laurence. Laurence bolted back up the lane as fast as his four legs would carry him.

"Larry!" Sophie called out, her pet name for Laurence.

Laurence was running too fast to respond, but he let out a loud bleat as he reached the top of the hill. Shep had been called back by the farmer, so he knew he was safe.

* * * * *

"Here endeth today's reading from The Young Person's Modern Parables."

Father O'Flaherty closed the book and took his seat.

The congregation sat in silence contemplating the story.

"Father, can I ask a question?" A young voice bounded from the congregation. It was a special youth service so nothing was going to go to plan.

"Why, yes, of course, Patrick. What is your question?"

Patrick, an eleven year old, asked what everyone was thinking.

"See, I know the story wasn't about real sheep, but what has it got to do with God?"

"A good question, my son," the priest replied. "God affects each of us in different ways no matter who or what we are. For some, his word is guidance, for some it's spiritual, for some it's literal."

He paused.

"You have to make a choice when you hear a story like this one, how you want to live your life. I'm not going to tell you and I'm not going to judge you, but you'll judge yourself and you will face the Day of Judgement. Now, will you be the good sheep or will you be the naughty sheep?"

THE RAP BEFORE CHRISTMAS

a comedy sketch by Elizabeth Parikh

<u>CHARACTERS</u>

in order of appearance

| JAMES | male, 27 | a rapper |
| BILLY | male, 27 | a rapper |

<u>Notes</u>

1. This sketch is written in rap and must be performed as a rap.
2. The whole sketch must be underscored with music to go with the rap.
3. The actors can improvise if they get the urge.

INT. LIVING ROOM. EVENING.

Shabby, cosy living room of a shared house that is dressed for Christmas. The tree has a pair of Y-Fronts hanging from a branch. There is large bikini model poster tacked on the wall.

JAMES is sitting in front of a real fire and knitting, he looks drunk on love. BILLY comes in from the snowy weather outside and takes off his outerwear.

MUSIC kicks in for the rap.

> BILLY
> Hey, James, my pal, how're ya going, my mate?

> JAMES
> Hi, Billy-boy, why you so late?

> BILLY
> I've fallen for this girl, she must be the one
> Her cute red nose was glowing by the sun
> The ice-skating she loved and surely so did I
> I can't believe it's after eight, my how time flies!

> JAMES
> It's catching dear friend, me too am smitten
> The love bug is about us and dear God it's bitten
> Her blonding hair, and slightly darker roots
> Her twinkling smile and Uggsome snow boots.

> BILLY
> Your date went well? I was asleep when you crept in
> Did she stay the night or was she averse to the sin?
> My One is a *Lady* no night she has stayed
> Apart from her thigh where my hand may have strayed!

226

JAMES

I crept in alone and she to her digs
But on our night out she did bare her nips
That is through her tight woolly top I mean
I could see two points looking frightfully keen!

BILLY

Tish is just great loves to sew *and* she knits!

JAMES

So does Tash what is it with these chicks?

BILLY holds up a nearly completed knitted tea cosy.

BILLY

I'm making her a cosy with a heart on the side
And across the back I REALLY LOVE YOUR
THIGHS

JAMES

I might join you old pal have you a spare couple of
needles?
I could make socks that read I LOVE THAT YOU'RE
INTO THE BEATLES.

BILLY hands JAMES some wool on needles.

BILLY

The Beatles you say? Tish likes them too
And Aerosmith, and Eva Cassidy and Betty Blue

JAMES

I think they'd get along like a house on fire these two
So much in common including me and you.

JAMES

You'll meet mine tonight she is coming to the house
I need to vacuum the carpet and shoo away the mouse.
And while we're at it your pants are on the tree
If she sees those ornaments I can't see her settling for
me

BILLY removes the pants and shoves them under the sofa
cushion.

BILLY

They're dry now matey the clothes rack was full
But yes if Tish stopped by I can kiss goodbye to a pull
You might want to rethink the old lady on the wall

JAMES

No problem there friend it's a problem I already
foresaw.

JAMES turns the bikini poster around, other side is cute
kittens. He then produces a carrier bag and pulls out the
contents. There is a tub of gel and for the table, stones,
candles and a book.

JAMES

I've bought special gel to mattify my hair
Some candles, some stones and this book on feng shui
– it's like yoga for chairs.

BILLY

I've an idea I'll send our address and invite Tish
The two can meet and stay over – I'll insist!
We'll do the gentlemanly thing and sleep here instead
I'll turn the heating off so they'll feel bad and make us
join them in bed!

JAMES

A splendid idea please do text away
A double date shall be had and matted hair is now on
its way
A dollop of this and a quick snip of some body hair
Mistletoe is hung and by our charms we are ready to
dare.

BILLY

I'll say it if you say it –

BILLY/JAMES

I think I'm in love!

JAMES

Tell the angels and saints

BILLY

I feel like a fluffy turtle dove!
Now tell me old chum and be as honest as you can
Should I marry my lady could I elect you to be my best
man?
I'd want a Christmas wedding to capture this time
And if you were to marry Tash best man would be I.

JAMES

Ay and ay yes and yes should the ladies hearts be ours
then to you I'll be Best!

BILLY

In fact would you be open to a double wedding day?
Half the price on things like the priest and the cake?

BILLY

If and if this is to happen I will need to seal the deal
and fast
How much for an engagement ring and how much is
left on my overdraft?

JAMES

Retail beckons as always internet is the key
Cheaper engagement rings search under buy one get
one free.

BILLY

Cheapy cheap right here import from Estonia
Ooh this is a bargain it's called cu-bi-ca zir-conia?

JAMES

Perfect that's the one I'll bookmark this page.
Fingers crossed they receive my order within a few
days!
Whilst I'm here would you like to see
My one and only blushing bride to be?

BILLY

Yes of course I'll be delighted to look
But nothing can hold a candle to my darling dear duck

JAMES

I think after seeing this you'll agree
Surely there can be no better looking than she.
That's my Tash!

BILLY

That's my Tish!

BILLY/JAMES

But she's what? With you!

JAMES

The harlot!

BILLY

The bitch!

JAMES

Stringing me along like some sad young twit!

BILLY

I knew in that moment she must be a shit!

JAMES

She'll be here any minute

BILLY

Our addresses will have matched

JAMES

Her wall of lies has now crumbled my heart is now smashed.

BILLY

She shall not be offered a bed for the night the cruel hearted tart

JAMES

Nor any eggnog but a black coffee to match her black heart!

BILLY

To think I wanted to have her as my bride

JAMES

And now all you're left with is this woollen ball poorly tied.

BILLY

Emasculating tools in the bin they shall be

JAMES

Or jam them through the hearts of any loving couple that share a path with me

231

BILLY
She shall not win though she has toiled with my cogs

JAMES
My princess of love has turned into a frog!

BILLY
She told me she cared for me!

JAMES
She told me that she was won!

BILLY
And now all that I am left with

JAMES
Is a memory of her shapely bum!

BILLY
Still she did steal my chips when we were on our first date

JAMES
And her laugh sometimes made me think of pigs over a slate.

BILLY
Did you notice that stench from her mothball vintage clothes

JAMES
And a fog horn was sounded every time she blew her little nose

BILLY
This has put me back years; I'm now on my guard

JAMES
There's nothing else for it. Let's watch Die Hard.

BILLY
With a Vengeance.

They slump back on the sofa. JAMES presses the remote
control at the TV.

THE END

A new beginning

a short story by Beth Heywood

The fresh breeze blowing off the sea whipped through Agnes' long blonde hair, lifting it momentarily before billowing around her forehead and shoulders. For the first time since she could remember, she felt free of worries and free of cares. Most importantly, she felt free of her past. She sighed. She'd get through today and it would be, as everyone said, a new beginning.

She raked her fingers through her tangled tresses, turning her gaze to the sand dunes and the treacherous emerald and turquoise water beyond them. Maybe it was the effect of her new medication, but today she could truly see and appreciate nature's beauty.

She turned around to survey her companions. Conservationists. Middle-aged, bespectacled tree-planters. Not one of them without the requisite stick, woolly hat, stout walking shoes. Not to mention the thick socks that went from knee to ankle. Even the women. But that was fine. Without her medication, she'd be angry even to be in their company.

"Lunchtime!" called the leader.

Just what she needed. The other tree-planters formed into groups. A thread of discomfort wormed its way to the pit of Agnes' stomach, the way it usually did when her medication was due. She glanced at her watch. 12.30. She should have taken it half an hour ago. But no matter. She searched her pockets. Nothing. She'd have to get through the afternoon as best she could. She could manage. She knew that.

Everyone else had planted a dozen trees to her one. She shrugged away any guilty feelings. This was only Community Service. Better than prison. And much, much better than wasting her time at psychiatric evaluation with

234

know-all, know-nothing do-gooders. The magistrate had been lenient on her. Bi-polar II, a form of manic-depression, was what the psychiatrist said she suffered from. She wasn't sure the magistrate held the same opinion. But whatever the label, she had made a good living and furnished the house she shared with her father.

There was one only other person in her age group. Jonathan. Thick dark hair sprinkled with grey. Chiselled features, a full and promising mouth, but an apology for a body. The silent type. Like her, he was excluded from the group. Like her, he was sitting on his own. Unlike her, he wore the uniform.

She wondered what he was like in the throes of passion. Would he sweat and pant like a stallion, losing all control as he powered into her? Or would he gently slip it in, pull it out, and wipe it?

Or would his tastes be different? The kind that make an ineffectual man the master of his own universe? The kind where such a man could imagine a woman subjugated to his sexual will. The kind where he called the tune and paid for such pleasures. The kind where he could avenge his past hurts.

Agnes shivered. Past hurts could be resolved with plenty of good sex. She had proved that time and again with her many clients.

She needed to look into this more closely. He was a real challenge. It would certainly be different from the mind-murdering boredom of planting native trees in barren soil.

She stood up quickly, and slowly, oh so slowly, brushed the grass from the seat of her tight jeans, adjusting her top to show the beginnings of her cleavage. When she was sure Jonathan had noticed, she lifted her top higher and tucked it into her jeans. Tight enough to show the outline of her nipples. Not for nothing had her clients had called her "organ-stops". Agnes knew what she needed, and fully intended to get it.

Smiling, and forcing a blush, she sashayed over, took

his left hand through her arm, and walked him away from the rest of the group.

"My name's Agnes," she smiled.

For a moment, Jonathan was startled. Mummy had always told him to keep himself pure for the Right Woman. And he'd tried. He'd really tried very hard. Sometimes, it had been harder than others. Those had been hard times. Times when he'd been unable to stop from touching himself. He looked down into Agnes's wide sapphire eyes.

He wanted to touch himself now. But he remembered Mummy – how she'd beaten him when he'd done that. This woman shouldn't be touching him. Mummy had said so. But she might be the Right Woman. He was a big boy now. He'd make his own mind up. He smiled. "Er, thank you."

"Let's go for a walk. I'll look after you for a while."

Jonathan suppressed the gasp that rose to his lips. As Agnes took his hand and they walked up the gentle grassy slopes, away from the rest of the group, he could hardly believe his good luck. All his life he'd been waiting for an opportunity like this. He could trust Agnes. "I've had dreams."

"Of course you have." Agnes was warm, reassuring. "We all do."

Relief flooded through him. And with it, a warm stirring in his loins. He knew now Agnes was the Right Woman. He still needed to touch himself. Needed to press the palm of his hand against his length, even if it was through thick trousers. But he mustn't. He hoped Agnes wouldn't notice. He didn't want to spoil things. He also needed to touch her. For forty years, he'd waited to touch a woman other than Mummy.

He glanced down at Agnes, at the outline of her young breasts thrusting through her tee-shirt. She wouldn't be wrinkled like Mummy. She wouldn't be floppy and smelling of fish like Mummy had been. She'd be firm and soft and warm.

Jonathan was happy. He'd be a proper man now. "Really?" Then with an effort, "What are your dreams about?"

"Let's discuss both our dreams later." She squeezed his hand and smiled.

Jonathan's breathing quickened. He thrust his right hand into his pocket, searched with his fingers, found the secret hole at the bottom. He badly needed to touch himself, just for a moment. It was him or her. He had to have relief.

Agnes was looking at him. She smiled again. That all-knowing smile. "Off you go into the bush. I'll turn my back. It's okay. I'll still be waiting for you."

She understood! That was wonderful!

He had scarcely turned his back to her before his fingers fumbled clumsily at his zip. His member shot out, hot and hard. He waited a moment before placing his fist around it. That was good. He quickly stroked, his breath coming in gasps. He used his fingers to erect a warm tunnel around his tip, his stroking became a frantic rubbing until he could feel his ecstasy coming upon him. He tightened his fingers around his tip, just as Mummy had taught him, sending his juices back down his shaft, and gasped.

He'd be all right now. Mummy had taught him well. Agnes truly was the Right Woman, the Understanding Woman that Mummy had told him would come along.

Satisfied, he returned his subsiding shaft to its home, zipped up his trousers, returned to Agnes.

"Better?" she asked, as they continued their journey. Jonathan was going to be a most interesting challenge. She knew what he'd been doing, of course. She'd seen that old trick with some of her clients. It would be fun to cure him of it. As they walked and talked, Jonathan told Agnes about his work at the solicitor's office, how Mummy had died, leaving him the family farm and the inheritance.

Agnes lied about her work with handicapped children and told the truth about her hopes for the future.

"Poor dear," he stroked her hair, "Life hasn't been easy for you, has it?"

Agnes shook her head. Jonathan might be a nerd. But he was an innocent nerd. And decent. She didn't need her medication to understand that. Maybe she could make something of him.

Jonathan stood back from Agnes, admired the sunlight shafting through her wind-blown hair, her deep blue eyes, her smile that lit up her face. Admired her thick-lashed eyes set in creamy porcelain skin, the kindness and compassion that he thought to find only in his dreams. And a body that he'd fantasised about since he was twelve. When the girls had laughed at him.

His face contorted in rage.

Agnes watched the tidal wave of love and desire break across Jonathan's face. Maybe, with his unknown help, she could turn her life around – as the magistrate had said.

She stretched out her hand to his and, bringing it to her lips, kissed it tenderly. "Will you be my friend?"

Again, a warmth stirred in his groin. Agnes was all he'd hoped for. Could he be her friend? He'd never been this close to a strange woman before. He needed to touch himself again. He struggled, pushing thoughts of pleasing himself aside, as Mummy had taught him. Before, the thoughts made him hard as wood and he had to attend to himself again.

"I've some demons to fight." Like the lies about his work at the solicitor's office. His inheritance. What had happened to Mummy.

"We'll face them together, darling. Sometimes they might win. But I'll always be with you."

"Do you promise?"

"Truly and faithfully with all my heart."

They reached the top of the hill and stood a moment. Beneath them, the waves thundered as they broke on the rocks at the base of the cliffs.

Agnes needed a man. She was different from the other women, who could go for weeks, months even, without a man. Agnes knew now, with absolute certainty, that the medication wasn't going to make her well. It was merely intended to relegate her to the ranks of withered, dried-up prunes of women who lived without men in their beds.

Maybe, it was as well for her that she hadn't brought her medication. Truly, today the Lord had blessed her and she could see things for what they really were.

With their arms around each other, their bodies so close they were almost one, Jonathan pressed himself fully dressed into Agnes' soft body.

And as the fresh breeze blew off the sea, billowing Agnes' hair around her face, its perfume filling Jonathan's nostrils, he felt happiness and joy like he'd never known before. His breathing grew laboured. He ran his hands up Agnes's arms, touched the swell of her breasts, caressed her tender neck.

Agnes knew Jonathan was a shy man. A restrained man. She could take her time with him. Tease him. Play with him. Teach him to play with her.

She settled back into his body. He was obviously smitten with her. She could do worse. Snuggling even closer, she knew that, given time, she could become fond of him. Maybe even give him the children he said he wanted. This would be a new beginning. For both of them. She didn't mind when she felt his maleness against her back. Caressing, loving, she'd give him what he wanted. It was a small price for her to pay for his money, farm, and the social prestige of being a solicitor's wife. She could turn out decent after all.

Jonathan liked the warmth of Agnes' body as she pressed into him. He wanted more. He pulled her closer, moving his loins away, just to be sure. He needed to touch himself, and this time the need was much worse than the last time. Touch. He had to touch. He allowed his fingers to creep around to her breasts, close over them. They were hard and high. Much better than Mummy's. She was the Right Woman. This was the Right Time. The time Mummy had told him would come. His breath was coming

239

hard now, almost choking him, like when he'd been running. Would she mind if he slipped a hand under her tee-shirt? He had to feel flesh.

Agnes didn't mind. Her hand helped him.

He moved a hand to rub down his trousers. This wasn't like the pictures in his magazines. His loins bucked, and he fought for control. He couldn't take care of himself now as Mummy had taught him. He would have to be a man. She turned around, her tee-shirt rucked up to her arm-pits, her breasts jutting for him to touch. He needed to touch himself, and her, too. He watched, his excitement mounting as her eyes moved to his trousers. He didn't want to send his juices back down again like Mummy had taught him.

Slowly, the girl smiled.

Was she laughing at him? She was, the bitch. She was laughing at him with her eyes. She was dirty. She'd make him dirty. But she was the Right Woman, wasn't she? He looked again. She stood before him and placing her hand on his trousers, started to unzip his flies. It was too much. She was giving him sinful thoughts.

The rage mounted in him. He knocked her to the ground, and kneeling on her legs, tore open her jeans, and threw himself upon her. His shaking fingers fumbled at her panties and they came free. They pried nosily at her entrance. She was damp, like Mummy had been.

Then she did the unthinkable. She grasped his manhood. He bucked violently and was inside her, in the place Mummy had said he mustn't go.

Again and again, he thrust into her, grunting his rage, unable to stop. Suddenly he was big, powerful, and stretching and stretching, and his juices were out. All of them. And inside her.

She'd made him a bad boy. A bad, bad boy. He'd be punished for letting his juices go. But it was her fault. She'd made him do it. He'd spilled his seed and Mummy would be cross, and that wouldn't do. That wouldn't do at all.

240

The girl, not him, should be punished.

As his fingers closed around her neck, he knew he was doing the right thing. He was punishing her for pretending to be the Right Woman. She wasn't. She was one of those whores, one of those harlots Mummy had warned him about. She was the Wrong Woman.

Beneath him, Agnes knew he'd a lot to learn. But there was the savage in him, to be drawn out, tamed and trained. She smiled.

Jonathan looked down at her, her legs splayed wantonly, presenting herself for all the world to see. His cock stirred into life again, turning him from the Path of Righteousness. With a bellow of rage, he powered into her once more. Agnes gasped and thrust her hips up to meet his.

She was ruining him and he couldn't allow that.

His fingers closed round a rock by her head, and he gripped it tightly as he felt his soul, with his seed, slipping away. When he was done, his body shook, with rage and fear.

His fingers tightened around the rock. He had to save himself. He had to. He knelt in front of her, the rock firmly in his grasp, and pounded it into the tuft of hair between her legs. This would stop her unseemly behaviour.

He pounded and pounded with the rock, heedless of the blood and bone flying in all directions. When the smell of excreta reached his nostrils he knew she was dirty and what he was doing was right.

He pounded at her face until, finally, she lay still, a bloody indecipherable mess, like the roadkill he'd seen when big people who could drive cars were careless on the roads.

He stood up. He needed to attend to himself again. With his bloodied hands on his organ, he pulled and tugged and thought of Agnes lying on the grass – just like Mummy had been. He didn't stop his juices this time. As they flew over Agnes' bloodied remains, an awareness of the blood also covering him crept into his consciousness.

241

With a sob, he knew what he had to do now. He had to treat Agnes with the same dignity and respect he'd treated Mummy. Fastening up his trousers like the good boy he was, he went and gathered some fallen branches, smaller twigs, and pine cones. He assembled them the way he had been taught in the Scouts. Then he put his hand inside his shirt pocket, and pulled out a small box of matches. He'd never been a smoker – that would waste money – but he was always prepared – something else the Scouts had taught him.

Withdrawing a single match, he scratched it on the emery paper, and touched it to the twigs. There now. While he waited for the fire to take, as he knew it would, as surely as he knew now he was a Good Boy, he turned his attention to Agnes' remains.

Separating the limbs from the torso was easy. He had the strength. Breaking them into smaller pieces was more difficult, but not impossible.

When he'd finished – and it didn't take long – he carefully arranged the pieces of meat on the twigs above the glowing embers.

Behind him, someone shouted.

He turned.

Two men were rushing up the hill.

"Come along, Jonathan," one of them called. "The bus is waiting to take you back to the hospital."

Jonathan burst into tears.

"But we can't go back yet," he wailed. "I thought you'd be hungry and I've cooked us a roast."

He paused, his face clearing.

"Did you bring some vegetables?"

it is most mad and moonly

a short story by Michael J Richards

Vice Chancellor, my lords, ladies, colleagues. Friends. I end this, my valedictory lecture, on a personal note.

It is well documented that I have dedicated my career at this university to the question, "What is love?"

In my early years, I postulated that love is the emotional bond tying human beings together to become a force for good, causing me to pass a decade swimming in the dark fathoms of meanings of the word "good", never appreciating that greater and nobler minds than mine have failed to sail across that semantically shark-infested ocean.

I progressed, if "progressed" is the *mot juste* (I fear it is not), to the proposition that love is the one sentiment separating us from God's other sentient beings. Yet, if that is so, why do gibbon apes mate for life? What prompts one black vulture to attack another black vulture caught straying from his partner? Within the human species, how can feckless celebrities declare eternal love only to acrimoniously separate a short time later?

I concluded there are as many explanations and theories to this seemingly unanswerable question as there are people providing them. As critiques of *Hamlet* tell us more about the critics than the play, those explanations and theories tell us more about the writers than love.

If that is true, then what do my attempts to unearth the secret of love tell us about this man who stands before you? You see an aging Professor of Philosophy. You see a man who dallied in his youth with demoiselles of sure or uncertain virtue with wobbling effect, who for a protracted period, believed he might, underneath his apparent *savoir faire* and despite himself, prefer handsome hirsute young men. Failure to connect with either brought equal dismay.

I sought. I bought. I failed to find love. Not until my

fiftieth birthday did it dawn on me that I would not recognise love if it came on a bright summer's evening bearing a bouquet of red roses, a bottle of 1893 Veuve Clicquot and a bed the size of the Giardino Giusti in Verona, where Romeo and Juliet were said to have met.

How does one know when one has found love? However much philosophers rant or theologians rail, it is poets to whom we turn for eternal truths. Shakespeare has Romeo tell us:

"Love is a smoke raised with the fume of sighs;
Being purged, a fire sparkling in lovers' eyes;
Being vexed, a sea nourished with loving tears.
What is it else? A madness most discreet,
A choking gall, and a preserving sweet."

Love is not, as St Paul would have it, seen through a glass darkly. It is as the poet e e cummings wrote:

"it is most mad and moonly"

When I first read these words, I did not understand them. But I knew they were true.

Compared to the love of a young man or woman, an academic's life is sterile. While the philosopher flails about in contrived words for baseless meaning, the lover searches his or her heart, the organ that keeps us alive and breathing. Love is not what we mean. Love is what we feel. Love is a prism through which we see the world.

Yet I have published to great acclaim. *Amo, amas, amat: on the meaning of love* was that rare phenomenon, a philosophy book that sold a million copies. My *No sacrifice can be too much: reflections on love, language and Wittgenstein* earned me the Kyoto Prize in Arts and Philosophy. The most surprising of all – to me, at any rate – *Where is love? A philosopher wanders the desert of the psyche* became a $74m film starring Brad Pitt, Jennifer Lawrence and Alex Pettyfer.

And then, two years ago, after thirty-two years of barren searching, I declared myself redundant of my quest to find why the human heart needs what Cole Porter calls "this thing called love".

Instead, I turned my attention to the significance of death. To my Beckettian dismay, the questions were identical to those I had posed about love.

Why does the human race attach such weight to part of the natural cycle of all things? Planets, stars, rocks, insects come into being, exist, atrophy, transmute, cease. Why must we feel the need either to refuse to take responsibility for our own life-cycles or to accept that we are nothing more than a mote in the eye of the gargantuan, Heideggeresque Being and Time? Why is there an interminable need within us to ascribe our miniscule grubbing about to an unknown, unseen, intangible, unnameable, indescribable *qi*?

But, in the course of my research, I met Carina, a funeral director from Sydenham in Kent.

Through her, I experienced the swirling headiness of compassionate care, a baffling need to please, a constant urge never to be parted. But most of all, I felt – *felt* – beauty. It is the sun rising over a buttercup meadow. The smile in the eyes of a puppy at play. A liqueur and cigar after a French chef's tasting menu. The inner glow after a rainy Wednesday afternoon's intimate and secret love-making.

"it is most mad and moonly"

I now understand it and embrace it. I am bemused to declare I fell in love and married this most beautiful, wondrous, wise and caring woman.

In my life, I never embraced love, only tried to define and capture it, possibly in so doing, to smother it out of existence. Now, my life shrinking into mellowing dotage, I have become the hunter trapped by his prey.

Surrounded by death, I find life. How can it be, I ask

myself, that when searching for love, I never found it? And the moment I stop, love attacks me, fells me to the ground and takes me hostage?

Were I to live the infinity of the universe, I will never dream that love could be like this.

What has my life been worth if at its nearing end, I deny everything I have stood for? What is my new life worth if for all of my previous life I sought to prove it has no worth?

For my years at this university, I thank you all. For my coming years of fathomless happiness, I thank Carina, whose name means "beloved". For a life of pointless anguish, I apologise.

Skin

a dedication by Pat Aitcheson

Skin, warm and smooth.

Tiny hairs clothe the inside of your arm, pale and velvet soft. Purple veins sit under the surface, tracing jagged patterns wrapped around your fingers. My fingertips brush yours. Trail fingers upwards to the soft curve of your shoulder, brush my lips against your collarbone and follow it, swooping down, up. Your throat pulses against my mouth as goosebumps stand to attention, your hair a waving cornfield. You tremble and I inhale softness, musk and vanilla, peach fuzz. When you speak, I do not hear. Instead I absorb your words, transmuted in vibration. I feel sound, rest my ear against your heart to understand life, strength, constancy. I am drowning, cocooned by memory, caught by anticipation, hypnotised, ensnared by the possibility of you.

Skin, taut and strong.

Long glossy hairs clothe the hills and valleys of muscles restrained and defined. Soft, corded veins contain the heat of blood and life. Your flesh retreats beneath my hand, then rises up to meet me, first shy, then bold. I map these contours of a strange and well remembered land. Your breath holds steady while mine catches in my throat. On a journey of discovery, I travel these many roads, to find and lose myself. I search this country of you, in the light and dark, on the wide plains and ridged fields, for the particular place that smells like home.

The Perfect Match

a short story by Gordon Adams

It wasn't possible, Jeremy Thomas told himself. He couldn't be in love again. Not now – surely not! Not with a woman he hadn't even met.

But something was definitely there, nonetheless: that extra bounce in his step; a slow smile spreading across his face whenever he thought of her; the tingle of excitement each time a new message popped up on his phone. And now (at last) he was going to meet her for the first time.

Science had triumphed here, it seems. He found that a little hard to accept, being the arch-sceptic that he was, but he had to concede on that particular point. When the university had invited him to take part in "a unique dating experiment", to see "whether science can bring about a perfect match", he'd acquiesced, but fully expected to be telling funny stories for years about how badly he'd been hooked up.

All of the so-called scientific "compatibility tests" they'd done at the university seemed no more than the usual pseudoscience you get with dating websites these days. Pretentious stuff! Stupid online questionnaires forever more, covering all of the usual ground. He'd completed standard psychometric tests and quirky personality tests: how quick was he was to anger or praise, how did he react to criticism, did he believe in UFOs, did he prefer cats to dogs and was he a morning or evening person? He'd detailed his hobbies and interests and been intimately probed by researchers (for that's how it felt) for clues about why his past romances had bloomed or died.

The so-called hard science element of it was little better. Genetic testing (what did they really do with that sample of his blood they extracted: did they really do a sophisticated DNA test or did it go straight in the bin?)

The brain scanning procedure was admittedly pretty impressive – certainly the equipment they used looked shiny and new – but what did it really show? All they had were a few fancy-coloured pictures showing parts of his brain lighting up whenever he was shown a photo of someone he fancied.

But then he was introduced to Miranda and she was something else! It was hard to put his finger on it. She just seemed to be in tune with him, from the very outset. He hadn't been shown a picture of her or told anything about her. As the rules of the experiment said it needed genuinely to be a blind date, he was only allowed to correspond with her (at first) by email.

He opened with: So, tell me something about yourself.

– *You go first – tell me something interesting about Jeremy Thomas.*

Ah, now you've got me on to my favourite subject!

– *You should definitely go first then. Keep it quick though. One thing you need to know about me is I've got a short attention span. Exam question here: who is Jeremy Thomas in 50 words or less?*

Well, I'm a Londoner. 40-something – actually it's a big something, I'm a bit closer to a major celebration than I'd really like. Happily divorced – I mean, happy to be divorced now, although it wasn't much fun at the time. No kids, thankfully. I like kids but it made it a lot easier for me and my wife to split up. I like art and film. Been self-employed most of my life. Probably pretty much unemployable now – I've been running my own business for so long and find I like making my own decisions.

– *Sorry, Jeremy, but you've failed. You've exceeded your word count there!*

OK, so you tell me something about yourself now, Miranda.

– *I'm a Londoner too. Similar to you in age (but hey, I'm not telling either). I like theatre and cinema, particularly French movies with happy endings. You know, real life dramas but where there's a bit of warmth in the characters? And I admire self-starters who make things happen for themselves. Life is too short, don't you think?*

* * * * *

Over the weeks, the two of them got to know one another pretty well. Miranda always seemed to understand his feelings. She always seemed to surprise him and make him laugh. She knew instinctively how to puncture his mood whenever he started to get overly serious, pompous or self-important.

– So you told me the other day you enjoy art. Do you enjoy it really, or were you just trying to impress me by sounding cultured?

I like it in a kind of non-traditional way I guess. They say all true art is a distortion of reality. So I love abstract art. And I love the French Impressionists, but then who doesn't?

– Depends who they're doing their impressions of, I guess!

They'd been given subjects to speak about each week (including the controversial ones like religion and politics) and were asked to keep an online diary of their feelings about their match. Each week they sent feedback to the university, scoring how well they thought the online relationship was going. To his surprise, Jeremy found the marks he was giving increasing each week.

Miranda always had a knack of summing him up.

Religion.

– Jeremy, from all you've said, it sounds to me like you're a self-made man who worships his own creator!

Politics.

– Ah, I get it, now! You're a left wing radical living a conventional right-wing lifestyle and you vote Liberal to salve your previous conscience.

Sport.

- You like sport in theory, not in practice, don't you, Jeremy? You enjoy it so long as it is somebody else getting

hurt.

Sense of humour.

– You're always joking, aren't you, to hide your own insecurities?

Now she was quizzing him about his previous relationships. Six serious girlfriends, one rather bitter ex-wife.

– Sounds to me, Jeremy, as though recently you've chosen to be alone rather than risk getting your heart broken again.

That's pretty much it, yes.

– I can understand that. That's me in a nutshell too.

* * * * *

It was about four weeks after their online relationship had begun that the subject of what they each looked like came up.

So tell me something you've not told me yet about yourself. For instance, what do you look like, Miranda?

– Would you believe: petite, slim, blonde, blue eyes and with a smooth unblemished skin?

No, I wouldn't.

– OK, how about short, fat and warty?

Now that sounds more like reality to me. But come on, you haven't even told me how old you are!

– Pah! Don't you know that age is in the mind, Jeremy? I feel like 40 going on 25... or perhaps I mean 25 going on 40?

Be serious for a moment. Tell me something about yourself that's true.

– I want someone to love me for who I am, Jeremy, not what I look like. Oh, and I wish I had more of a social life: I don't get out much. I don't really get out at all.

Me, too. I've only been out once in the last month, apart from work. I used to go to the gym once a week and the cinema every couple of weeks. Perhaps make it to the theatre every few months. But I haven't done any of that for ages. I'm 80% housebound these days. That's me being honest, Miranda. So tell me some numbers about yourself.

– Oh, you want my vital statistics now, do you?

OK – go on!

– Would you believe 34-26-34? Oh, but that's just my bank sort code, I don't know why I'm telling you that!

You know, Miranda, I'm never sure if what you tell me is true.

– You realise this isn't a test by the university of how well matched we are, Jeremy? It's really a test of our credulity! So far the university has probably got us both classified as impossible dreamers. At the extremely gullible end of the spectrum. But go on then, answer your own question: what do you look like?

Think of Clint Eastwood in his prime. But with a wide centre parting (my comb took redundancy a few years ago). Moody, blue eyes. Lots of laughter lines. Lovable but misunderstood. Broad mind, narrow waist (actually, I think I got those last two the wrong way round).

– You know, Jeremy, I'm not sure how much of what you tell me is true! But at least I found the comb bit convincing.

* * * * *

Miranda certainly knew how to keep him engaged and curious. He couldn't wait to meet her. Today was finally going to be the day. All the participants had been invited into the university to meet Dr Ringel, the organiser of this dating experiment.

Jeremy had looked around on arrival. All of the participants were drinking tea or coffee before meeting the academics, but none of them could be Miranda. He felt sure he would know her – *he would sense who she was –* on sight.

Soon it was his turn to meet Dr Ringel, in his office.

"So where is she?"

"Who?"

"Miranda, of course. I've been really looking forward to meeting her!"

"I'm afraid that won't be possible," said Dr Ringel.

"Why not?"

The doctor smiled. "Mr Thomas, did you really expect to meet Miranda today?"

"You said in your letter that all the participants of this experiment were being invited here today. So, yes, of course I expected to meet Miranda. Where is she – couldn't she make it?"

"She's here, but you can't meet her."

"Don't play games with me! I've taken part in your stupid experiment so I have a right to meet her. In fact, I demand to meet her!"

"Mr Thomas," said Dr Ringel patiently, "I'm sorry to disappoint you. But I have to explain to you: you can't meet Miranda today, because she doesn't exist."

"What?"

"Miranda is a computer program, an early AI program, an Artificial Intelligence program. All of the participants have been communicating with different variants of our AI program, to see how long it took them to realise that they weren't conversing with a human intelligence. It seems Miranda has passed our test with flying colours!"

* * * * *

As he drove home, Jeremy laughed out loud at the absurdity of the situation. So he was in love with some software, then, was he?

It suddenly dawned of him that he would be alone, for certain, for the rest of his life. His perfect match wasn't a person, she was a computer program. And not just any old computer program. As the good doctor had explained, Miranda was a 'mirror program' set up to reflect his own personality back at him.

The reality, it seems, is that he was in love with himself. Ah well, he thought, at least he'd be spending the rest of his life with someone he loved!

Things we do for love

a short story by Michael J Richards

"Hey, Jack," I say. "Look at these. I got them off eBay. Not bad, eh?" I sort through my fishing-tackle box. "What do you think? £6.38 for five." I hold up my fishing-floats. I smile. "Porcupine quills."

Jack leans forward. As ever, his black hair falls over his eyes so he can't see what he's looking at. He never combs his hair. I've tried to get him to get it cut but he doesn't. To shave it off, like me.

"Where'd you get them?"

"Saw 'em in town," I tell him. "Went in. Took a look. Came home. Got 'em off eBay."

"How much were they in town?" he says.

"6.99."

"And how much postage did eBay charge you?" he says.

"Two quid."

"So how was eBay cheaper?" he says.

I work it out. "Oh yeah," I say. "What a dipstick."

Jack straightens up and looks around. The early morning sun gets in his eyes. He squints. "Here okay? It's as good a spot as any."

We take off our coats. I take off my beanie. Jack puts his shades on. We pull out our fishing-gear, our flasks and sandwiches and set about sorting the day's fishing.

"Good of you to give me a lift, Sean," he says as he feels in his trousers. He pulls out a hanky and a scrap of paper. He puts the scrap away, wipes his nose and shoves the hanky away. "Dominique's got the car at the moment."

"No problem, mate," I tell him as I turn towards the river and look at the current. "Off on a trip, is she?"

"You could say that," Jack says. He bends down, searching his box.

I turn away. I size things up. "Where do you wanna go? There" – I point to a small clearing by the river, where someone has sat before – "or there?"

"You choose," he says, pulling out his reel.

I go down. "Only a few yards apart. Doesn't matter. I'm here now. That okay?"

He looks up. "Yeah, yeah. Fine." He picks up his open tackle-box and heaves it down the bank.

I watch him. I can help but don't bother. Like seeing him struggle. His problem is he's got no muscles. He's as weak as a soggy milk pudding. "You okay, mate?"

"Got a few things on my mind, haven't I?" he says.

* * * * *

For the twenty or thirty minutes or so, neither of us speaks. Occasionally, I catch Sean watching me. I smile. He winks back. We place our seats, position rod rests, connect up landing-nets, put bait and keep-nets within easy reach. Setting up rods comes last, of course. Finally, everything is in place and we stand back and pour hot drinks from our flasks.

"We're in for a good day," he says, opening his cigarettes. As he pulls out a lighter from his faded jeans, he strokes his bald head. "Yeah," he says, letting out a cloud of smoke, "it'll be good."

I stand and watch, waiting until he has smoked it down to the filter.

He catches me staring. "What?" he says.

I avoid his eyes. I feel queasy. I can't look at him. I rub my boots against the grass.

"You're like a horny horse," he says. He throws away the dog end. As long as I've known him, he's always enjoyed my discomforts. "Hoofing at the grass like that."

But I take no notice. I carry on, concentrating on my boots. I can feel him his eyes on me. Finally, I look up at him. Against my will, I go for it. I smile at him, hoping it's friendly. "You're sleeping with my wife, aren't you?"

* * * * *

I look away. Look at the grass. Trees. Anything except Jack. I can feel my earring swing about and my face go red. I open my mouth to speak. Close it. Reach into my jeans for my fags. Realise I lit up a few minutes ago. Light up again.

"Well, mate," I say, "it's like this – "

"So you admit it," he says.

I look him in the eye. "Dominique is a very beautiful woman," I say. "You know that more than me, mate. And French. Who can resist a beautiful French woman?"

"She's my wife."

"And we're mates, Jack," I say. "And always will be... Yeah." Thinking about Dominique gets me excited. And Jack, he stands there, going red in the face, doing nothing about it. Wimp. I feel like a dog on heat. I carry on smoking.

He says, "Do you love her?"

I don't know what to say. We've been mates since we were eight years old, right through school. When he married Dominique, I was his best man. But he doesn't understand. When you're adults, things take over, you're not always in control. I let out some smoke.

"Christ almighty, Jack," I tell him. "She's the world to me – I'd do anything for her. I'd give up everything I own to see her happy. Sorry, Jack, but that's how it is."

We look each other up and down. We're waiting for the other to move or speak. It's like that game we played when we were kids and had nothing else to do – trying to make the other blink first. He stands there. Like always. His trouble is, he thinks too much. Never done anything on the spur of the moment. Not like me. Never gets angry. Not like me. I don't think I've ever seen him angry. That's probably why Dominique was such a push-over. She was bored. Dead bored.

I throw the dog-end into the grass. I tell him, "Look, Jack, if Dominique were my wife, I'd be knocking the shit out of you. But you – I mean, look at you – you're like a rabbit caught in the headlights."

Jack takes off his shades and pushes the hair out of his eyes. "Yes, well, you're not me, are you?" he says.

"No, mate," I tell him. "No, mate, I'm not. At least get angry with me. Thump me or something. Don't care what you do. But, for fuck's sake, man, do something."

He shakes his head. "And what good would that do?" he says. He laughs. "You'd have a bloody nose, me a bruised knuckle. Do you know how much it hurts when you hit somebody?" He laughs again. "Yeah, you do, don't you? And you'd still have Dominique."

I get my fags out. Fiddle with the flip-up top. "Doesn't seem right, mate. I mean… Don't you at least want to fight me for her?"

"You mean, fists and grunting and blood and rolling in the grass and things?"

"Why not?" I light up another fag. Jack leans forward and lifts one. I light it up for him. As we stand close to each other, drawing on the fags, I tell him, "If it were my wife, you'd do the same, wouldn't you?"

"Maybe," he says. He looks out over the river. "Look at that beautiful swan."

"For fuck's sake, Jack, fuck the swan – "

"Anyway, you haven't got a wife, have you?" he says. "Well, not one of your own, that is… Oh… Let's get on with why we're here, shall we?" He puts his shades on. Then he turns away, walks down to his spot, baits a hook and casts out. He sits down, puffing his fag. He doesn't move. I watch him and then, when it's clear he's not going to do anything, I go over to my tackle, bait up, cast out and sit down.

It's like this for nearly an hour. He doesn't move a muscle. He gets a few bites but he takes no notice. Once he stands up and pees into the river but that's the only time he moves.

Me, more or less the same. I get a few bites and I play them. Take a leak. My mind's not on the job. I've knocked off his wife and I feel I'm the cheated husband.

I put my rod on its rest and walk over. "Jack, we gotta do something," I say. "Now it's out in the open." I give him a fag. He never has his own fags. Always smoking mine. We light up. "So what do we do?"

"Oh… " he says. "Oh, I don't know… " He stares out over the river, scratches his nose, looks at me, sighs again. "What do you think?"

"Well, don't ask me," I shout at him. "She's your wife. Remember? I'm the one who's been fucking her. Remember?"

"I don't see what I can do about it."

"Well, you could put up a fight," I say. "You could throw her out, you could – you could – fuck it, you could at least get angry. For fuck's sake - "

He stands up. "Okay, suppose I hit you, what then? Will anything have been resolved?"

"Well, no," I say.

"So what's the point?" he says, staring out over the river.

I'm starting to boil up. For me, the point has changed to getting him to do something. "So," I say, "do I walk away or does she walk away with me?"

"That's up to her," Jack says. "Let her choose."

"No," I say, "I don't think so. It's up to us. If one of us isn't here for her to choose from, then that's it, isn't it?"

He turns. "So what – you wanna toss a coin? Heads, you can fuck her, tails, she won't let me near her. Is that what you want?"

I shake my head. "Don't be stupid," I tell him. "You know I didn't mean that."

"Have you got any better ideas?" Jack says.

"No," I say.

He sits back at his rod. I stand behind him. We say nothing. Wait for inspiration, I suppose.

After a few minutes, while nothing happens, he says, his back to me, "All right, if it makes you feel better – I'll fish you for her."

"What?"

"Fish," says Jack. "You're so bloody proud of your porcupine quills. Let's see how good they are. Four hours. Match rules. The one with the heaviest total catch at the end gets a shot at Dominique, loser walks away."

I don't believe it. He's flipped. I always thought there was something weird going on inside that head of his but this… bloody stupid. "That's what you wanna do, is it?" I say. "Let a few gudgeon decide the rest of your life?"

"It's better than thumping the living daylights out of each other," Jack says, getting up and turning towards me. "And we get some fishing out of it, too. That's why we're here, isn't it?"

My fag is stuck to my lips. I don't know what to do. I scratch my head. Rub my nose. Feel under my armpits. Fidget a bit more. I wanted him to challenge me. He's done that and now I'm cornered. For the first time in his life, he's made a decision. He's barmy. I shrug. I say nothing.

* * * * *

Sean holds out his hand and we shake on the deal. We measure twenty paces and place the pegs. We toss a coin. Sean wins and chooses the upstream peg. A minute ago, he was thoroughly confused and now he's full of himself.

He thinks he's going to win with those quill floats and take Dominique from me. I can see him thinking I'm off my head trying to resolve my marital problems like this. Maybe he's right. But chance brought Dominique and me together; chance can decide whether we part.

He's laughing his head off. "You'll see," he says. "Upstream, I'll get the big bastards, you'll get the tiddlers I throw back. I'm already on a winning streak. Jack, me old mate, kiss your wife good-bye."

We move our tackle to the appointed pegs. We synchronise watches. Four hours, 3:16pm, then the weigh-in.

"Rounding up and down?" he shouts.

"If you like," I shout back, not caring whether the weigh-in is measured precisely or not.

For the first hour, neither of us moves, neither of us makes a sound. Neither of us acknowledges the other is there. I sit and watch my plastic float and the flowing river. The occasional elegant swan, mallard or coot swims by. My bites are minimal.

Seventy minutes in, Sean gets his first catch. He lets out a triumphalist cry as I hear splashing and swearing. It seems to take some landing but after a while, he goes quiet.

Then he shouts, "Fuckin' hell, what a size." He's exaggerating, of course, like he always does when he's stressed. He's always been competitive. Targets, victory, winning, that's Sean. Even when we were nine years old, a game of conkers was a matter of life and death for him. Me, I'm a negotiator. I want everyone to get on with each other. If it means compromising, then that's the price you pay for an harmonious life.

Of course, I can't see exactly what he's got and I don't go over to have a look. Before all of this, I would've gone over, as he would've done if I'd landed something, supporting and encouraging each other, basking in the other's successes. But today, things being what they are, we don't.

After that, I land them about every thirty minutes or so. I think I hear Sean doing the same but he's uncharacteristically quiet. Maybe he's realised there's more at stake than having someone else's – my – wife. He's 38, never found a woman for himself and he's never asked himself why.

We're three hours in now. I dare to look through the rushes and the long grass. As I do so, Sean looks in my direction. He grins. I grin back. I can read his face even at this distance. If he had been nearer, he would have hugged me. He would have said, this is why we're mates, Jack, this is what it's all about. He would've reminded me that

261

we share fishing-kit without having to ask. We take each other's cigarettes without permission. You bring coffee, I bring tea, and we drink either as we want. Women don't come between mates. He would have said.

At this precise moment, he pulls a perch – so I congratulate him, as we'd done in the past. He waves at me. He's focussed on fishing for its own sake. For Sean at least, the reason for our conflict – women – is temporarily forgotten.

Later, he shouts, "Ten minutes."

"Agreed," I shout back.

"I've got a heavy net," Sean shouts. "We can call it off if you like."

"Up to you," I shout back.

His reply is immediate. "If you want to – "

"Do you want to?"

"Only if you do," he shouts. Then he's landing another and putting it in his keepnet as he shouts, "Time."

* * * * *

I sweat like a bull's bollocks. Jack has crept up like a ghost behind me and stands with the scales and his sling. He puts the hook into the handle and checks the scales. I've caught five. I empty my keep net into the sling.

"That's a good haul," Jack says. We watch the scales move around to 6.84 kilos. He pulls out his scrap of paper and a pen and writes it down.

"Still not too late to call it off," I say.

"No, it's okay," he says.

"I know but – "

"Let's get on with it."

We put the fish back into my keep net and go over to his peg. He's got eight. They weigh 6.77 kilos. Jack writes it down and studies the figures.

"Rounding up and down," he says, "your 6.84 becomes 6.8 and my 6.77 becomes – " he looks up at me – "6.8."

A true and fairly fought combat makes us equals. Jack

looks down and I don't know where the fuck to look. I get out my fags and light up two and hand him one. He takes it.

"What now?" I say.

He's staring at the figures. At last, he looks at me. "Don't know... Could have a penalty fish-off. First to catch anything wins," he said.

"Not after four fucking hours," I say. "I've had enough, mate."

"Me, too," he says, folding the paper up and putting it back in his pocket, along with the pen. He takes off his shades and breathes deeply. "Well, okay" he says. "As technically, your catch was heavier than mine, you win."

But I won't let him. "For god's sake, man," I say, "this is Dominique we're talking about, your wife. Are you giving up? C'm' on!"

"I don't understand," he says. "Why are you fighting my corner for me?"

"Dunno, mate," I tell him. "I want Dominique yet you're my mate. I want to fuck your wife but I don't wanna let you down. I'm confused."

"Pity you didn't think of that before," he says.

He's right, of course. To be honest, there are always other blokes' wives. The first time I fucked Dominique, I should have known no good would've come of it. But she was so good – so, so bloody good. And she loved it as much as I did.

Nothing wrong about that, 'cos to begin with, that's all I wanted. But then, for me, it changed into something else. It didn't take me long to work out that at last I'd found the woman I wanted to spend the rest of my life with.

And I didn't give Jack a thought. While I was fucking my mate's wife, I didn't give him one single solitary thought. But, to be fair, neither did Dominique. I never heard her speak his name. Trouble is, I'll never find another mate like Jack. Not at my age.

* * * * *

I turn away and walk a few yards away. As usual, Sean has given up trying to sort things out. Whenever he has a problem, he gives up and comes to me. Even this. He has an affair with my wife and he expects me to sort it out for him.

I need time to think. I crouch down and pick at some buttercups. I put them in my mouth and chew. I can feel him watching me. The buttercups are tasty. I don't hurry. I make him wait. I spit out the flowers, stand up, put on my dark glasses and face him.

"Do you love Dominique?"

He nods slowly. "I'll do anything for her."

"Okay. This is what we're going to do," I tell him. "And this will be the end of it. No arguments. You can go to Dominique – with my blessing – and tell her she's yours. If she'll have you."

"Just like that?" he says.

"On one condition," I say.

"Oh yeah?"

"You said you'd give everything you owned to see Dominique happy," I say.

He nods. "Yeah, that's what I said." But he's not sure.

"So that's my condition," I tell him. "You hand over everything you've got here – your fishing-kit, your car – everything – and Dominique is yours."

"Whoa," he says, stumbling backwards in the grass. "Hold on a minute. We shouldn't trade women for things. That's not right, mate."

I walk up to him. Our faces are so close our stomachs lean again each other, our lips are nearly touching. "A few minutes ago," I say, "you would've traded my wife for fifteen pounds of crappy carp. And before that? Did you give her chocolates? Did you send her flowers? How much did you fork out on condoms? So how much did you trade to get your hand down her knickers? What's the difference?"

He licks his lips with exaggerated care. I step back. "Doesn't seem right," he says.

I force the point. "What would you give up to be with the person you love? How much does Dominique mean to you? Are you telling me that heap of fifteen-year-old metal you call a car is worth more to you than the woman you claim to love? What will you do for love?"

Sean sweats more than ever. I've got him. He opens his cigarettes, looks and screws up the packet. "I gotta get some more fags."

I stay where I am while he walks slowly to his car. I start packing away my things. Out of the corner of my eye, I watch him reach into the glove compartment and get some cigarettes. He's never without. He takes off the wrapping, lights up and sits, smoking. He's trying to think. He smokes to the end, throws the dog-end out the window, gets out, slams the door, locks it and walks slowly back.

* * * * *

"Jack," I say, "this is really weird."

He doesn't look at me. He's tidying up his tackle-box. "Thirty years we've known each other," he says, not looking at me, "and I find you've been knocking off my wife and you think this is weird?"

So," I say, "you keep my stuff, we drive home and Dominique and I – and you – "

"Something like that," he says, still not looking at me, taking his rod apart.

"But what if Dominique doesn't agree?"

"Not my problem," he says, putting the rod pieces in their bag. "Once we've done here, you can tell her what you like."

I'm playing with my earring. Then I decide. After all, as Jack says, what's a rusty shitheap of a car compared to Dominique? I rub my head all over. Pull at my ears. "Okay," I say, suddenly really thirsty. "It's a deal."

Jack holds out his hand. "Good luck, mate," he says as we shake. "You're gonna need it. Let's pack our stuff up – "

"Your stuff."

I watch him pack up his stuff. I don't help. Then he packs mine. His.

"No hard feelings, mate?" I say.

"We sorted it out," he says. "That's all that matters."

He's got my stuff. But I've got Dominique. I should feel really happy. But I feel like an abandoned animal. Something new's starting for me. Something else is ending. I unlock the car and watch him load up. I can't move. When he's done, we step back from it, like we're buying it from some bastard dealer.

Jack holds out his hand. "The keys," he says.

"Oh yeah, sure." I hand them over. "Let's get going, shall we?"

I get in the front passenger seat.

* * * * *

I go to the driver's door, open it and put my leg in and then get out. "Um, Sean – "

"Yeah, what?"

I go round and open the passenger door. "Can you get out for a minute?"

"What?" he says. "What now, mate?"

I hold the door open. "We're not finished."

Sean gets out and stands a few paces away. His hands are on his hips, ready for the fight he's wanted all along.

"You're handing over everything here that you own – right?" I say.

"Yeah," he says. "I've done that."

"Not quite." I wave my hand at him. "Your clothes."

"What?"

I say, "They're mine."

Sean steps back. I can see he's shocked. Which is good. "You want my clothes? You want me to strip off for you?"

"How many times have you stripped off for her?" I say. "Ten, twenty, thirty times?"

"Seventeen."

"So pleased you've been keeping records," I say.

266

"When you next see her, you can tell her you stripped off for her for an eighteenth time, can't you?"

"Mate," he says, going from one foot to the other, breaking out into another sweat. "Okay, I'll give you my clothes, okay, but let's wait until we get home, eh? Do the decent thing, eh?"

"You said you'd give up everything to see her happy," I tell him. "That was the deal. You shook on it."

I see him squirming. Which is very good. What is he prepared to do for love now?

"Are you trying to humiliate me?" he says.

"No," I say. "I'm succeeding. And it's nothing like what you've been doing to me for the past few months."

"But, look here, mate – "

"They're mine," I say. "Give them to me."

He's like a statue. He's staring at me with half-closed eyes. Then we're staring at each other, waiting for the other to blink. I know if I blink first, I've lost. But as I'm wearing my dark glasses, it doesn't really matter because he won't see, anyway.

"You bastard," he says, red-faced. He's backed down. I've won. I've finally won. I stand with folded arms and watch as he slowly undresses and places his things in a pile at his feet. "What would you have done if the weigh-in hadn't been a dead heat?" he says.

"You can keep your credit cards," I say. "No use to me. I'll take the rest of your wallet, though. A bit of extra cash'll come in handy. And your mobile. You can keep the fags and lighter. You'll need them."

"Thanks," Sean says.

I open the car boot and throw his things in. I open what has been his fishing-box, take out the porcupine quill floats and close the boot.

"You can have these," I say, handing them over. "They didn't do you much good. I'd ask eBay for your money back. And you might as well have this." I pull out the piece of paper. "Our weigh-in scores. A souvenir."

I get in the car and shut the door as Sean stares at the

figures. I lean over, pull shut and lock the passenger door. I half get out the car.

"If you turn it over," I tell him, "you'll see you've been wasting your time with her. Go on, turn it over."

Sean looks at me, not understanding.

"Sean," I say, explaining things to a child, "that's the note Dominique left me a couple of days ago before she drove off in my car. She's met some French woman at her Spanish class. She says they're in love. Still, I suppose that's what she told you, didn't she? She's taken us both for a ride, Sean. She's going to book their flights for Marseille tonight. Good bit at the bottom. She sends you her love and says sorry."

Sean grips the floats, fags and lighter as he reads the note again. Then he reads it again. And again. "But why didn't you tell me in the first place?" he whines. He looks up. "You planned this, didn't you?" he says. "Right from before we got here, you knew what you were going to do, didn't you?"

"I had no idea," I tell him. "Everything came from you. What you said, what you did. I told you I had a few things on my mind, didn't I?" I leaned on the car roof, taking off my dark glasses. "I kept asking myself whether you're to blame. You aren't, of course. But then again, you sort of are, aren't you?"

"But the fishing," he blubs, the reality of it finally dawning on him, "and taking my car – my mobile – my clothes, for fuck's sake, Jack, my clothes – "

"I'd got nothing to lose," I say. "As for the fishing – well, I wanted to see what would happen – wanted to see what you'd do. Anyway, whatever the result, I'd already won, hadn't I? You said you'd give up everything you owned to see her happy. You did that and you've seen her happy."

I look at the naked man standing in the field in the middle of the summer's afternoon, clutching his few possessions. For a brief moment, I feel sorry for him.

"You and me, Sean," I say, "I always thought we had

something. Sean and Jack. Jack and Sean. We loved each other like brothers, didn't we? We looked after each other. Do anything for each other. Like lovers."

He looked at me. "You're not leaving me here, aren't you?"

"Yep," I tell him. "Good luck... Mate."

I get in and start up the engine. I adjust my dark glasses, shove the car into gear and rev more than I need. I adjust the mirror and drive off.

CONTRIBUTORS

Gordon Adams is a marketing consultant living in Buckinghamshire. He is the author of two non-fiction books on career change, both originally published by Infinite Ideas: *Overcoming Redundancy* (first published 2009) and *The Great Mid-Life Career Switch* (2010). The second edition of *Overcoming Redundancy* was published by New Generation Publishing in 2015. Gordon's four short stories in this anthology are his first published works of fiction.

Pat Aitcheson has always been in love with words. Her writing life was greatly enlivened by joining Northants Writers' Ink in 2015. She finds group meetings encouraging and supportive, and motivate her to write regularly. Her reading and writing tastes are similar: science fiction, fantasy and contemporary. Her sci-fi novel *Looking for Heaven* was long-listed for the 2016 Bath Novel Award. She now seeks an agent to represent her while she works on the sequel. She has also completed a fantasy novella *Heart of Fire* as well as numerous short stories and poems. At her blog **2squarewriting.com**, she posts weekly thoughts on writing, as well as occasional shorter pieces. She fits her writing around her family, garden and a busy full-time job.

Deborah Bromley is a hypnotherapist specialising in Life-Between-Lives (LBL) hypno-therapy, a deep trance process that connects you with memories of your life as a soul, in between incarnations. She trained with Dr Michael Newton, bestselling author of *Journey of Souls* and *Destiny of Souls*. Deborah contributed to Dr Newton's subsequent book, *Memories of the Afterlife*. She is the author of two novels, *The Channelling Group* and *The Walk-In*. Both are self-published and available from Amazon. She is currently working on the final part of this trilogy entitled *The End of Earth*. Deborah wants to reach out to a wide audience who love paranormal fiction and share an interest in alternative realities. She has a passion for reading and is never without a stack of books on her bedside table – most likely to be either crime thrillers or romantic fiction. She has discovered the pleasure of writing short stories from her membership of Northants Writers' Ink and hopes to assemble enough material for a collection in the future. Deborah is Secretary of Northants Writers' Ink.

Beth Heywood has lived in the South Pacific for 35 years where she taught creative writing. She has now retired to Wellingborough in the UK with her husband and a house full of books. She publishes poetry, short stories, and novels. When Beth is not writing she enjoys walking, reading, gardening, and sailing the seas on merchant ships.

Nick Johns lives largely in his imagination and, since retiring from a life of crime, rescues orphaned words and tries to find them literate homes. Some of his work is scattered around the internet and also on Amazon (other retailers are available – no, honestly!). He is not working on a novel.

Jason McClean is married with two fantastic children that fill up his days with more happiness than he ever thought possible. Name checks for Gaelen and Ariane, not to mention his much loved wife, Lyn. Jason enjoys mountain biking in his spare time and the older he gets the bigger the jumps he is completing. He enjoys riding on the roads as well. With a background in motorcycle journalism (Chief Reporter at *Motorcycle News* and Editor of *Inside Line*, the Motorcycle Trade Magazine), Jason wrote the biography of his friend and triple British Superbike Champion John Reynolds, published by Haynes in 2008. Jason is currently writing short stories and building up his voice and writing style for fiction novels. He reads a lot and enjoys thrillers, horror, sci-fi, fantasy and young adult genres. Jason is a Director at www.thepropertyinsurer.co.uk and manages Northants Writers' Ink's website. He likes cinema (a brief spell as a cinema critic when training as a journalist was one of the best jobs in the world), travelling, theatre, eating out, property investing and meeting interesting new people.

Elizabeth Parikh is a writer from Lancashire and works as a teacher of Religion and Philosophy in North Bedfordshire. She has a particular penchant for eighties music and writing comedy. Elizabeth first came to love the genre whilst watching the sitcom *Bottom* as a young girl and, while she was too young to truly appreciate the genius of vodka margarine, a seed was planted to one day create comedy of her own. She was encouraged as a candidate at the Media Guardian Television Festival where she learnt how to master comedy sketches with writers from Baby Cow Productions and went on to co-write two plays for the Edinburgh Fringe Festival (*Plot Holes and Advert Breaks* and *Murder We Wrote*) which received four star reviews from Three Weeks magazine. Elizabeth then worked for five years as a script reader for the Manchester Library Theatre. Her latest project is an all-female sit-com which she hopes will contain at least four philosophy-based jokes but is guaranteed to include a minimum of three references to The Human League.

Michael J Richards is founder Chair of Northants Writers' Ink. He is also Chair of Northampton Literature Group and leads its Writing Circle. He is a Deputy Chair of Northampton Writing Group and a member of Northants Authors. In 2014, he published *Afterwards Our Buildings Shape Us*, a comic horror novel. In 2015, he edited Northants Writers' Ink first anthology *Tales of the Scorpion*. Both are available on Amazon. In 2015, he wrote and directed *The Isolated Essence of a Subject,* a twenty-minute film. He is currently engaged in his first professional ghost-writing commission.

Allan Shipham is a founder member and Treasurer of Northants' Writers Ink. He occasionally takes the lead chair on meeting nights. New to writing as a hobby, he uses the support from the group to develop his skills, exploring new ideas and undertake challenges set by the other members of the group. When *Tales of the Scorpion* was published, Allan developed a single short story he had already written. In this anthology he shares a wide scope of his work for your enjoyment.

Lightning Source UK Ltd.
Milton Keynes UK
UKOW01f1236021116
286691UK00002B/9/P